*"But now, O Lord, thou art our father;
we are the clay, and thou our potter;
and we all are the work of thy hand."*

—Isaiah 64:8 (kjv)

Love's a Mystery

Love's a Mystery in Sleepy Hollow, New York
Love's a Mystery in Cape Disappointment, Washington
Love's a Mystery in Cut and Shoot, Texas
Love's a Mystery in Nameless, Tennessee
Love's a Mystery in Hazardville, Connecticut
Love's a Mystery in Deadwood, Oregon
Love's a Mystery in Gnaw Bone, Indiana
Love's a Mystery in Tombstone, Arizona
Love's a Mystery in Peculiar, Missouri
Love's a Mystery in Crooksville, Ohio

in

CROOKSVILLE
OH

JOHNNIE ALEXANDER
& DANA LYNN

 Guideposts

Scripture references are from the following sources: *The Holy Bible, King James Version* (KJV). *The Holy Bible, New International Version* (NIV). Copyright ⓒ1973, 1978, 1984, 2011 by Biblica, Inc. Used by permission of Zondervan. All rights reserved worldwide. www.zondervan.com.

Cover and interior design by Müllerhaus.
Cover illustration by Dan Burr at Illustration Online LLC.
Typeset by Aptara, Inc.

ISBN 978-1-961251-63-2 (hardcover)
ISBN 978-1-961251-64-9 (softcover)
ISBN 978-1-959633-58-7 (epub)

Printed and bound in the United States of America

The Potter's Design

by

Johnnie Alexander

Does not the potter have the right to make out of the same lump of clay some pottery for special purposes and some for common use?

—Romans 9:21 (NIV)

CHAPTER ONE

Crooksville, Ohio

Summer 1938

Jasper Kane stood beneath the hickory tree and stared at the sign above the two-story structure with the same unsettling mixture of pride and guilt he'd felt every day since the funeral.

KANE POTTERY

OUT OF FIRE COMES STRENGTH

The manufacturing company wasn't the biggest in the region, appropriately christened the Pottery Capital of the World, nor was it the most innovative or competitive. But its founding focus on manufacturing utilitarian pottery—dishes, serving bowls, pitchers—for utilitarian purposes at a utilitarian price had kept the pottery wheels turning and the kilns burning throughout the worst years of the Great Depression. Not a single employee had been let go, an accomplishment old Edmund Kane attributed solely to his superior business acumen.

Perhaps he'd been right. But Edmund now rested in Crooksville Memorial Cemetery, and the mantle of responsibility now rested on Jasper.

Who hoped to implement the product line his father had forbidden.

In what had become a morning ritual, Jasper took a deep breath, adjusted his hat, and strode toward the concrete steps leading to the brick building's thick wooden doors. Once inside, he greeted everyone he met on his way to the mezzanine office with the half wall of glass that overlooked the warehouse floor.

He paused outside the door, placed one hand on the frosted glass pane that bore his name, and shut his eyes. When he opened them again, his name was still on the door. Rightfully so—this was his office now.

Yet it didn't seem right. Until only a few weeks ago, the name Edmund Kane was printed in big block letters as a subtle means of intimidation for all those who entered the boss's private domain. Jasper went with a smaller, friendlier font as a subtle message that he wasn't his dad and his door was open to anyone.

Especially anyone with new ideas for a shift from the utilitarian mundane to more artistic products.

He entered the office, still feeling like an interloper, and set his briefcase on the broad desk. His suit jacket went on the coat hook behind the door, and then he rolled up the sleeves of his white dress shirt. Time to work. Time to plan. Time to call Vernon Spears.

During a long and sleepless night, Jasper had tossed and turned, pondered and prayed, and finally risen before sunrise with a pathetic plan.

He wanted to give Vernon the benefit of the doubt, to believe that the owner of Spears Ceramics would have a logical explanation for his latest venture. But the knot in Jasper's stomach told him those hopes were as fragile as the most delicate porcelain.

The direct approach—one he didn't want to take—was the only way to find out for sure.

Almost as soon as the operator connected the call, Vernon's baritone voice roared through the line loud enough that Jasper held the receiver a few inches from his ear.

"What can I do for you, Jasper? Need my advice now that your daddy's gone? I'm telling you again, son, you should think about liquidating. Best thing for you to do. I'll make you a fair offer on your equipment and your inventory. Then you can put that building to a more profitable use."

Jasper envisioned the older man—sweat glistening on his bald pate, thick fingers gripping the phone, feet propped on his desk as he leaned back in his chair.

"Thank you for your concern, Mr. Spears, but I have no plans to close these doors," Jasper replied. "There's only one thing bothering me right now."

"What would that be, son?"

Jasper pulled the pamphlet from his briefcase and opened it. "This new line of decorative ceramics you're advertising to your retailers. You're calling it 'Autumn Decor.'"

"Aw, yes. The ladies in this fair land have denied themselves for too long, if you ask me. They want something new and pretty to put on their mantels. As proof to their neighbors that they've got more than two dimes in their change purses again. You know how it is." Vernon's voice didn't reveal even the slightest tremor. The man had no shame. "What do you think of our new pieces?"

"Those are my designs." Unfortunately, Jasper's voice did waver. He closed his eyes and inhaled a silent breath. He dared not sound weak. He firmly enunciated each word. "You have no right to them."

"Well now, son, I don't know what you're talking about. I bought those designs fair and square, which means I can do whatever I want with them."

That wasn't possible. "Who did you buy them from?"

"You don't think I'm going to give you the name of my designer, do you?" Vernon let out such a loud guffaw that Jasper moved the phone away from his ear again. "You have a lot of gall, son, to claim my designs as your own. A lot of gall. Didn't your daddy teach you anything about this business before he headed to the great beyond?"

"You must not have heard me, Mr. Spears." Jasper did his best to push down the growing pressure against his chest. "*I'm* the designer. Whoever sold you those designs stole them, but they belong to me. You can't manufacture that line."

"Seems to me that you're the one who isn't listening. I *bought* those designs. They're mine. And the first run of that line is already on its way to my distributor in New York City. Even if I believed you came up with those fine designs, it's too late to stop my production. And, son, just so we're clear. I *don't* believe you. Kane Pottery never sold anything like what I'm selling now."

A cackling laugh reverberated against Jasper's ear.

"I'm telling you again, and I'm telling you this for your own good. You might as well close your doors. You may have your daddy's business, but you didn't inherit his sense or his guts."

The slam disconnecting the call reverberated through the line.

Jasper gripped his receiver then set it on the cradle. Those designs, ones he'd created and tweaked over several years, were meant to propel Kane Pottery into a new era. His father had refused to even consider them, but Jasper was certain that as the Depression eased, demand for new products would rise. As Vernon had said, an optimistic country would be interested in decorative items. Unfortunately, Vernon had decided to give the customers what they wanted with Jasper's ideas.

What to do now?

Jasper pushed away from his desk and stared through the glass to the factory floor below and the beehive of activity occurring there. Most of these employees had been at the company for years. They'd watched Jasper grow up, and now they counted on him.

Hard to imagine that one of them could have betrayed him.

Vernon had made it clear that he wanted Jasper to fail. Then there would be one less competitor in the Pottery Capital of the World. But Jasper wouldn't go down without a fight. He couldn't stop Vernon from going forward with the stolen designs. But he'd do whatever it took to find out who'd stolen them and make sure it didn't happen again.

He returned to his desk, pulled the latest edition of the *Crooksville News* from a shelf, and flipped through the pages until he found the advertisement he wanted. The P&I Detective Agency based in nearby Zanesville promised professional service and discreet confidentiality.

Exactly what Jasper needed. He picked up his phone.

Roll the stacked sheets—paper, carbon, paper, carbon, paper—into the Underwood typewriter. Type, type, type. Remove the completed report. Separate the pages from the carbons and place them in the appropriate boxes for filing. Repeat.

After all of Polly Matthews's intensive training with the renowned Pinkerton Detective Agency, this was now her life.

She once again questioned the wisdom of joining her brother in opening their own agency. The proposed business arrangement had sounded perfect when he suggested it. After all, he'd been a Pinkerton man for a few years, and Polly had completed her training with impeccable scores.

"Together, we can build the most reputable detective agency in this part of Ohio," Isaac had said. A dream he still believed in and, to be fair, one that could still come true.

But Polly had expected to be working cases with him—she'd envisioned sleuthing for clues, sneaking into forbidden places, and solving crimes in the grand traditions of Edgar Allan Poe's C. Auguste Dupin and Sir Arthur Conan Doyle's Sherlock Holmes.

Instead, Isaac did the detective work while she filed reports and balanced their books. She'd told him more than once that if she'd wanted to be a secretary, she'd have finished secretarial school instead of quitting after her first year. But Isaac insisted someone needed to keep them organized. Since he didn't type and his penmanship was too atrocious for him to write in the accounting ledgers, those roles naturally fell to her.

If only she'd stayed with the Pinkertons. The famed agency had the foresight to hire Kate Warne, their first woman detective, in 1856—before the Civil War—and had valued her contributions enough to hire even more women. They recognized, as Isaac apparently did not, that women made excellent detectives.

As Polly rolled another sheet of paper into the typewriter, she imagined the thrilling cases she could be working on right this very minute if she hadn't agreed to Isaac's plans. She might be trailing a counterfeiter or hunting a jewel thief or posing as a femme fatale to gain access into a secret society intent on overthrowing the government. Isaac would laugh at that last scenario, but during her training, Polly had proved herself adept at transforming into either a glamour gal or an insignificant spinster.

Yet here she was, stuck in the P&I Detective Agency's storefront office, typing and filing, filing and typing.

Isaac emerged from the inner office—another bone of contention, at least from Polly's point of view, since she longed for an inner office of her own—and perched on the edge of her desk.

"I just got off the phone with the owner of a pottery company down in Crooksville." He handed her a piece of paper covered with his chicken-scratch handwriting. Polly might be the only person on the globe who could decipher it. "Something about one of his competitors stealing designs for what he called 'artistic pottery.'"

Polly leaned away from the typewriter and studied the paper. *Jasper Kane. Pottery. Who cares?* Beneath the smart-alecky question, twice underlined for emphasis, was a telephone number. If Isaac wanted to grow their partnership into an agency that would someday rival Pinkerton's, *he* needed to care about the problems of any potential client.

"What does he mean by 'artistic pottery'?" she asked.

Isaac shrugged. "No idea, and I didn't ask."

"Are you going there this afternoon?" Crooksville was about fifteen miles south of Zanesville, which meant Isaac could be gone for over an hour. Probably two. She'd be alone in the office and could practice her self-defense moves without him around to offer his unsolicited comments.

He picked up her desk calendar and flipped through the pages. The summer months had brought with them a lull in business. Either people committed more crimes in cooler months or potential clients cared less about pursuing the miscreants in their lives when sapped by the heat.

"I'm not going there at all," he said.

"Why not?" Polly demanded. "You know as well as I do that we need every case we can get right now." Even one her brother deemed boring.

"Pottery manufacturing may be an important industry around here, but this sounds like a case of petty rivalry to me. After all, a vase is a vase is a vase. Who's to say who came up with what design?"

"I'll call him and get more details." She picked up the handset and started to dial, but Isaac depressed the button.

"Don't bother with that." He ambled to the front window and peered through the glass. "We might have a client with deep, deep pockets in need of our special investigative skills."

Despite herself, Polly couldn't help but be intrigued. "Who's that?"

"I read about it in the *Chillicothe Gazette* this morning. A woman found an intruder in her home a couple of nights ago. He took off when she confronted him, but he left behind a jar of buttons. Police are stumped."

"That sounds intriguing. When do we leave?"

Isaac's thick brows met in the middle. "Not we. Me."

"But you said '*our* special investigative skills.'"

"I meant *our* as in the agency." Isaac twirled his finger as if to encompass the office then waggled it between him and Polly. "Not *our* as in you and me."

She should have known. He'd never give her a chance to prove herself. Her eyes lit on the scrap of paper. "What about Jasper Kane? If you don't want me calling him, why did you give me his number?"

"So you could call one of your contacts at Pinkerton and find out if there's anything to this design-stealing business. I mean, how could this Kane even prove that he and this other fella didn't come up with similar ideas at the same time?" Isaac gave an exaggerated shrug as if to say there was no plausible answer. "Then call him with whatever you find out and send him an invoice. That's about all we can do, but at least we'll make a little money along the way."

Polly didn't appreciate Isaac's indifference to Mr. Kane's situation, but he was right. Any help they offered was better than none. Though if Isaac wasn't interested in pursuing the matter, perhaps... butterflies swooshed in her stomach.

"When are you going to Chillicothe?" Polly asked, careful to keep her tone indifferent.

"I'll leave on the early morning train. You can take care of things around here while I'm gone, can't you? It may be several days before I return."

"You know I can," Polly said, miffed he'd even ask such a question. Though in this case, taking care of things would mean closing the office while she took a trip of her own.

Since Isaac refused to help this Jasper Kane, Polly would take off her secretarial hat and don a deerstalker's cap.

In the grand tradition of Sherlock Holmes.

CHAPTER TWO

As soon as Isaac left for the train station, Polly scrambled to clean the kitchen. She had sent her brother off after a hearty breakfast of eggs, sausage and gravy, toast, and hash browns with a cheery farewell. She wanted him in a good mood as he walked out of the house because he definitely would not be happy if he returned before she did and found her gone.

He'd fly off the handle all the way to the moon when he discovered the where and the why. She regretted that…but not enough to forfeit her plan. Jasper Kane, whoever he was, needed the professional services of the P&I Detective Agency. Since Isaac wasn't interested in Mr. Kane's troubles, Polly now had a chance to prove her worth to their company—and to her brother.

Once the kitchen was tidy, she retrieved her already-packed suitcase from her upstairs bedroom, put on her hat and gloves, and tucked her purse under her arm. The butterflies from the day before swooshed in her stomach once again as she embarked on her first solo case.

With the suitcase tucked in the boot of their blue 1930 Oldsmobile Coupe, Polly slid into the driver's seat. She'd consulted a map the night before. All she needed to do was stay on Roseville Road from Zanesville south to Crooksville. She maneuvered along the town's streets then navigated the right turn onto the highway.

The drive took her through Roseville—hence the name of the road—another town known for its pottery manufacturing. Polly knew little about the industry, but she didn't need sharp detection skills to deduce the region's clay must be valuable. Otherwise, the Pottery Capital of the World designation would have gone somewhere else.

While she drove, Polly rehearsed her plan, though admittedly it was more of an outline than a one-two-three approach to the potential case. Before she contacted Jasper Kane, she needed to know more about him and his company. That meant stealthy research and secretive sleuthing—the skills she had excelled at during her training and the same skills that Isaac eschewed.

She slowed as she entered the town, crossed over a narrow stream, passed the Crooksville Cemetery, and turned left onto Main Street. Few people were out and about in the downtown area, which wasn't a surprise. Children were out of school for the summer, and many were probably working on family farms or maybe even in the pottery business.

If Crooksville was anything like Zanesville, it boasted a diner where longtime citizens gathered for coffee and gossip. Polly spied the Bisque Biscuit Diner as she crawled down Main Street and noted the various businesses. She parked the Olds not far from the diner's entrance and checked the flip of her hair along her shoulders, the tilt of her hat, and the brightness of her lipstick. Pleased with her appearance as a confident traveler, she slid from the vehicle and strode to the diner.

Most of the morning crowd, if there had been one, had already dispersed to conduct their day's business. Only two or three tables were occupied by lingerers. Polly eyed the interior then purposely chose a booth by the front window. A pencil-thin waitress with a quick smile and blond hair tucked beneath a hairnet appeared with a coffeepot in one hand and a menu in the other.

"Welcome to the Bisque Biscuit Diner," she said as she poured steaming hot coffee into one of the thick cups that was already on the table. "Haven't seen you in here before. Are you passing through, or staying a spell?"

Polly pulled off her gloves and laid them across her purse on the bench beside her. "Staying, but only for a few days. Is there a hotel in town or a room I could rent?"

"There's a boardinghouse out on Ceramic Road. A brick house with a red door known around here as Reed's Mansion. You can't miss it." The waitress provided the directions. "Tell Miss Marla that Lavonne sent you her way. She'll set you up just fine."

Polly thanked her then studied the menu. She had sat down to breakfast with Isaac but only nibbled at the food on her plate. How could she eat when she was eager for him to leave so she could begin her own adventure? Now that she was here in Crooksville, ready to get started on her solo case, she was starving.

She ordered a breakfast similar to what she'd fixed for her brother, but chose bacon instead of sausage and gravy. Lavonne left with the order, returned a moment later with a glass of water, and then was gone again to greet newcomers who perched on the stools at the counter.

Polly immediately regretted that she hadn't chosen a stool. Her polished persona of an assured, independent woman had directed her to the booth. But she realized now that a seat at the counter would have given her more opportunities to chat with Lavonne. A learned-on-the-job trick to tuck into her arsenal.

When Lavonne returned with two sunny-side up eggs, bacon, hashbrowns, and toast, Polly smiled a thank-you and started to ask her a general question about the pottery companies in the area. But Lavonne jumped in with a question of her own.

"What brings you to our little corner of the world?" she asked as she set a metal holder containing two jars of jam on the table.

"My mother left me a couple of ceramic vases," Polly enthused, thankful that this tidbit of information was true. She'd brought the smaller of the two with her in case she needed it to substantiate that potential cover story. "I know so little about pottery, but everyone talks about Crooksville's pottery companies. I decided to come and see the process for myself."

"You've come to the right place then." Lavonne tucked the now-empty tray under her arm. "Spears Ceramics is the largest manufacturer around here, and you can tell what pieces come from there by the special SC stamp on the bottom."

Wanting Lavonne to stay engaged in their conversation without realizing that she was being subtly interrogated, Polly focused on spreading blackberry jam on her toast and keeping her tone light.

"I don't remember what the stamp on the bottom of Mama's vase looks like," she said as if astonished to learn of its importance. "Or even if it had one. Though I believe someone said something about a Kane Pottery company."

"Why, all of our coffee cups are made by Kane Pottery," Lavonne exclaimed as she pointed her pencil to Polly's cup. "Including that one. It's not as big a manufacturer as Spears Ceramics, but the product is just as good. Maybe even better."

"Do you know the owner?"

"Sure do. That'd be Jasper Kane, though he only took over a month or so ago. His father—that would be Edmund Kane—keeled over while introducing the contestants for Miss Teen Clay City at our summer festival. Old Doc Bryant said his heart gave out that very moment. Such a shame for Jasper and Elsie."

Polly raised her eyes to the waitress. "Elsie? Is she Jasper Kane's wife?"

"Oh, no, honey." Lavonne chuckled as she tapped Polly's shoulder with her pencil. "Jasper isn't married, though, between you and me, it's not for the lack of any number of young ladies willing to have him slip a ring on their finger. Elsie is his sister. She's about your age, I'd say, and busies herself with keeping the house. There's only her and Jasper living in Stone House now that Edmund passed along. Their mama died around fifteen years ago, when they were still in school. What a sad event that was for everybody."

Polly slid the jam-smeared knife across the toast's edge then angled it on her plate. "I'm sure it was," she said, her tone somber and without any pretense. That kind of heartache never quite went away.

"Why, look at that. There he is now." Lavonne pointed the eraser end of her pencil toward the window. Her voice turned flirtatious. "If I was ten years younger, I'd be inviting that man to supper to ease his grieving."

Polly peered through the pane glass between the etched letters announcing the diner's name. Despite the summer heat, the two men standing in front of the hardware store next door wore suits and homburg hats. Though the brims of their hats shaded their faces, both appeared to be attractive men in their late twenties.

"Which one is Mr. Kane?" Polly asked.

"The one with the green tie. Jasper's eyes are a delicious light brown. Almost amber if the light is right."

"You seem to know him well." As Polly studied both men, she wished she could use the tiny binoculars she carried in her purse to get a closer look at their faces. Jasper's hair appeared to be a sandy blond while dark curls escaped from beneath the other man's hat. The cuffs of the second man's pants were frayed, and a fresh coat of polish didn't hide the scuffs on his shoes. Like almost everyone else in the country, the dark-haired man probably made do with what he had.

Use it up, wear it out, make it do, or do without.

The saying appeared on posters and was often repeated on the radio during the past few years. Little went to waste when goods were scarce and money even scarcer. The economic tide was slowly turning, but the rhyme remained popular for many.

"Jasper comes in often," Lavonne continued. "At least he did when his father was alive. This booth"—she indicated the one Polly occupied—"was old Mr. Kane's favorite. He liked to see who was out and about. Come to think of it, I don't think Jasper has been here more than two or three times since the funeral."

"Who's the other man?"

"That's Mark Gleason. He grew up here then left, oh, I don't know. Several years ago. He came back to town for the funeral and has been around ever since. He and Jasper were best friends growing up, so maybe he plans to stay in town for good. He's such a dreamboat, I hope he does. Brightens the day when a good-looking young man pops in for a bite to eat."

Polly didn't interrupt Lavonne's prattle as the two men held her full attention. Boyhood friends reunited by grief. Jasper, the heir to a local business, Mark...what? Jasper, quiet, his body still and attentive. Mark, animated, almost boisterous, as he talked nonstop and clapped Jasper's shoulder.

Both laughed, but Jasper didn't seem to find the story as amusing as Mark did.

Perhaps it was too soon for laughter. Perhaps sorrow clung too close.

Jasper laughed at Mark's anecdote, more to be polite to his longtime friend than because he found the story funny. He knew from experience that if he didn't laugh, Mark's account would only get more outlandish. Ever since they were boys, Mark had loved to embellish the simplest of events into humorous yarns. He might have become their generation's Mark Twain if he'd ever learned to sit still long enough to put pen to paper.

That task was as impossible as expecting the famed frog of Calaveras County to jump after lead shot was poured down its throat. The thought of pouring lead shot down Mark's throat to get him to stay in one place amused Jasper more than the story his friend had told. He looked away to hide his grin and fastened his eyes on a vision staring at him from the Bisque Biscuit's window.

His grin froze, his pulse raced, and his heart stopped.

Though it was difficult to make out her features through the diner's paned glass, her image filled his chest with a sudden warmth, making it difficult for him to breathe. He blinked, and when he opened his eyes, her profile was turned to him.

It had been a while since he'd been to the diner. Perhaps now was a good time to stop in. He wouldn't mind a midmorning snack of whatever pie was available today. He was about to step off the sidewalk when Mark grabbed his arm and pointed down the street.

"Isn't that Elsie?" he asked. "I thought she planned to spend the morning with the church missionary society. That's what she told me when I asked her to go canoeing on the river with me. You don't suppose she said that just to get out of going, do you? Why would she do that?"

Jasper shifted his gaze to where Mark pointed.

"Looks like Elsie."

"Is she going into the telegraph office?" Disbelief deepened Mark's usual frivolous tone. "Why would she be going in there?"

"I guess she wants to send a telegraph."

"To who?" Mark demanded.

Surprised by the change in Mark's mood, Jasper stared at him. A scowl replaced Mark's sometimes jovial, sometimes sardonic, but almost always present grin.

"Who knows?" he answered. "Maybe she's picking up a telegram."

Mark's scowl darkened.

Jasper grew perturbed. "Elsie has her own little secrets. They keep her busy, I suppose." Why should Mark care what Elsie was doing? Was he that miffed she'd refused his invitation to canoe? Such a strange thing to invite her to do in the first place. Mark knew better than just about anyone that Elsie wasn't fond of the water. And he knew why.

She'd almost fallen into the pond that winter Mark dared her to race him to the other side. The ice cracked between her feet, and one of her legs dropped into the freezing water. Thankfully, Mark had pulled her away from the break before she slipped in the rest of the way.

"What kind of secrets?" Mark demanded.

"The newest way to can preserves? The fastest way to make a bed?" Jasper darted his glance to the diner, but now the booth was empty. Where had the woman gone? She couldn't have come out the door—he would have seen her. "With Elsie, one never knows. Not that it matters. I need to get back to the office."

Without waiting for Mark to respond, or even waiting to see if he tagged along, Jasper strolled toward the factory. A cloud hung over him. One of suspicion and frustration and self-doubt. A cloud because of the burden he now carried as the sole owner of Kane Pottery. The suspicion because of the stolen designs. And frustration because the wrong setting on a mold almost ruined an entire run of mugs that morning. He couldn't afford for mistakes like that to happen. Something similar had happened with a run of bowls only last week.

A mistake? Or sabotage?

He shivered at the thought that one of his long-time employees could be capable of such a thing. That man, Isaac Matthews, from the P&I Detective Agency, had promised to return his call. Perhaps Jasper should ask him to look into that too, even though the very idea of accusing any of his employees stuck a dagger in his heart.

How could any of them try to harm the company when his father had done everything possible to keep them all employed during the leanest of times?

Perhaps they didn't trust Jasper to run the operation as efficiently and competently as his dad. And there was the self-doubt. Dogging his every step and his every decision.

When he got back to the office, he'd call Isaac Matthews again. He needed help.

Chapter Three

A confident but unassuming air. Hair pulled into a tight bun at the nape of her neck. Wire-rimmed spectacles. Goodbye, Polly Matthews, co-owner of the P&I Detective Agency. Hello, Polly Martin, lowly office clerk and newest employee of Kane Pottery.

That was, if she successfully balanced her "I belong here" persona with a humble demeanor meant to lower the guard of anyone who might challenge her.

Polly stared at her reflection in the speckled mirror over the sink in the diner's restroom, tilting her head first one way then the other. Satisfied with her appearance now that she'd removed all traces of rouge and lip color, she rolled her shoulders into what she called her "spinster slouch." From experience, she knew that few people would give her a second look as she walked right past them.

Since she'd already paid the bill before discreetly asking Lavonne if she could please use the facilities, she made her way out the diner's back door. Not long after, she drove across the railroad tracks on the outskirts of town, parked in the Kane Pottery lot, and entered through the big double doors.

She took a second to get her bearings, quickly noting the bespectacled receptionist speaking into a telephone on her left, the short hallway in front of her that led to closed metal doors, and the row of desks to her right where three women tapped on typewriter keys.

Polly strode to the door as if she'd been doing so every day of her life. From her peripheral vision, she noted the receptionist's expression change from surprise to puzzlement to uncertainty. She could practically read the woman's thought processes. *Stop the interloper. Don't be rude to the person on the other end of the line. I don't recognize that woman heading for the factory floor, but she seems to know where she's going. What to do, what to do?*

Before the woman could settle on a decision, Polly passed two rooms opening off the hallway and was through the metal doors. Once again, she quickly assessed her surroundings. Here, everyone was too busy focusing on their own tasks to pay her any mind.

The factory floor was huge but appeared to be divided into separate work areas. The central space rose two stories with a mezzanine along one side.

Across the space, Polly spied exactly what she needed. A woman about her own age and carrying a stack of folders was coming her way. Polly pretended to be interested in a framed print on a nearby wall until the woman was almost next to her. With a perfectly timed step, Polly turned into the woman, and the folders skidded from her arms onto the floor.

"What did I do?" Polly covered her mouth and widened her eyes in horror. "I'm most sorry for my clumsiness." She dropped to her knees and gathered the folders and loose papers into an untidy pile. "This is what I do on my first day. I should leave now before I get thrown out." Her voice dropped as she mumbled, "Oh, no, oh, no."

"Don't be so hard on yourself." The woman, an attractive brunette wearing a blue dress and black heels, knelt beside Polly and tried to stack the pile into some semblance of order. "No harm done.

I can straighten these out in no time." The slight edge in her tone indicated she didn't look forward to that task, but helpfulness and courtesy won out over her frustration.

Polly had counted on that based on the woman's kind eyes and quickness to smile. Another type of woman, one with a hard set to her chin and wariness in her eyes, would have castigated Polly with a verbal barrage. Not that Polly wasn't prepared for that response. She'd have pretended to be cowed to give the woman the sense of power she obviously craved.

But with this kindhearted woman, Polly played the friend in need. The ploy worked.

"Your first day," the woman exclaimed. "Welcome to Kane Pottery. I'm Vivian Ayers."

"Polly Martin," she replied. By using her mother's maiden name, Polly honored the woman who'd encouraged her imagination and playacting throughout her childhood.

"Have you been employed to work in the office, or in the factory?"

"The office." Polly allowed a small smile while she handed the woman a folder that had skidded behind her. "I've been hired on a temporary basis to help with filing and organizing records now that Mr. Jasper Kane has taken over the company."

Polly needed to tread carefully here. She didn't want to inadvertently insult her new friend in case this woman was in charge of the files, and she wasn't that interested in what were probably invoices, correspondence, and production data. The idea of pretending to be an employee had come to her while she stared at Jasper through the diner window. This cover would allow her to move freely around the company so she could evaluate security and gain an understanding of how the employees felt about their new boss.

After all, the most likely thief was someone who worked for the company.

"Let me put these where they belong, and I'll take you to Mr. Kane." Vivian led the way back through the metal doors.

"There's no need to bother Mr. Kane," Polly said. "I'm sure he's busy with other matters. It can't be easy, after his father's recent passing, to suddenly be the one in charge."

"It's a heavy responsibility, to be sure. But he's doing as well as he can. We've only experienced a few snags here and there."

Polly's detective antennae alerted. "What kind of snags?"

"I'm not sure, except that a couple of recent runs had to be halted because of quality control issues."

"That's unusual?"

Vivian shrugged and opened one of the hallway doors. "It happens, but very rarely. No one thought too much of it happening once. But two times so close together is odd. I suppose it's the kind of thing that happens when people are nervous."

The door opened into a square room lined with filing cabinets. Wooden tables holding stacks of folders and papers were arranged in the middle of the room. Polly silently congratulated herself for choosing a file clerk as her cover story. The business obviously needed help in that area.

"Why are people nervous?" she asked. "Don't they like the new boss?"

"We all like Mr. Jasper. I mean Mr. Kane." The woman gave a light, self-deprecating chuckle. "It's not easy calling him something different when he's been Mr. Jasper all his life and Mr. Kane was, well, Mr. Kane. Everyone respected Mr. Kane, especially when he made sure none of us lost our jobs or went hungry during these awful years. Not everyone could have done what he did. In fact, not everyone did. But the son is a good man too."

Polly waited, trusting that in the silence the woman would complete her unspoken thought. But if Vivian had doubts about Jasper's ability to run the factory as efficiently as his father, she was prudent enough to keep them to herself. Out of loyalty to the company, or to the father, or to the son? Polly couldn't say which.

Vivian placed the unwieldy stack she carried on one of the tables then divided it into two piles. "Have you had a tour of the facility yet?"

"No, but I'd love one."

"Great." Vivian tapped the files. "These can wait a few minutes. I'll show you around and introduce you to a few folks."

Polly did her best to remember the names of the people she met while Vivian chattered about the process. They went from one station to another, following the path from raw clay to finished product and ending in the warehouse where orders were packaged for shipping. Afterward they returned to the room with the filing cabinets and Vivian explained the different sections.

"I'll put those files we dropped back in order while you get started with those." Vivian pointed to another table. "They've already been sorted, so now they only need to be filed. I'll be here if you have any questions."

The work wasn't difficult. Look at a file, determine where it needed to go in the huge bank of files, and shove it in. But the repetition of the task was mind-numbingly boring. Polly got through the long hours by playing mental games and reminding herself that this was only temporary. The job-that-wasn't-a-job got her into the factory. Filing the paperwork provided her with a glimpse into the operations of the manufacturing plant, though it didn't take long for her eyes to glaze over.

She found examples of the different kinds of paperwork—receipts, inventory information, employee records—needed to keep a business running, but she didn't come across any files or any paperwork at all that had to do with designs. Perhaps those files were kept somewhere else.

Lunchtime came, and Polly politely refused Vivian's invitation to join her and the women from the typing pool at a picnic table under a covered pavilion. Though she wouldn't have minded the opportunity to learn the local gossip, she didn't want to answer any questions about her own background. Not yet anyway, despite having a cover story ready.

Instead, she went to the Reed's Mansion boardinghouse, told Miss Marla that Lavonne from Bisque Biscuit Diner had sent her, and was warmly welcomed as a new guest. When she learned that Polly was on her lunch break from her new job at Kane Pottery, Miss Marla even fixed her an egg salad sandwich.

Later that afternoon, Vivian gave Polly a few folders to take to the shipping department. On her way, Polly passed through the factory and glanced up at the mezzanine area. From her angle, there was no way to know if Jasper was in his office, since he wasn't standing by the glass and looking down on his workers.

She walked past the shelving that held recently glazed pottery. Vivian had told her that the items on these shelves were rotated to the inventory area and from there to the shipping department as needed.

Drawn to the rich blues and greens, the vibrant purples, and the luscious yellows, Polly wandered up one aisle and down the other to admire the lovely bowls, cups, pitchers, and serving dishes. These items were similar to ones she'd seen in department stores and catalogs. She'd rounded the end of one aisle when the murmur of voices caught her attention.

Unable to resist the lure of a whispered conversation, Polly quietly approached the sound while staying hidden by the shelves.

"It isn't fair, Jasper," a feminine voice said. "We have to find a solution."

"I'm not trying to cheat you, Elsie," a masculine voice replied. "But you're asking me to do the impossible."

Elsie? She was Jasper's sister.

Upstanding and honest Polly knew she should leave instead of eavesdropping on the private conversation.

Polly the Pinkerton-trained detective wasn't about to move.

"I know more about how things work than you think I do." Elsie's harsh whisper was filled with frustration. "Since I don't have a say in how anything is done around here anyway, you should buy me out. Then the company will be all yours."

"You haven't been listening. I don't have the money to buy you out. Why can't you understand that?"

"I don't believe you. This is a profitable company. If the only option for me to have my money is to sell it, then that's what we need to do."

The only reply was a heavy sigh.

"Say something, Jasper. Say you'll at least try, or I'll…I'll…talk to an attorney."

"An attorney?" A pause. "Is that who you're sending telegrams to?"

"What are you talking about?"

Without even seeing Elsie's face, Polly knew from her defensive tone that Elsie was up to something that she didn't want Jasper to know about.

"Mark and I saw you enter the telegraph office this morning." There was no triumph in Jasper's voice. Only a weariness. Maybe even sadness.

Polly's heart went out to both siblings. She knew the difficulty of mourning parents who died too soon. And she knew the tension that an inheritance could cause even between siblings who were otherwise close.

Elsie didn't reply, but light footsteps hurried away from the area followed by Jasper calling his sister's name. His own, heavier, footsteps sounded, leaving Polly alone in the shelves.

If Elsie had indeed contacted an attorney for advice on forcing her brother to sell, could she also be desperate enough to steal her brother's designs?

Chapter Four

Jasper couldn't remember a time when he and his sister had been so at odds. After a silent supper where Elsie barely responded to his compliment on the meal, Jasper retired to his study.

Not to his father's study, which smelled of oiled leather, old books, and the aftershave his dad favored. Jasper hadn't stepped foot in that room since the dramatic reading of the will that occurred a few days after the funeral.

Father would have appreciated each moment of the production. The family attorney, who could have played a memorable Ebenezer Scrooge in any production of *A Christmas Carol*, presided over the proceedings. He sat ramrod straight in Father's chair, folded his hands on Father's desk, and eyed each of those in attendance before clearing his aged throat.

"We are gathered here this day," he'd intoned in his rich baritone, "for the formal reading of the last will and testament of Edmund Halverton Kane, Esquire." The words had sent shivers down Jasper's spine.

Someday he'd need to get over the irrational sense that he didn't belong in that study. But for now, Father's presence loomed too large within those four walls for Jasper to feel comfortable within them. It was difficult enough to close his eyes to his father's lingering presence in the factory office.

One step, one day, at a time.

The study he preferred, which he'd claimed as a teen, was on the opposite side of the large stone house. Where Father's study had a view of the road leading from town and the formal driveway, allowing him to note the comings and goings of others if he had a mind to do so, Jasper's study overlooked the gentle slope into the valley behind the house. The weeping willows lining the stream that meandered through the meadow and the far woods inspired him with their seasonal colors and changing features.

Jasper settled on an upholstered couch and flipped through his sketches of another potential line of artistic pottery he hoped to manufacture, a spring-inspired line of soft tones featuring hummingbirds and butterflies. But the sketches did nothing to soothe the uneasiness in his soul or give him answers for any of his many problems.

Which, at this moment, centered on his sister.

Jasper was almost five when Elsie came into the world. He could remember his first peek at his only sibling as if it were yesterday. She wore a pink gown trimmed with lace and satin ribbons. Blond fuzz covered her head, and she was screaming her displeasure. Jasper touched her soft cheek with his finger and whispered, "Don't cry, Elsie. I'm your big brother, and I'll always take care of you."

As if she'd understood each word, her eyes blinked open and her sobbing ceased. Somehow, she'd grabbed hold of his finger and clutched it in her tight fist. He was smitten.

But that was a memory Elsie didn't have. Or, if she did, it was locked too deep in her heart for her to recall it. The most he could hope for was that she remembered the feeling of always being safe, always being cared for, that he'd spent his lifetime trying to give her.

A feeling that was shattered when their father's will was read. Beside him on the leather sofa, Elsie's body had stiffened when the attorney announced the pittance she'd inherited. Her mouth opened, but she said no words, made no sounds. A solitary tear slipped from the corner of her eye and trailed down her cheek.

She'd been betrayed, and Jasper felt the betrayal almost as deeply as she did.

"It should be more," he'd said to her. He then repeated the words to the attorney, who gave a *Bah! Humbug!* shrug.

"This is Edmund Kane's last wish." The attorney made the pronouncement and pressed his lips together while Elsie quietly stood and left the room.

Jasper started after her, but the attorney stopped him. "Our business is not yet complete. The formality must continue."

As obedient to the odious man as he'd ever been to his father, Jasper returned to his seat and endured the monotonous listing of the remaining bequests.

He wished now, as he'd done so often since then, that he'd remembered that the attorney worked for him, not the other way around. He should have gone after Elsie and provided her the comfort and assurances she'd needed. If he had, perhaps she'd be more understanding of their present predicament.

Jasper closed the sketchbook and tossed it on a nearby table. A spring-focused line could wait for a few months anyway. Right now, he should be focused on a Christmas line. If he wanted to produce one, the molds needed to be made, the designs tweaked, the glazes formulated, the photographs taken, and the marketing materials and order forms created in the next few weeks, or he'd have to wait until next year.

His head hurt thinking of all the tasks that needed to be accomplished to take advantage of the holiday shopping season. He'd put off his plans long enough. Though perhaps that had turned out for the best. Otherwise, Vernon Spears might have gotten his Christmas ideas instead of the ones for the autumn line. That would have been disastrous.

Leaning forward, and with his elbows propped on his knees, he rubbed his temples. Twice during the day he'd called the number to the P&I Detective Agency, but no one had answered the call either time. Perhaps he should drive there tomorrow. Zanesville wasn't that far away, and if he left first thing in the morning, he'd be back before his luncheon appointment with a longtime supplier.

Any action was better than no action, as Father had been fond of saying.

Jasper tapped his knees and walked to his desk. He'd call the agency first thing in the morning, but if no one answered, he'd make the drive. Even if no one was at the detective agency's office or they couldn't provide him the help he needed, the trip wouldn't be a waste of time. A leisurely drive on a nice summer day, all by himself, would give him time to think and plan and perhaps even figure out answers to a few of his more pressing problems.

Since he wanted to go alone, he needed to leave early. Mark had a habit of dropping by without an invitation, both here at Stone House and at the factory. If he found out Jasper planned a trip to Zanesville, no doubt he'd want to tag along.

Jasper hadn't yet told his friend about the theft or his fruitless conversation with Vernon Spears. He definitely didn't want to have that conversation all the way to Zanesville and back again. Especially since Mark was almost as upset as Elsie at the reading of the will. Though his presence had been requested, he'd received nothing except a box of memorabilia. A cruel trick from beyond the grave, and one Jasper didn't understand and couldn't even try to excuse. After his initial shock, Mark had put on a brave front. Even said it didn't matter that the bequest wasn't a monetary one—he hadn't expected anything anyway.

But how could he not have? Why else was he asked to attend? After all, the box could have been shipped to him.

Besides, there would be no Kane Pottery if not for the initial investment provided by Mark's father at the company's beginnings. When Mr. Gleason moved to North Carolina to start his own pottery company, one that later failed, the partnership between him and Edmund Kane was dissolved. Though the relationship between the partners had soured, Jasper and Mark had managed to remain friends. Jasper had traveled to North Carolina a few years ago to support his friend when Mr. Gleason died in a drowning accident.

Still, sometimes friendships flourished best at a distance. Jasper was grateful for Mark's support in recent weeks. But he wasn't sure why he was still in town. Scouting out business opportunities, Mark had said, but he never gave any details. Jasper had the sense that he'd made an insincere promise to the wrong young lady and was staying away from home until her family's ire lessened.

Jasper didn't want to spend the drive to Zanesville listening to Mark brag about his romantic entanglements any more than he wanted to talk about Vernon Spears. But avoiding Mark was only one reason not to go into the factory in the morning. If he showed up, he'd inevitably be drawn into conversations and maybe even a phone call or two, which would delay his leaving, which might delay his return.

He needed to have everything he wanted to take with him packed and ready to go tonight. Which meant a late-night trip into town.

He found Elsie in the front parlor embroidering a pillowcase while listening to *Mercury Theater on the Air* on the radio. Orson Welles hosted the program's dramatizations of literary classics. As soon as he entered, Elsie's cheeks flushed and she slipped an envelope beneath the pillowcase. Though he was tempted to ask what she was hiding, he wasn't in the mood for the argument that would surely follow such a question.

"What novel are they performing?" he asked instead, more as a peace offering than because he was interested.

Elsie didn't look at him. "*The Thirty-Nine Steps* by John Buchan."

"I've read it. It's—"

"I'm trying to listen to it."

"Right." He waited a beat then spoke quickly. "I'm going to the factory, but I won't be gone long."

"Why now?" She clipped the question as short as if she were cutting a piece of floss with her tiny golden scissors.

Jasper paused, inwardly debating how to answer. Like Mark, she didn't know about Vernon's unethical move. He'd dreaded telling her when she was already so upset about the factory. And also, truth be told, because he didn't want to hand her any ammunition she could use against him. Elsie wanted the family business sold to whoever would buy it. It wouldn't help his cause for her to know that an interested party was waiting in the wings for him to fail.

The thought made Jasper ill. He dreaded being the one who lost Kane Pottery, especially after his father sacrificed so much to keep it going through the worst of the Depression.

The company might not be in the best shape right now. But Jasper had to do whatever was necessary to keep them afloat until they could make a decent profit again.

"I need a few papers I forgot to bring home."

She glared at him over her half-moon spectacles. "That can't wait until tomorrow?"

"Afraid not." He turned and left the room before she could ask him anything else.

A short time later, he unlocked a side door at the factory and used a flashlight to make his way through the familiar building. He decided not to turn on any lights because he didn't want anyone driving by to see them and report a possible break-in to the sheriff. That kind of publicity wasn't in his best interests.

As he entered the factory floor, a beam of light swept across the upper half of the vast space. Startled, he instinctively retreated into the shadows and flicked off his flashlight. The beam came from his office.

Had the thief returned to steal more of his designs?

If so, the miscreant was in for a surprise.

Jasper bent over and trotted to the stairs. Being mindful to bypass the familiar creaks, he climbed the steps to the second floor and peered around the corner. His office door stood ajar.

He crouched below the molding that separated the half-wall's solid lower section from the upper section of glass and raised his head enough to see inside. A small figure dressed in black rummaged through a stack of papers on his desk.

Still crouching, Jasper made his way around the corner and along the wall to the door. When he reached it, he straightened, threw open the door, rushed inside, and flicked on his flashlight.

The beam shone on his desk, but the figure was gone. Bewildered, he started to scan the office when gloved fingers gripped his wrist, the flashlight was tugged from his hand, his body spun around and up and over as if he'd lost all control, and he fell flat on his back. He groaned and tried to sit up, but a black boot pressed against his chest.

He peered up at his attacker, but a bright light blinded him. He closed his eyes and turned his head.

The figure gasped and stepped backward. The flashlight beam slanted across him.

"You're Jasper Kane."

He must be unconscious and dreaming. The black-clad attacker sounded like a woman. A young woman. Once again, he tried to sit up. This time, the black boot didn't stop him. He peered through slitted eyes at the darker shadow near his desk.

"Who are you?"

"I'm so sorry." The woman knelt beside him. "You weren't supposed to be here. Are you all right? I didn't hurt you too badly, did I? That wasn't my intent."

Jasper arched his back and rubbed the ache where he'd hit the floor. "Are you sure about that?"

As he rose, the shadow took him by the arm and helped him to a chair. "Whoever you are," he continued, "you're not supposed to be here either."

She took the seat beside him and positioned the flashlight to direct the beam toward the ceiling. In the meager sidelight cast by the beam, a pale face emerged. She pulled a black cap from her head, and blond waves framed her wholesome features.

"I don't know much of anything about being a thief," Jasper said, "but I don't recall ever hearing about one who stayed around to chat with the victim instead of running away."

"Oh, I'm not a thief," she exclaimed, her eyes wide. "I'm here to help you discover your thief."

Jasper stared then tilted his head. There was something familiar about this woman. Where had he seen her before? He stared at her, and she stared back at him.

"I know you," he said. "You're the woman I saw this morning at the Bisque Biscuit Diner."

But what in the world is she doing here?

CHAPTER FIVE

Polly almost dropped the flashlight and stumbled to set it upright again. "You saw me at the diner?"

"Through the window." A slight grin lifted the corners of Jasper's mouth. "Then I blinked, and you were gone. I never expected to find you in my office." He glanced at the desk. "Or to find out you're a criminal. Breaking and entering is a crime, you know."

"I shouldn't have done it, that's true." Isaac would never forgive her. "But I was testing your security. And perhaps being a bit nosy."

"A bit?"

"Perhaps too much."

Jasper tried to feign exasperation, but Polly believed he was secretly amused. That was a point in her favor because she definitely did *not* want to be arrested.

"Please tell me who you are."

"I'm Polly Matthews, the *P* in P&I Detective Agency, at your service. *P* for Polly."

"But you're a woman."

Polly bit the inside of her lip and pressed down the irritated sigh that threatened to erupt. "Yes, I am," she said primly. "That is an astute observation on your part."

"I didn't mean any—"

"I am also a graduate of the Pinkerton Detective Agency's training course, where I took top honors. You are familiar with the Pinkertons, I assume."

Jasper's eyes sparkled with amusement. "I've heard of them."

"I know you talked to my brother yesterday. He's the *I* in P&I Detective Agency. *I* for Isaac."

"That's right. He said he'd be in touch, but I haven't heard from him."

"Unfortunately, he was unavailable." She smiled her most engaging smile. "So I came instead."

"Instead of returning my call?"

"Like I said, I wanted to test your security. Find out more about your company before I made my presence known."

While she talked, Jasper's expression shifted from surprise to interest to something she couldn't quite name. Perhaps understanding mingled with regret? But regret about what?

"You mean you felt the need to prove yourself," he said. "Because you were afraid that I'd prefer to have your brother take my case instead of you."

"Another astute observation."

"One, I'm sorry to say, that I wish wasn't true." He shifted in his seat and stared at the darkened glass. His thoughts no longer seemed to be with Polly, but somewhere else entirely. Perhaps his sister? Though Polly was glad to have firsthand knowledge of their family dynamics, since a good detective *needed* to know such things, she wished she hadn't eavesdropped on their argument. She wouldn't have wanted anyone to eavesdrop on her and Isaac when they had their spats.

The detective profession had its downsides. This was definitely one of them.

Suddenly Jasper turned back to her. "I'm glad I showed up tonight. You saved me a trip to Zanesville."

Polly gave him a questioning look.

"I planned to drive there in the morning, since no one answered my calls today," he explained. "But now that you're here, illegally in my office, I guess I need to decide whether to call the sheriff and have you arrested or hire you on the spot."

Polly's heart dropped to her stomach when Jasper said *illegally* and to her knees when he mentioned *the sheriff* and to her toes when he said *arrested.* She was so eager to prove herself to her client that she'd made at least two mistakes.

First, Jasper Kane wasn't yet her client. Second, until she'd gotten caught, she hadn't considered the consequences of getting caught.

"I didn't expect you to come back once you'd left," she said.

"Normally I wouldn't have except in an emergency. But I needed to pick up a few items so I could leave from home in the morning instead of stopping by here."

"What kind of items?" Polly tilted the vertical flashlight beam toward Jasper though she was careful not to blind him. If she did anything to annoy him further, he might just make that call to the sheriff. Then Isaac would have to bail her out of jail and he'd forbid her from ever taking on another case for the rest of her days.

She shivered. How dull life would be if she could never have adventures like this one. Adrenaline energized her, sharpening her senses and testing her mettle. She had to admit that the thrill of danger had more to do with her nighttime foray into the depths of the mammoth structure that made up Kane Pottery than any other excuse her imagination could offer up.

Jasper's hand closed around the flashlight. As he took it from her, his fingers brushed against hers. Even through her thin gloves, his touch ignited something within her stronger than adrenaline. She wanted to see his face, to know he'd felt it too, but he'd shifted to point the beam to a nearby lamp. He turned it on, and a soft pool of light surrounded them.

"That's better." Jasper switched off the flashlight and smiled at Polly.

Heat warmed her cheeks. He must think her mad, the way she was dressed in a black jacket that reached past her hips and thick tights. Her unruly waves probably sprang out in all directions after escaping the dark cap. She removed her gloves, more for something to do than any practical reason, and settled deeper into the chair.

Jasper left the circle of light to pull a thin catalog from a shelf behind the desk. He handed it to Polly as he returned to his seat.

"This is the latest retailers' catalog from Spears Ceramics," he said. "Vernon Spears, the owner of the company, sent it out to his buyers not long ago. That means he's now taking orders from department stores, gift shops, and probably a few grocery stores. Any place that wants to sell something he manufactures. He even sent samples to his showroom in New York City."

Polly listened intently as she opened the catalog. The first page displayed a thank-you letter signed by Vernon Spears. He promised quality products, timely delivery, and prices guaranteed to allow his buyers to make a profit.

The next page featured photographs of a variety of figurines and vases beneath a heading that read *Autumn Decor. Invite fall into your home.*

"These are lovely." Polly gathered the courage to raise her eyes to Jasper's. "I expected the catalog to show more practical items. Like dinnerware and serving platters."

"Those products are in the catalog too." Jasper pressed his finger against the open page. "But this is the first time that Vernon has ever offered what we call 'artistic pottery.' It serves no particular function except to be decorative."

"His first time," Polly murmured, thinking about the note that Isaac had placed on her desk two days before. "These are your designs?"

Jasper's finger trailed down the page. "They were. Until someone sold them to Vernon."

"Who would do that?"

"Maybe one of my employees, though I find that hard to believe. Maybe Vernon stole them himself, though he denies it."

Polly listened carefully while Jasper recounted his telephone conversation with his competitor. She couldn't help but laugh a few times at Jasper's gift for mimicry. Mr. Spears sounded like a bombastic bully. But Jasper, chuckling himself, assured her that his imitation accurately portrayed the older man's speech.

"Shortly after hanging up," Jasper said, "I remembered seeing your agency's advertisement in our local paper."

"So you called us and talked to Isaac."

"That's right." Jasper released a quiet sigh then stood. "I should be getting home before Elsie starts to worry. Why don't you come back in the morning and I'll show you around the factory? We can talk more then."

Polly feigned a guilty expression. "Vivian Ayers gave me the tour today," she confessed. When Jasper's eyes narrowed in confusion, she enthused, "It's an amazing process. I wasn't aware of all the steps and decisions that go into making even the simplest bowl. I find it fascinating."

"Why would Vivian give you a tour? She didn't say anything to me about that."

"Because..." Polly twisted her gloves and put on the contrite expression she'd practiced during training. It wasn't that hard to pretend. To her surprise, she did feel sorry for her deception. Naturally, she wanted to make a good impression on her client—though she supposed he was still a *potential* client, since they hadn't discussed terms and fees—but the regret went beyond Jasper as client. She was sorry she'd deceived Jasper the man. The theft of his designs obviously affected him more deeply than simply anger at Vernon's nefarious attempt to make money from products he had no right to produce.

She stared at the page again and imagined Jasper putting pencil to paper to create the artwork that preceded the delightful images in the catalog. This theft was personal. That realization deepened the effect this case had on her too. Now it was personal to her in a way it hadn't been before.

When she first came to Crooksville, her goal was to solve a client's case to prove to Isaac that she was a competent detective who shouldn't be stuck behind a desk.

But now she wanted to solve the case for Jasper.

That desire breached one of the ground rules for any competent detective—don't become personally involved. Doing so was a sure path to losing objectivity.

Polly refused to believe it. In this case, wanting to help Jasper meant she'd do whatever was needed to uncover the thief's identity. Wasn't that what any good detective would do? Wasn't that what Isaac would do?

"Miss Matthews?" Jasper's voice pulled her from her thoughts. "Why did Vivian give you a tour?"

At least his question sounded merely curious and not accusatory.

"Because she thinks I work here." The words came out almost as if she were asking a question. Which, unfortunately, didn't demonstrate the professional demeanor of a highly-trained Pinkerton graduate.

Jasper appeared momentarily stunned. "Why would she think that?"

Polly rose from her seat. Though the top of her head barely reached his nose, at least he no longer towered over her. "I wanted to get an inside view of your business. So I told her I'd been hired as a file clerk."

Jasper's eyes grew bigger.

"She gave me a tour, and then I spent most of the day filing." No need to tell him, at least not yet and maybe never, about how she'd eavesdropped on his conversation with his sister. With the turn this conversation had taken, he'd probably order her off the premises and out of town. That was, if he didn't decide to call the sheriff and have her arrested.

"Filing?" Jasper sputtered. "You spent the day filing?"

"You don't need to worry. I know how to file." A year of secretarial school had taught her the basics of typing, filing, and even shorthand. "Nothing got lost or misplaced. Vivian said I was a natural."

She said the last sentence with pride, even though Vivian's compliment wasn't the kind she wanted. Not when her ambitions were so much higher than having a clear grasp of the alphabet.

Jasper stared at her. Then a strange gurgle seemed to grip his chest, crawl up his throat, and burst forth into a bout of laughter that soon had him perched on the edge of his chair, his hands covering his face while tears poured down his cheeks. A few moments later, the laughter slowed. He took one look at her, sputtered something about filing, and the gurgle burst forth again.

"It's not that funny," Polly declared, unsure if she should feel insulted or simply appreciate his good humor. After all, no one who laughed that hard was likely to have her arrested.

The second time Jasper's guffaws subsided into chuckles, he strode to a filing cabinet behind his desk and opened a drawer. He pulled out a couple of forms, stuck them in a folder, and handed them to Polly.

"This is a job application. Fill it out and bring it to me first thing in the morning. We'll talk more then." He pulled a watch from his pocket and checked the time. "Where are you staying while you're in town?"

"Lavonne at the diner suggested Reed's Mansion. Miss Marla rented me a lovely room." Though Polly hadn't spent much time in the small room, her first impression had been favorable.

Jasper simply nodded as if he had other things on his mind now that he'd come to his senses. "I didn't see a car outside. How did you get from the boardinghouse to here?"

Polly couldn't have kept from smiling even if she'd been promised a new frock in exchange for a frown. What was the fun in driving from Point A to Point B when one could slink along dark alleys, hide in the shadows, and sprint undetected from one building to another? True, she'd probably done more slinking, hiding, and sprinting than was absolutely necessary, since the streets of Crooksville were deserted at this time on a weeknight. Still, she'd relished each nerve-tingling minute.

"I came on foot."

"Dare I ask how you managed to get inside?" Jasper asked.

Polly pulled her lock-picking kit from her jacket pocket and held it up with a sheepish grin. "The back door, the one by the loading dock, took less than ten seconds to open."

Reluctant admiration gleamed in Jasper's light brown eyes, which were as attractive as Lavonne had suggested. He returned Elsie's flashlight then flicked his own beam on. "We have a great deal to talk about in the morning," he said as he switched off the lamp. "Come on. I'll drive you to Miss Marla's."

Polly aimed her flashlight at the ground as she accompanied him out of the building. When they reached his car, a gorgeous late-model Packard, he opened the passenger door for her. She started to get in then hesitated.

"Thank you for not having me arrested. It might have been more prudent for me to simply enter your office and introduce myself."

"Maybe." Jasper lifted his shoulder in a careless shrug then winked. "But not nearly as much fun."

CHAPTER SIX

When Jasper entered his office and spied the young woman standing by the picture of his father taken at the ribbon-cutting ceremony for the opening of the factory, he did a double take. Instead of a tousle-haired, black-clad sprite, the woman in front of him wore a frumpy skirt, stretched-out cardigan, and wire-rim spectacles. Her blond hair was pulled back into a tight bun that downplayed her attractiveness. Still, she was adorable in his eyes. Too adorable for a man who'd devoted his life to a father, sister, and pottery company.

"Miss Matthews," he said, "I almost didn't recognize you."

"It's Miss Martin," she gently corrected. "I'm using my mother's maiden name while I'm undercover."

"Good idea," he stage-whispered. As he rounded his desk, he gestured to a chair. "Please, have a seat."

She perched on the edge of the chair and slid a folder across the desk. "My application, as requested."

He pushed it aside. "Good. You're hired."

"As Miss Martin, or as Miss Matthews?" Her teasing grin warmed a place in his heart that he never knew existed. Having discovered it, he longed to hold on to it.

Despite that distraction, he responded with a grin of his own. "Both."

"We haven't discussed fees."

"Or wages," he countered.

Her gentle laugh somehow made him think of Tinker Bell, the fairy from Neverland who drank poison to save Peter Pan's life. Father and Mother had taken Jasper and Elsie to see the play once when they were in Louisville for a business trip. Father's business associate had arranged for the family to go backstage after the play to meet the cast.

Jasper was about eight or nine at the time, and he immediately fell for the actress who'd played Tinker Bell and laughed with such mischievous abandon. The memory warmed him even as Polly now enchanted him.

A feeling he needed to set aside no matter how difficult or how lonely it left him. Their relationship was a professional one and should stay that way. Despite how impossible it had been to push her out of his mind since he'd first laid eyes on her at the diner. And more than impossible after their unexpected meeting the night before.

She'd insisted that he park a block away from the boarding-house so no one would see her get out of his car. He'd obliged but stayed parked beneath a giant oak to be sure she got safely inside. Not that there was much danger of anything happening to her. Not in Crooksville—despite its name.

Instead of going through the front door, though, she stopped beneath a maple with low-lying limbs, gave him a pert wave, and then climbed up the tree and inside the boardinghouse through a second-floor window. Another wave, and then the window closed and the curtain was drawn.

Jasper had sat in his Packard and laughed out loud then driven home, chuckling to himself all along the way.

Incredible to think that same woman now sat across from him, as prim, proper, and strait-laced as a maiden aunt whose only beau never returned from the war.

"I'm undercover," she said. "No wages needed. Our fee is a daily rate plus expenses."

Jasper readily agreed to the amount she quoted. "How do you plan to find the thief?"

"First by asking you questions. Who knew about the designs? Where did you keep them? Who had access to them?"

Jasper swiveled his chair to the credenza behind him and retrieved a stationery box from an inner shelf. After swiveling back, he placed the box on his desk and removed the lid.

"They're in here. All of them for the Autumn Decor line anyway." He pushed the box toward Polly, who set it on her lap. As she scanned through the drawings, he continued. "As you can see, I even came up with the name that Vernon used in his catalog."

"If they're still here, then how..." Her voice trailed off. "The thief must have taken photos of them. Or copied them, though that would have taken a great deal of time."

"Apparently anyone who knows how to pick a lock and wield a flashlight could spend hours in my office at night without anyone knowing." Even to his own ears, Jasper's tone seemed an odd mixture of frustration and teasing.

"Crooksville is a small town where everyone knows everyone," he continued. "Most of us were born here to families who were born here. Sure, we have the occasional bit of vandalism, usually teenage boys with more spirit than sense. It's an open secret where a man can get his hand on a jug of moonshine if that's his pleasure. But few doors are locked during the day, and I never would have thought I'd need to do more than lock down this place at night."

"Isaac and I grew up in a town like that," Polly said. "East of here, in Noble County. We'd probably be there now if we'd decided to do something other than open a detective agency."

"I wouldn't think Zanesville is a hotbed of crime and corruption."

Polly's lips turned up in a faint smile, and her eyes sparkled. But anyone looking into the office through the glass window would immediately peg her as what she still presented herself to be with the curve in her posture and her hands clasped on top of the stationery box—an unassuming woman other people tended to overlook.

Jasper admired the self-discipline it must take for her to maintain that demeanor. He couldn't help thinking how enjoyable it would be to learn more about all the various facets of Polly's personality. Such a hobby might take a lifetime. He didn't think he'd mind that.

"Zanesville is a fine town," she agreed. "It offers more opportunities for detecting than you might think. Besides, neither of us wanted to be small fish in a big pond. Too many other rivals. Our office is centrally located in a region with hardly any competitors."

"Which makes you the big fish in a small pond."

"You could say that. Isaac can easily travel by train to Cincinnati or Columbus when we get a lead on a potential case. Even Cleveland if necessary. He's in Chillicothe now."

"And you? Do you take cases in the big cities too?"

For the first time, the prim facade wavered, though only for a second or two. If Jasper hadn't been closely watching her, he might have missed it.

"I prefer less crowded places," she said.

Jasper nodded, signaling his acceptance of her excuse. But deep inside, he knew that was all it was. What was the real reason Polly was left behind to solve the mystery of stolen pottery designs while her brother covered what he must have considered a more exciting assignment? Jasper didn't need to be a detective to answer that question. Guilt stabbed his conscience as he recalled his recent argument with Elsie.

"Who else knows about this box?" Polly's question brought his attention back to the purpose for their meeting.

"You mean that the designs were in that box?" Jasper shrugged. "I don't know, but the designs aren't a secret. I've wanted to manufacture a decorative line of pottery for years. Father wasn't in favor of the idea though."

"Why not?"

"He didn't think the sales would be worth the investment."

"Vernon Spears must not have agreed. Or he wouldn't have gone to such lengths to steal your designs. I wonder why he did that instead of creating his own."

"You'd have to ask him."

"I might do that."

Jasper shot her a spontaneous grin. He didn't doubt she had the gumption to go toe-to-toe with the bombastic blowhard. Probably more than he did. In his own confrontation, he'd sounded almost apologetic, as if he were in the wrong.

"Aren't the designs copyrighted?" Polly asked.

"Not officially." Jasper shrugged as he explained. "Because of the expense and time involved, I wouldn't take those legal steps until I'd decided which designs I wanted to use. Maybe not even then unless a design became especially popular. The factories around here have always had a gentleman's agreement not to infringe on each other's work. That is, until now."

Polly nodded in understanding. "You said Mr. Spears bought the designs. But he refused to say from whom."

"That's right."

"Are you sure he's telling you the truth? Maybe he paid someone to steal them."

"I suppose that's possible. But even if he did, he'd never admit it."

Polly tilted her head as if in thought, and Jasper didn't interrupt her. He didn't want to stare, but he found it difficult to keep his eyes off her. He still couldn't get over how different she appeared now than last night. True, the lighting had been much dimmer then. Neither the flashlight nor the lamp had provided much light in the dark office.

The more Jasper watched Polly, the more he appreciated the subtle contours of her features and her command of her facial expressions. Such a gift to transform her appearance in this way. She probably would have made it big in Hollywood. An actress to rival Irene Dunne or Vivien Leigh. He wondered if Polly ever had such aspirations. Would it be unprofessional of him to ask her? Probably.

"Do you have other designs you could put into production?" Polly asked.

"Yes, but it might be a risk."

"A risk Vernon Spears is willing to take, but you aren't?"

Jasper would have been offended if anyone else asked him that question. But Polly managed to do so with no hint of judgment. She simply wanted to know, and that approach allowed him to consider his answer instead of responding in a defensive way.

"I think people are tired of making do. In recent months, we've seen an increase in orders for a few of our more expensive products. Even so, I have to admit that Vernon is more of a risk-taker than I am." He swiveled in his desk chair and glanced through the glass. From this angle, he could see Linus Vaughn inspecting a recent run of their classic bean pots.

Linus was the first employee Father hired when he opened the doors of Kane Pottery, and over the years he'd worked in practically every aspect of production. Even Father often said that Linus knew more about the hands-on operation of the pottery business than anyone else at the plant.

Jasper didn't doubt it, and he was grateful for Linus's expertise and his loyalty. Especially since he was another who'd seemed disappointed by the small bequest Edmund Kane had left him. Not that Linus said anything. Perhaps Jasper thought it was so because of what Linus hadn't said. And because of how Linus no longer whistled while he monitored the factory's workflow.

Jasper shifted back to Polly and folded his hands on his desk. "It was a point of pride with my father that none of our employees went without a paycheck during these past years. No one got a raise, but they maintained their jobs. Father could do that because he'd accumulated savings in our more bountiful years. These people deserve a raise, but if I put money into a new line that doesn't sell... It would be not only my loss but theirs too. And yet, if I don't take a chance now, Kane Pottery might lose any competitive advantage it may have. I can't let that happen either."

Polly didn't respond, but her steady gaze spoke volumes. Unlike most people he knew, including himself, she didn't have a need to fill a silence with words. Instead, her eyes told him that she understood the obligation he felt to his employees and how that obligation warred with his dreams.

He'd shared with her the thoughts he wrestled with on sleepless nights but had always kept to himself. He supposed Elsie, who was a witness to multiple discussions—even arguments—over the years between him and Father, had an inkling of how he felt. But he'd never discussed the issue with her.

So why was he baring his heart and soul to this stranger who one minute was a black-clad sprite and the next a dowdy file clerk?

No, not dowdy. At least, he could no longer see her that way. Intelligent, clever, and irrepressibly cute. That was how she appeared to his eyes.

A movement outside the glass caught his attention, and he turned to see Linus limping toward his door. Linus had come home from the Great War, his uniform adorned with medals that were now hidden away somewhere and an injury that never quite healed.

The man's face was set in a grimace that would do a stone troll proud as he flung open the office door without knocking.

"Young Jasper," Linus said, using the same form of address he'd used since Jasper was a child, "there's a matter needin' your attention."

He completely ignored Polly's presence, almost as if he didn't see her. For a quick second, Jasper wondered if she'd made herself invisible. Was that another trick she had up her sleeve? With one part of his mind, he chided himself for being ridiculous while the rest of him had the good sense to stand up and address his unwelcome intruder.

"Somethin' done messed up the glaze," Linus exclaimed. "Don't know how it could have happened, but you best come see."

He limped away before Jasper had a chance to respond. Jasper turned to Polly, who had stood and placed the stationery box on his desk. "I should go. We'll talk more later."

"Do you mind if I tag along?" she asked, then quirked one side of her mouth up in an adorable grin. "Or should I join Vivian in the filing room?"

"Come along with me," Jasper replied. "I think we need to find you a different job. You won't uncover much about the thievery if you're stuck with the filing cabinets."

He needed her on the factory floor, talking to his employees. Though he couldn't imagine any of them stealing his designs, what other explanation was there? Polly had asked him who had access to them. The better question might be who didn't.

CHAPTER SEVEN

As they descended the stairs, Polly's mind whirled with all the information she'd gleaned from talking with Jasper and with how much she still didn't know. It appeared that almost anyone employed at Kane Pottery could be a suspect. She needed to narrow down that list as quickly as possible. But Jasper was right—how could she do that while stuck in the filing room?

"I agree with you. I need a different cover story," she murmured to Jasper, who was one stairstep ahead of her.

He glanced back, eyes wide. "Any ideas?"

"Have you thought about creating a tribute to your father? I mean a kind of compilation of the company's history and his contributions to the community. That would give me an excuse to talk to, well, everyone."

"Excellent idea," he whispered over his shoulder. He stopped on the bottom step and turned back to her. "What will we tell Vivian? From file clerk to company historian in two days seems extraordinary."

"The truth might work. That I wanted to get a feeling for the atmosphere, how the place operated, before revealing my true reason for being here."

Jasper grinned. "Except you're still not revealing your true reason for being here."

"I'm only postponing it a little longer."

"I like the idea," he conceded. "Not just as a cover but as something we should do."

"I'll take careful notes then," she said, pleased that she'd come up with a suitable idea. Plus, it was another trick to tuck into her arsenal. She could easily imagine herself in the role of company historian for any business that the P&I Detective Agency needed to investigate.

Perhaps she would wear a pair of those pince-nez glasses instead of her wire rims and a cardigan that wasn't quite as faded as the one she wore today. A less severe bun would work too. Professional yet unintimidating. An overly large brooch and multiple rings would give her a look of eccentricity.

When they arrived at the glazing station, Linus pointed to two bean pots on a rack. The first resembled a bean pot that Polly had in her own kitchen. A deep, luscious brown glaze covered most of the round pot while the upper rim was covered in a creamy tan that flowed into the brown, creating a unique wavy line. She had a gravy boat and a fish tray with a similar design. The second bean pot originally had been dipped into the same brown glaze, but a hideous yellow tinged the creamy tan overflow.

"What happened here?" Jasper asked.

Three or four workers stood nearby, but none of them attempted an answer.

"The wrong pigment was obviously added to the glaze." Jasper's gaze shifted around the group. "It wouldn't be the first time. Who mixed this?"

A thin woman in a patterned flour sack dress, who appeared to be in her midthirties but could have been younger, hesitantly raised her hand. "I did, sir." Her voice faltered, and she rushed her words. "But I followed the instructions exactly, I know I did. But then this came out." She was almost in tears.

Linus glared at her. "You had to have made a mistake," he declared. "And now the entire batch will have to be thrown out. I'll make the new one myself so this doesn't happen again."

"You don't need to do that," Jasper said to Linus then switched his attention to the distraught woman. "Mrs. Pearson, please make up a new batch of the proper glaze so we can finish this run of bean pots."

"What about the ruined batch?" Linus asked. "A waste of money that was, and someone needs to be held responsible."

"I agree that it's not a very attractive glaze." Jasper eyed the bean pot then stepped closer and studied the odd coloring. "I may be able to do something with it though."

"Like what?" Polly blurted. The color was dreadful, and she couldn't imagine any housewife wanting it in her kitchen. When she realized that all eyes had turned on her after her outburst, she feigned a nervous smile. "Please forgive me. I know nothing about pottery, though I am anxious to learn."

"I have a few tricks up my sleeve." Jasper favored Polly with a smile and carried the pot to a different worktable.

Once Jasper was out of earshot, Linus scowled. "Always wantin' to fix what don't need fixin', that one."

He jerked his head toward Jasper and worked his mouth. Polly was fairly certain that if he'd been chewing tobacco at the moment, a stream of the vile juice would have already flown to the cement floor. Such a dirty habit but one too common among the older men in the region. A couple of the elderly women too, who made their homes way back in the hollows of the Appalachian foothills.

Polly pasted on her prettiest smile and softened her gaze. "But something does need fixing," she said calmly. "Isn't it worth trying to make it better if he can?"

Linus grunted. "His pappy was fine with doin' what we did year in and year out. Old Edmund never took to young Jasper's ideas when he was alive, and I don't see how his dyin' changed much. This company needs to stick with what's worked to get us through the hard days instead of wastin' time and money on newfangled folderol ideas."

As he talked, Polly maintained her pleasant composure even though her detection sense was on full alert. Interesting that Linus was against implementing Jasper's ideas. Was he against the new line enough to sell the designs to his boss's competitor?

Maybe. Maybe not.

What mattered most was that Polly had her first suspect.

"Miss Matthews," Jasper called. "Come and tell me what you think of this."

Polly inwardly cringed that Jasper had called her by the wrong name, but to correct him would draw too much attention to the mistake. All she could do was join him at the table.

Linus hadn't been included in the invitation, but he limped along beside her, the scowl still darkening his features. The others joined them too. Apparently, everyone was interested in seeing if Jasper had improved the glaze.

As Polly stepped beside him, he beamed at her then let his gaze scan the others, including Linus, who surrounded the worktable.

"I added a tiny bit of black," Jasper said, "to get rid of the brightness, then a dollop of blue. Roy, grab a few of those mugs over there, will you?"

A paunchy man wearing a long apron over a short-sleeved striped shirt and denim trousers shot an exasperated look at Linus then hurried to a nearby rack. He hooked his forefingers and thumbs into four unglazed mugs and brought them to Jasper.

"These have been fired," Jasper explained to Polly, who still pondered the look Roy had given Linus. "They're usually sold like this, but we can experiment to see what the glaze looks like now. If it works, perhaps we could offer a few mugs as a limited run."

"You don't got enough glaze there for any amount that would matter," Linus said. "And you won't be able to duplicate it, since none of us here knows how that yellow got made."

Polly glanced at Linus. Was he protesting too much, or was it his job to be the company's official naysayer? She'd need to ask Jasper about him later.

"You're right," Jasper said with a frown.

"Don't matter none about that," Roy said. "The mugs don't all need to be glazed the exact same. We can add them as a kind of bonus to our best customers. That'll make it seem like it was done on purpose. A one-of-a-kind mug unlike any other."

"I like that idea." Jasper slowly nodded, his lower lip tucked in thought.

"Or sell them as an eclectic set."

Polly turned toward the familiar voice. Vivian stood at the end of the table, a stack of folders tucked in her arms. Her cheeks were slightly flushed, as if she feared she'd spoken out of turn. "That's an interesting idea," Polly said to encourage her.

"What do you mean by 'eclectic'?" Jasper asked.

"It's like Roy said. Make it look like the differences in the glaze were done on purpose. They can be packaged in sets of four or eight. As long as the overall color tone is the same, there may be interest."

"You can market them as limited editions too," Polly added. "Only a few sets available, so get yours now."

"Those are all great ideas." Jasper's huge smile beamed at everyone. "Perhaps we should have these informal meetings more often."

Roy picked up one of the mugs. "It's in all our best interests for Kane Pottery to stay in business. New ideas will help to make that happen."

"I agree," Jasper said quietly.

Polly resisted shooting Linus a *so-there* look, though she was thankful to know that not everyone thought as he did.

"Let's try this." Jasper nodded to Roy, who dipped the top of a mug into the pot of glaze then expertly pulled it out and set it on a rack. A pan about the size of a baking dish held the rack and would catch any drips.

Polly gasped. "That's a lovely shade," she exclaimed then turned to Vivian. "What do you think?"

"I really like it too," Vivian said.

"It needs to dry," Jasper said. "Go ahead and do five more mugs, Roy, then seal the remaining glaze until we decide what to do with it. I'll return in a couple of hours to see what they look like. Thanks, everyone. Let's all get back to work now."

Linus had already left the area. Polly wondered if he'd even stayed around long enough to see what the glazed mug looked like.

Jasper took her arm and stepped away from the others. "Does this seem as strange to you as it does to me?"

"I'm afraid so."

"I need to have a private word with Linus. He's been here since the beginning, and I hate to think…" Jasper's voice trailed away.

"If you're going to ask him questions, then I—"

Jasper cut her off. "He doesn't have the respect for me that he did for my father. I won't learn anything about how this…mistake… was made if you or anyone else is with me. Believe me, this is already hard enough."

Polly lowered her voice. "Because you don't believe it was a mistake?"

"I don't know what to believe. Not anymore." He let out a heavy sigh that tugged at Polly's heart. In the thrill of the hunt, it was too easy to forget that his grief was still raw.

"Father wasn't supposed to die," he continued, and she sucked in a breath, surprised how their minds were in sync with one another. "Vernon wasn't supposed to steal my designs."

His gaze landed on her, and he smiled. A sad yet gentle smile that sent her pulse racing. "And the detective who answered my plea for help was supposed to be the *I*, not the *P*, in the P&I Detective Agency. It seems that my only recent good fortune is that you were the one who came."

Polly, for one of the rare times in her life, had no words. A soothing warmth flowed through her that weakened her knees and clouded her mind. Something she couldn't allow to happen. Not when she needed to prove to Isaac that she could solve this case on her own as a professional.

Jasper turned, and Polly followed his gaze. Vivian stood at the end of the table as if wanting to be inobtrusive while waiting to be noticed.

"I like the idea you presented to me earlier, Miss Matthews," Jasper said, his voice raised enough for Vivian to hear.

Miss Matthews? Oh, no, no, no. He'd done it again. As difficult as it was, Polly kept her expression impassive. So much for using her mother's maiden name as a cover.

"We should talk more about it later," he said. "But for now perhaps you could give Vivian a hand in the filing room."

His gaze implored her to go along with his request though she was hardly in a position to do otherwise. After all, Vivian believed Polly to be a new file clerk. And file clerks didn't argue with the owner of the company if they wished to stay employed.

Neither did fledgling detectives argue with their clients. At least not in front of witnesses.

"I'd be happy to," she said cheerfully. Her direct gaze sent a different message.

Amusement briefly sparked in his eyes, and he seemed about to touch her elbow then stopped himself. "We'll talk again soon." He waved farewell to Vivian then walked away, his back straight and shoulders stiff.

Linus must be more formidable than Polly considered him to be. His lengthy tenure at the company no doubt gave him a feeling of indispensability. Perhaps one he'd earned during the years he'd risen in the ranks and watched Jasper grow from a toddler into adulthood. Did he feel entitled to an even more responsible position now that ownership had passed from father to son?

Polly made a mental note to find out as much about Linus as she could. Starting with asking Vivian about him once they were alone in the filing room.

But Vivian had a question of her own, and she didn't wait for the privacy of the filing room to ask it. "Did I hear Mr. Kane refer to you as Miss Matthews?" she asked as they walked side by side toward the filing room. "Why didn't you correct him?"

"Did he?" Polly kept her gaze straight ahead. "He must be confused."

"I suppose he must."

The words sounded as if Vivian accepted Polly's explanation, but her tone sure didn't. What would Vivian say when Polly got promoted from file clerk to company historian after only two days?

CHAPTER EIGHT

After a couple of hours of filing, Polly's muscles ached from bending over and forcing file folders into already overstuffed drawers. Her neck, back, and knees might never be the same, and she looked forward to soaking in the tub at the boardinghouse later that evening. That was, if she could lay claim to one of the shared bathrooms before anyone else did.

She also looked forward to Jasper rescuing her from this dreary task. But as the minutes clicked their way around the face of the huge clock on the wall above the door, she wondered if that rescue would ever happen. Had he forgotten his promise to come for her? Or had something else been more important?

Though what could be more important than finding the thief who wanted to destroy his business within weeks of his taking over?

Which led her thoughts back to Linus, the ugly yellow glaze, and the possibility of sabotage. Hopefully Jasper had found out enough from the old warrior to know if the glaze mixture had been an accident or a deliberate act. Maybe what he learned was the reason he still hadn't come for her.

As if being stuck here wasn't bad enough, her plan to gently interrogate Vivian hadn't worked out well either. Vivian had assigned Polly the folders that belonged in the files on one side of the room while she busied herself with files on the other side. There was no easy way to have a conversation about such popular topics as the weather or farm commodities or even Vivian's upcoming wedding—a topic the bride-to-be had eagerly engaged in the day before—when they'd have to practically shout across the room at each other. Polly could forget about finding out what Vivian might know of Linus or any of the other employees.

Instead, she focused on the task at hand while quietly singing the old hymn that seemed perfect for a pottery factory.

Have Thine own way, Lord, have Thine own way;
Thou art the Potter, I am the clay.
Mold me and make me, after Thy will,
While I am waiting, yielded and still.

The familiar words soothed her heart with the "peace that passeth understanding" as the song became a prayer for her and Isaac, and also for Jasper and Elsie. Two sets of wounded, orphaned siblings in need of the Potter's guidance.

A few minutes before noon, Vivian broke her silence. "Mr. Kane, what a surprise. Is there something I can find for you?"

Polly popped up and made her way to the door.

"I'm on my way to see how our experiment turned out before the mugs are placed in the kiln queue." Jasper shifted his gaze from Vivian to Polly as she rounded the table. "I thought both of you might want to join me. Before we go, though, I wanted to tell you, Miss Martin, that I've given your proposal a great deal of consideration."

Polly breathed a quiet sigh of relief that he'd finally gotten her cover name right while resisting an urge to take a peek at Vivian's reaction. Surely she'd noticed.

"Could you start that project this afternoon?"

Even though she'd anticipated this—after all, how else was she going to be able to sleuth around the factory without raising suspicion?—she broke into a spontaneous smile as if she'd just been handed the Christmas gift of her dreams.

"Absolutely."

"What is this?" Vivian asked.

"Miss Martin will be interviewing several of the employees, especially those who have been here the longest, to create a kind of tribute to Father along with a short history of the company."

"How clever of Miss Martin." Vivian managed to keep her voice even, but Polly feared she'd unwittingly made an enemy by being the focus of Jasper's attention. She regretted that, though it probably hadn't helped that Jasper had earlier made a point of thanking Polly for her ideas but didn't mention Vivian's innovative suggestions.

Polly resolved, if at all possible, to invite Vivian to tea after the case was solved in hopes they could regain the camaraderie they'd first experienced.

"She's not the only clever woman who's hiding her talents in this stuffy room," Jasper said. "I was impressed with your ideas, Miss Ayers, on how to market the mugs as either one-of-a-kind items or package them together as an eclectic set."

Vivian blushed as Polly inwardly shook her head. How had it happened once again that she and Jasper shared similar thoughts?

"I don't think I would have thought of it," Vivian said, "if Roy, I mean, Mr. Watkins, hadn't made his suggestion first."

"Roy is another one of our employees who has hidden talents," Jasper said. "I can't help wondering what other ideas are going unnoticed, and I want to find a way to bring them out into the open. My name may be above the door, but everyone here plays an important role in our company's success."

"We believe that, Mr. Kane." Vivian extended her smile to include Polly. "If there's anything I can do to help with the interviews, please let me know. Though I promise I won't let that interfere with my filing."

"I appreciate the offer," Polly said, unsure of how she could accept it. Unless Vivian was able to decipher Polly's shorthand…

As much as Polly wanted to help Jasper with a tribute to his father, the thought of transcribing her notes from a steno pad to typed pages made her want to keel over from boredom before she'd even started.

A detective's life was only glamorous on Hollywood's silver screen.

Jasper waited on the front porch of his family home to see who would arrive for supper. The spectacle-wearing file clerk turned company historian. The shadowy sprite with a black cap covering her blond hair. Or the genuine *P* of the P&I Detective Agency.

He guessed she'd come as the first, determined to maintain her cover even in the safety of his home. A few minutes later, a 1930

Oldsmobile coupe entered the long drive and parked to the side of Stone House, one of the oldest homes in Crooksville.

Before the Kanes became known for their pottery, they'd been farmers whose ancestry traced to the Revolutionary War. After the colonial victory, a huge tract of land located north of the Ohio River and west of the Scioto River designated as the Virginia Military District was set aside for veterans of the war. The first Kanes came to the region to claim their share of the land in the late 1700s.

About twenty years after Ohio became a state in 1803, a branch of the Kane family moved east to Perry County, named for Oliver Hazard Perry, a hero of the War of 1812. This was another war where members of the Kane family fought bravely and with distinction.

As the years went by, sons and daughters sought their fortunes by heading west, crossing the Wabash and the Mississippi Rivers. Others headed south into Georgia and Florida. But Jasper's ancestors stayed on the farm they'd staked out over a century before. Acreage was divided and sold until now only the house and enough acres for a small cattle herd remained.

Jasper jogged down the broad steps and opened the coupe's door after it came to a stop. He grinned as the spectacle-wearing prim and proper spinster emerged from the driver's seat. However, she wore an attractive shirtwaist dress instead of a dowdy skirt and cardigan. Her hair, though still pulled back into a bun at the nape of her neck, wasn't as severe as it had been earlier.

"Welcome to Stone House, Miss Martin. Or should I call you Miss Matthews?" He chuckled. "I had difficulties with that today."

"I noticed. Perhaps you should call me Polly."

"Only if you call me Jasper."

"I'll do that here. But not at the office." Her sweet smile turned his insides wrong side out. Not that he minded.

She took in the view of the valley and the woods beyond the house as she removed her gloves and appeared pleased with what she saw. Jasper found a deep satisfaction in that, though he hadn't realized until that moment that her opinion of his property mattered to him. He followed her gaze as she scanned the horizon, wanting to see the vista through her eyes.

He loved this place, and he suddenly, desperately, wanted her to love it too.

"It's beautiful. How long has your family been here?"

"I'll bore you with the family history over dinner. That is, if you're interested in the story and not just being polite."

"I'm interested," she said. "Curiosity may have killed the cat, but it has yet to kill me."

Jasper wasn't sure how to respond to that, so he simply laughed and cupped her elbow in his hand. "Come on in and meet my sister. She's anxious to meet you."

"I hope she doesn't mind having a last-minute dinner guest."

"Not at all." He guided her up the stairs to the wide veranda. "For one thing, we have a cook who always makes more than enough. Father often brought home guests without giving any prior notice. And for another thing, Elsie loves any excuse to bake. I have it on good authority that she's made her amazing blackberry tart for dessert, and there may even be homemade ice cream to go along with it."

"I envy anyone who can bake," Polly said. "My cakes always fall, my piecrusts are always soggy, and I couldn't bake a tart if my life depended on it. I'm already looking forward to dessert."

Jasper escorted Polly into the parlor, where Elsie waited for them. Since their mother had died only a few years after Father founded the pottery company, Elsie had taken on the role of hostess at an early age. She had a gift for hospitality, which Jasper appreciated now and realized he'd taken for granted way too often. He introduced the two women, and Elsie warmly greeted Polly.

Once they had taken their seats, Polly and Elsie in matching wing chairs separated by a hefty round table and Jasper across from them on the sofa, Polly's gaze swept around the room. "How lovely this is," she exclaimed. "And so comfortable."

"Father loved his comfort," Elsie said with a polite laugh. "Though he always said this room was meant for women. He enjoyed his study, which is a much more masculine room."

A noise in the hallway brought the conversation to a halt. Jasper rose as his friend Mark sauntered into the parlor.

"I wasn't expecting you this evening," Jasper said. "Why didn't you let us know you were coming?"

"I invited him," Elsie said, her tone cool. "To even our numbers, which is something you didn't consider."

Jasper's ears burned at the unexpected reprimand. He'd thought Elsie was over being angry with him. She'd readily agreed when he told her that he wanted to invite a last-minute guest for supper. He didn't understand, though, why she'd kept her invitation to Mark a secret.

"Please have a seat, Mark, and you too, Jasper," Elsie continued. "You're hovering like a mother hen when you should be introducing our guests to one another."

"Forgive my lack of manners." Jasper forced a smile and made the introductions. Once again, he said Matthews instead of Martin.

Not that it mattered. He'd invited Polly here because he wanted Elsie to know as much as he did about what was happening at the factory. Now Mark would be in on the secret too.

For reasons he couldn't explain, Jasper felt uneasy about that. Probably because Mark seemed so restless lately, as if he were impatiently waiting on shore for his ship to come in instead of rowing out to meet it.

After greetings were exchanged, Jasper and Mark settled on the couch. Elsie shifted toward Polly.

"Jasper tells me you're here to talk to our employees so you can write a tribute to Father," she said. "That sounds like an unusual occupation. Not that I'm against women working, please don't misunderstand me. It's only I've never heard of anyone who writes tributes and company histories as a profession. I'm fascinated."

"It is unusual," Polly agreed, though she seemed uncertain what else to say. She glanced at Jasper, her gaze sending him a quiet plea for assistance.

When he'd invited her to dinner after they'd inspected the newly-glazed mugs—which had turned out beautifully—he'd told her his plan to include Elsie in their secret. She must be wondering if he still intended to tell his sister the truth, especially since Mark had now joined them. He gave Polly a reassuring smile.

"I'm afraid I haven't given you the entire story," he admitted to Elsie. "I wanted you to meet Polly before you learned her true occupation."

"So you're not writing a tribute?" Elsie's eyes grew cold as she folded her hands in her lap. "What is it you do, Miss Matthews?"

Polly's pleading gaze became a glare. She obviously expected Jasper to explain the situation to his sister.

Mark feigned a good-natured grunt. "What's the big secret, Jasper? Are the two of you planning to elope?"

Polly's cheeks turned pink, but Jasper couldn't help but notice her glare had disappeared. Mark's comment had embarrassed him too, but Polly's reaction was worth his slight discomfort.

"Nothing as daring as that," he said. "Polly is a private detective. I hired her to help me solve a mystery."

A myriad of emotions flitted across Elsie's features—too many for Jasper, who knew her so well, to interpret them. Her gaze darted from Jasper to Polly and back to Jasper.

"A private detective," she said quietly. When she spoke again, her tone sounded almost demanding, as if she struggled to maintain a polite facade in front of their guests when what she really wanted to do was shout at Jasper. Not that shouting was her style. But he could almost see the steam coming out of her ears.

"What is this mystery?" she demanded.

Instead of answering, Jasper retrieved the Spears Ceramic pamphlet from a nearby drawer. "I placed this in here earlier so I could show it to you. Look at the first page."

Elsie opened the cover and studied the decorative line of items displayed on the page. "'Autumn Decor,'" she murmured. She narrowed her eyes as she raised them to Jasper. "Didn't you once suggest this name to Father? How did Mr. Spears know?"

"Those are my designs, Elsie." It hurt that she hadn't recognized the individual pieces, since she'd seen the sketches before. He tried but failed to keep the hurt out of his voice. "Vernon said he bought them, but he won't tell me who sold them to him. But whoever it was stole them from me."

"I see." Elsie's features relaxed, as if she was relieved by Jasper's explanation. "You want Polly to find the thief. Is that right?"

"Unless Vernon is lying, and he stole them himself. He denied that when I confronted him, but he made it clear that he already has these pieces in production and will sell them as his own." He might as well tell her the rest, though he dreaded doing so. "Vernon would love it if we went bankrupt. He practically said so."

"That won't happen." The force in Elsie's voice and determination in her eyes, as if she knew something that Jasper didn't, baffled him. Perhaps he wasn't the only one who had a secret to confess. But would Elsie tell him hers?

He was relieved when Mrs. Bennett, their housekeeper and cook, entered the room to announce that dinner was ready. Elsie immediately donned her gracious hostess persona. She stood, smiled at their guests, and made a sweeping gesture with her hand. "Shall we?"

Mark rose, chuckling as he shook his head at Jasper, and then offered Elsie his arm. They led the way to the dining room, and Jasper followed with Polly on his arm. They took their seats and enjoyed a delightful conversation along with their delicious dinner of pot roast with mashed potatoes and gravy, green beans, and homemade rolls.

Elsie appeared genuinely interested in Polly's training at the Pinkerton Detective Agency, and even Mark didn't seem to mind not being the center of attention for once.

Generous slices of Elsie's blackberry tart, garnished with fresh mint, was served on pastel dessert dishes with scoops of vanilla ice cream that Mrs. Bennett's husband had churned earlier that day.

"This has always been my favorite dessert," Mark exclaimed. "No one's tart is as delicious as yours, Elsie."

"I agree," Polly said. "What's your secret? Or is it too much of a secret to tell?"

Elsie's cheeks flushed at the compliments. "This is a longtime family recipe, and I'm happy to share it. But the secret is in the blackberries. They grow wild along the pasture fence on the other side of the stream."

The conversation veered into other topics. Mark always had embellished anecdotes to tell, and Jasper was gratified to see Elsie and Polly getting along so well. Elsie had even smiled at him occasionally. For a few pleasant hours, he allowed himself to forget about the stolen designs and the troubles at the factory.

If only life could always be this pleasant.

✑ CHAPTER NINE ✑

The next day, Polly sent a telegram to Isaac in care of the Chillicothe lodging where he always stayed with the cryptic message: *I took the case.*

That alone would let him know she was in Crooksville and why. She didn't expect a reply, but sending the telegram alleviated the guilt she felt over avoiding him. After the previous night's dinner with Jasper, Elsie, and Mark, that guilt had deepened. Even though she and Isaac had their differences, she knew he'd be worried if he returned home and discovered she was gone with no word of her whereabouts. Just as she would be if the situation were reversed.

On Sunday, Polly attended church with Jasper and Elsie but declined their invitation to dinner. Instead, she drove to Zanesville. On the way home, she stopped at the office to gather the agency's mail. After a quiet afternoon, which included reading a book on the history of pottery that Jasper had lent her, she returned to the boardinghouse in Crooksville.

Over the next few days, Polly interviewed the employees of Kane Pottery and learned more about the process of transforming clay into functional dishware than she'd ever thought possible. For the most part, the employees took great pride in their work, whether they created molds, operated the kilns, mixed the glazes, finished the pieces, or fulfilled the customers' orders and shipped them out the door.

Jasper was right that the employees seemed grateful to his father for keeping them employed during the hardships of the past few years. Several had family members and friends who worked for the six rival manufacturers, and none of the others had managed to do what Edmund had done.

Even when Polly tried to dig a little, the employees were loath to say anything negative about Edmund. When they did, they couched the criticism with understanding. Sure, he could be abrupt at times, and he might think he knew best. But he was a busy man and, most of the time, he made the right decision even if no one realized it except in hindsight. He was a boss, not a friend, but he took care of his own. It had been a privilege to work for him.

Polly, true to her word, took copious notes using the shorthand she'd learned during her stint at secretarial school. She thought Jasper and Elsie would want to know the high opinion the employees had of their father. The employees might value a printed copy of the company history under its founder's leadership as much as his children. Her notes were a start to making that happen.

Except those notes were still incomplete.

Each time she approached Linus Vaughn, he grumbled he was too busy to talk. Twice she scheduled specific times for them to meet. He stood her up both times. During her evening debriefings with Jasper, he'd volunteered to talk to Linus. But Polly wasn't sure that was such a good idea.

Though she was enjoying her cover story very much, and even wondering if writing company histories might be an interesting backup in case Isaac never accepted her as a true partner in their detective agency, she hadn't neglected the primary reason she was at the factory.

Through small talk, and because she had developed trust with the employees, she learned that a mix-up in the glaze had happened before. Only that time, Roy had diluted the color and set it aside to be used for ornamental purposes. Jasper hadn't been involved and, this informant said, might not know about the blunder even though Roy said he'd tell him. This was shortly after the reading of the will, an event that had fed the factory grapevine for several days, so Jasper had more important things to worry about than a little mix-up in the glaze.

Polly also learned that the workers sometimes found the settings on their machines changed. Each one chalked it up to a mistake, but by the time Polly had heard the same story three or four times, she'd become convinced that someone was committing small acts of sabotage against the company.

Could Linus be that someone?

And if Linus was capable of purposely changing settings on the equipment to ruin a run or change a recipe to spoil a glaze, could he also be guilty of stealing designs and selling them to Vernon Spears? Her suspicions became even more pronounced when she learned that Linus's father had worked for Vernon a long time ago. Though Linus himself had always been employed with Kane Pottery, did he have a loyalty to his father's former employer?

Polly needed to find out exactly what Linus was up to…if anything. Since he had become adept at avoiding her, she planned to keep her eye on him. And she knew exactly how to do it.

The only question now was whether she should tell Jasper her plan.

Polly adjusted her binoculars as she peered out from the abandoned railroad car and watched the workers slowly emerge from the factory. A few headed to cars while most walked toward town. Two or three others, including Linus Vaughn, stabled horses in an outbuilding. She had learned that Edmund Kane had modified the building for the horses when he realized that a handful of his employees, even in the 1930s when automobiles were becoming more commonplace, needed that old-fashioned mode of transportation if they were going to get to work on time.

"This is so exciting." Elsie, standing on the opposite side of the boxcar's open door, practically squealed. She wore a black pullover and pants similar to Polly's. Both women hid their pinned-up hair beneath black caps. "I still can't believe we're doing this."

"Men shouldn't have all the fun," Polly said. "Besides, Jasper has a harder time being objective than you do. I think he'd simply ask Linus if he was involved, and when Linus said no, that would be the end of it."

"Jasper has a kind heart." Elsie's gaze shifted. She stared at the boxcar's dark interior corner, but her thoughts obviously weren't on whatever crawly creatures might be lurking beneath the dirt and the debris. She released a heavy sigh then lifted the corner of her mouth in a sad smile. "At least where the employees are concerned. He wants them to be as loyal to him as they were to Father. I think he fears finding out they might not be."

"I believe most of them are," Polly said, wanting to reassure Elsie of that at least. She wished she could assure her that Jasper's kind heart extended to his sister too. But she feared that Jasper took his sister for granted. He didn't mean to be unkind, but he didn't fully appreciate that she had dreams and aspirations that might not include him.

With a brother like Isaac—kind and caring but also blind to her abilities—Polly understood exactly how Elsie felt.

"But you don't believe that everyone is loyal." Elsie stared through the door again. "Otherwise, we wouldn't be here."

"Too many odd things have happened, and I'm not sure Jasper knows the half of them."

"Why wouldn't he? Are the employees afraid to tell him?" Elsie's mouth quirked as if she was puzzling out her own thoughts. "Or maybe they don't fear him enough. He isn't Father."

"Did they fear your father?" That wasn't the impression Polly had after her interviews. Respected him, yes. But feared him? She wouldn't have said so, but then again, would anyone have admitted that they did? Elsie would certainly have a better understanding of her father's relationship with his employees than Polly could have.

"Strange as it seems, they feared him too much *not* to admit to mistakes," Elsie said. "A mistake he'd forgive because he believed in second chances. But deception?" Bitterness crept into her tone. "He didn't mind telling his own tales even though he wouldn't forgive anyone who lied to him."

Polly tucked that information away to mull on later. She had a childhood friend whose father, an insurance salesman, bristled at any suggestion that he'd gotten a detail wrong when telling one of his many anecdotes but was quick to accuse others of lying when their only guilt was to misspeak. When Polly and her friend were teens, the man was arrested for insurance fraud. Over the years, he'd bilked his employer out of tens of thousands of dollars in fraudulent claims.

For now, Polly wanted to share her insights with Elsie in hopes of getting a clearer picture of the different relationships at the factory. Plus something deep inside her wanted to help Elsie understand that her brother had depths she might not see.

Could that be true of Isaac too?

Polly immediately hushed that intrusive, unwelcome voice. This wasn't about her and Isaac but about Elsie and Jasper.

"I don't think the employees are keeping information from Jasper out of fear," Polly said. "Or because they don't fear him or respect him. They want Jasper to succeed, and not only because their livelihoods depend on keeping the factory open."

"What other reason could there be?" The words expressed exasperation, but Elsie's tone was shaded with an earnest wish to know an alternative. She seemed afraid to hope that there could be another answer, but Polly had one to give her.

"They want to protect him."

Elsie darted her gaze to Polly. Though the sun was still a few hours from setting, the shadows cast by nearby trees and buildings made it difficult to see Elsie's eyes, but her expression spoke volumes.

"Protect him from what?"

"They know he's grieving. You both are." Polly momentarily closed her eyes as the memories of how it felt to learn a beloved father had unexpectedly died washed over her. More than ten years had passed since that tragedy, but there were moments like this one when the relief brought by time vanished, leaving her heart as fragile as it had been on that awful day.

"They're protecting him from what they see as minor day-to-day problems because they want to give him time to adjust to being the boss," Polly explained. "They like him."

"I'm not sure that's a good quality for a boss."

"It's not a bad one."

"Only as long as no one tries to take advantage of him," Elsie countered. "You wouldn't be here if that hadn't happened."

Polly couldn't argue with that. Neither woman spoke for a few moments until Elsie pointed. "Jasper is leaving."

He stood at the back entrance, the one that Polly had opened with her lockpicking tool, and jiggled the handle. Apparently satisfied that the new lock would hold—though Polly would have enjoyed the opportunity to test that theory—he pocketed his set of keys and whistled as he strolled to his vehicle.

"I didn't see Linus come out," Polly said. "Did you?"

Elsie shook her head. "What do we do now?"

"As soon as Jasper is gone, we make our way to the barn to see if Linus's horse is still there."

Before hiding in the boxcar, they'd visited the barn. The swaybacked mare stood in a lean-to, sheltered from the late afternoon sun, along with two geldings. Elsie had identified Linus's mare, saying that he'd had her as long as Elsie could remember.

"He and Penny have grown old together," she'd said. She wondered aloud how Linus would handle the loss if the horse died before he did.

Apparently, he had no family other than his fellow coworkers, who looked after him at Thanksgiving and Christmas and never forgot to celebrate his birthday. Elsie herself baked the cake each year and topped it with a candle.

"You go first," Elsie said as soon as Jasper's vehicle turned onto the main road. "I'll follow."

Polly nodded agreement, took one last look around to ensure no one was near, and then slipped to the ground and beneath the box car. As soon as Elsie joined her, she crept to the other side and trotted, back bent, from one tree to another, along a fence row, behind a hedge and more trees, until they reached the rear of the barn. She could feel the adrenaline flushing her face as they paused to catch their breath.

"That was exciting." Elsie's eyes sparkled. "I don't think I've had that much fun since we played hide-and-go-seek when we were children. Sometimes on a summer evening, it seemed all the children in town would join in the game. A few of the fathers too. Though now that I'm older, I suppose they played with us mostly to keep an eye on the teen boys who hung around their daughters."

Polly chuckled. "Did your father ever do that?"

Elsie rolled her eyes, but her good-natured smile remained. "He didn't have to. Jasper kept his eye on me, and I kept my eye on Bobby Stillman."

"Wait a minute. Is Bobby Stillman the same person as Rob Stillman? As in Vivian Ayers's fiancé?"

"He's her fiancé now, but we used to like each other years and years ago." Elsie's cheeks turned a deeper shade of pink. "It wasn't love though. Looking back, I think he always liked Vivian best, but her father was stricter than most about dating and such. So Bobby, that is Rob, went out with several of us girls but wouldn't let himself get too serious about any one of us. I can't say he broke any of our hearts. It's sweet, don't you think? That kind of devotion?"

Polly wasn't sure how to respond. She and Elsie were on a mission. How had the conversation taken this kind of turn? "I suppose it's what we all long for, though only with the right man."

Images of Jasper flitted through her head. How he'd stared at her through the diner window on her first day in Crooksville. The shocked look on his face when she'd tossed him on his back with her signature defense move. The pleased expression he'd worn when she arrived at his home for dinner the other night.

She shook her head to make the images disappear. This was not the time to be thinking of Jasper. Or to analyze the warm feelings flowing through her veins. Her cheeks burned, and she turned away before Elsie could notice. They were both in their midtwenties, past the blush of youth. Was it too late for Cupid's arrows to hit their hearts?

Instead of answering Elsie's question about Vivian and Rob's sweet love story, Polly rounded the barn. Penny nibbled grass in the paddock.

"Let's find Linus," she said.

CHAPTER TEN

Jasper drove to Roseville, another of the prominent towns in the region known as the Pottery Capital of the World and home to the Buckeye Dishware Company. The pottery manufacturing firm had managed to survive the Depression almost as well as Kane Pottery. The company's longtime customers were as loyal to Paul Nolan, the owner, as Father's customers had been to him. Even though their orders weren't as big as before, they still managed to purchase enough products to keep the runs going.

Paul had called Jasper earlier that day to invite him to supper at his club. The invitation was a surprise, but not an unwelcome one. Jasper liked Paul and hoped that their business relationship could be similar to what his father had experienced—friendly rivals who had each other's backs. Jasper didn't want to take anything for granted, and he was sure that Paul didn't see him as being the strong negotiator his father had been. But he didn't think Paul would try to take advantage of him either. The man had always had an eye to the future and a long view of events that many owners lacked.

Paul would want to build for that vision, not take advantage of Jasper for a temporary gain in the present. As he drove, Jasper prayed he was right about that.

At least Elsie had other plans for the evening. Otherwise, she might have asked to accompany him. Her disappointment with their father's decision to leave her a sliver of the business seemed to deepen as the days passed by. Jasper hadn't known the provisions of the will until the attorney read it to all of them. He was as surprised as Elsie by her inheritance. But he also understood Father's thinking.

At least he thought he did.

Elsie, whose marriage prospects dimmed with each passing year, would have a home with Jasper for the rest of her life. The percentage of the profits she would receive served as an annuity, an annual income, at least as long as the company remained profitable. Surely that was a wiser financial move in the long term than for Jasper to buy her out.

Though a lump sum was what she wanted, an argument they'd had again that morning before he went to work. Strange, how fine everything had been as they enjoyed the breakfast of poached eggs and bacon prepared by Mrs. Bennett.

Then the mysterious telegram arrived, one which Elsie seemed embarrassed to be receiving. She barely talked to him after that and quickly made an excuse to leave the table.

Even if Jasper had the money, which he didn't, Elsie had to see that he was only looking out for her best interests. That was what a good brother did for his sister.

He arrived at the club and was ushered into a small dining room. Buckeye Dishware must be doing much better than Kane Pottery for Paul Nolan to have a membership here. Perhaps in a year or two Jasper would be able to afford one too. It was possible, especially if he could get his decorative line going. He knew as certain as he knew anything that the utilitarian lines were their bread and butter, but a fine arts line was pie à la mode. Something special, something worth having, something worth leaving to one's children.

An heirloom. A keepsake.

That was how he needed to market such a line. Appeal to people's sense of tradition, of family. Their appreciation of beauty.

Paul Nolan rose from a corner table as Jasper approached, and greeted him with a hearty handshake. A carafe of tea stood on a silver tray, and a waiter immediately appeared to pour the amber liquid into their glasses. The two men made small talk, gossiping about village politics involving both Crooksville and Roseville. The two towns shared a similar history, similar economies, and were similar in size, so the distinctions between them were minor to outside eyes. But the citizens themselves were loyal to their own birthplaces, even though most of them had relatives who lived in the opposite town. Or in the rural countryside between the two.

The only boast Roseville had over Crooksville was its name. Even diehard Crooksville fans had to admit that *Roseville* sounded more charming, friendly, and welcoming than *Crooksville*. Their response was that the name of Crooksville was unforgettable and unique. There was probably a Roseville in just about every state in the Union. But there was only one Crooksville.

It might not be much of a defense, but it was theirs.

As the meal went on, Jasper relaxed. Paul was amiable and seemed as eager as Jasper to foster a friendship. Not with Jasper, Edmund's son, but with Jasper, the owner of a company in the same industry.

When the dessert arrived, Paul took a bite of his chocolate cake then cleared his throat.

"I'm glad we could meet like this," he said. "It's a pity to spoil it with shop talk, but I'm afraid it's unavoidable."

A sick feeling grew in the pit of Jasper's stomach. Bad news was headed his way, he could feel it. Worse was his feeling that he'd misread Paul's intention all along. He'd wanted this to be a friendly dinner. One that he would soon reciprocate. But to learn that Paul had an ulterior motive was gut-wrenching. Would he turn out to be another Vernon Spears, only dressed in sheep's clothing instead of revealing himself to be a wolf from the outset?

"I hope you're not expecting me to file for bankruptcy," Jasper said, the conversation with Vernon fresh in his mind. "We're nowhere close to having to do something like that. I don't plan on selling either. Father managed to get us through the Depression, and I intend to see us through the country's economic recovery."

Paul held up both hands and waved them as if to erase Jasper's words. "You misunderstand me if you think I want either of those events to happen," he said. "I wanted us to meet so I could warn you in private."

Jasper leaned back, confused. "Warn me of what?"

Paul leaned forward. "You have a traitor in your company."

Jasper tried to keep his expression impassive, but he found it impossible to do so. It couldn't be true. Polly herself had told him that his employees liked him. They wanted him to succeed. They were behind him in his efforts to try out new ideas.

Maybe Vernon had told Paul about the stolen designs. Maybe Paul didn't know that Jasper had already confronted Vernon.

"Why do you say that?" He braced himself for the answer, sure it was one he didn't want to hear. Though, in truth, there was nothing he wanted to hear about a traitor either. Except the person's name. And he wasn't one hundred percent sure he wanted to know that.

Instead of answering, Paul retrieved an envelope that must have been leaning against the table leg and slid it to Jasper. On the front, Paul's full name was written in block letters, an obvious ploy to disguise the handwriting. Below his name were the words *Private! For Your Eyes Only!*

"Go ahead and open it," Paul urged.

Jasper quietly exhaled then pulled a sheaf of papers from the envelope. They were onionskin pages, the thin paper used to make carbon copies of typed documents because they were lightweight and easier to erase than the thicker bonds. These particular pages were more translucent than other varieties Jasper had seen in the office. That translucence made them perfect for the thief's apparent purpose.

"These are my designs," he said quietly as he leafed through the pages. The sketches were of figurines that he had based on nursery rhymes and fairy tales. "Why do you have them?"

He picked up the envelope and turned it over, but nothing was written on the back. He scanned the pages again. "Who sent these to you?"

"I thought they might be yours," Paul said sympathetically. "I remember how your father used to talk about the ideas you had for ornamental pottery." He tapped the pages. "I take it these were stolen from your office."

"These are copies." Jasper held up the top sheet, a penciled tracing of Cinderella's glass slipper. On the original sketch, he'd imagined a delicate porcelain shoe trimmed in gold. "This sheet of paper was laid over my sketch, and someone traced it. Someone traced all of these."

"I wish I knew who that someone was," Paul said as he picked up the envelope. "This was found with the rest of our mail earlier this week. A few hours later, I got a phone call from someone who refused to identify himself. He said he wanted payment for the designs and for others in the same line."

"What did you tell him?"

Paul's eyes widened. When he spoke, his voice was tinged with disappointment. "I'm sorry you felt you had to ask that question, son."

"I'm sorry I did too." Jasper tossed the pages onto the table, not caring that the corner of the bottom page landed in his cake. "You're not the first person to get copies of my designs. I didn't find out about the first time until it was too late."

Paul slowly nodded. "Vernon Spears, right?"

Jasper didn't answer.

"Let me assure you, Jasper, that I don't operate my business the same way as Spears. I never have and I never will."

"I didn't mean to offend you. It's just—"

"We'll say no more about it." Paul sat back. "I saw Spears's latest catalog. The Autumn Decor line? That was yours?"

"It was. Apparently not anymore."

"Let me guess. Spears refused to tell you how he got the designs."

"He said he didn't steal them," Jasper explained. "But that he'd paid good money for them and there was nothing I could do about it. He knows I don't have the proof to press criminal charges or the money for a civil suit."

"I regret now that I didn't arrange to meet with the thief. That anyone would think I'd operate in such an underhanded way made me so hot under the collar that I couldn't think straight. I told him to never contact me again, and I hung up."

Paul took a long sip of his tea before he continued. "Later, after I'd cooled down a bit, I got to thinking about Spears's catalog and how these designs had a similarity about them. And I remembered how you were always sketching things and your father talking about how much he wished he could let you have your way to start a production line. That's why I asked you here tonight."

Jasper almost fell out of his chair. "Father said that? That he *wished* he could let me? Then why didn't he?"

"He knew people couldn't afford them. Not with the way the economy was in so much trouble. He was afraid to take resources away from the product that they would buy. That was his practical reason. But he was also afraid you'd be heartbroken when they didn't sell in enough quantities to keep production going. He didn't want to ruin your dream by making it happen too soon."

It was just as well that Jasper didn't know how to respond, since the lump in his throat prevented him from speaking. He'd had no indication from his father, ever, that he saw his ideas as workable.

"I don't know if you have the ability or the desire to put these into production," Paul said as he placed his forefinger on the top sheet of onionskin. "But if you do, I wouldn't wait too long. Vernon got the jump on you, but you can't let Spears Ceramics become synonymous with decorative pottery. That's rightfully your niche. If your father were still here, I believe he'd tell you the same thing."

Jasper raised his gaze to the older man and pressed his lips together. Once his emotions were under control, he extended his hand. "I appreciate your advice more than I can say. And your integrity."

"We're rivals," Paul said. "Not enemies. That's true of most of our competitors, though not all of them, I'm afraid." He clapped Jasper on the shoulder. "I'll make a few phone calls and see if anyone else has been approached by this thief. Discreetly, of course. Believe it or not, Jasper, there are many of us who believe that multiple companies in the same region strengthen our industry. We want to stay the Pottery Capital of the World, and we can't do that if people like Spears pull these kinds of shenanigans."

"That's encouraging to hear."

They talked more about the future of their industry as they finished their dessert then went their separate ways. Jasper's mind and heart were overwhelmed with all he'd learned from Paul.

Someone had taken the time to trace his sketches onto onionskin. Who and how and when?

His father's discouragement was a misguided attempt to protect him. Jasper couldn't be mad about that, but their lack of forthright communication while his father was still alive saddened him.

The other pottery company owners wanted him to succeed—except for those like Vernon Spears, who wore self-centered blinders.

On the drive home, Jasper determined to evaluate the costs and benefits of launching his proposed line. He'd honor his father by thinking with his head, and he'd honor his dream by thinking with his heart.

But he wouldn't risk financial ruin, especially not when so many people's livelihoods depended on him making wise decisions. He would first carefully consider the necessary steps to make his dream come true.

He was eager to share the evening's events with Polly. Maybe he could stop by the boardinghouse on the way home and invite her for a drive. Working together, they'd come up with a plan to identify the thief who, for now, had it in his power to ruin all of Jasper's future plans. He could not and would not allow that to happen.

No matter the cost.

৵৹ CHAPTER ELEVEN ৩৲

Polly stood guard while Elsie used her key to unlock the door that Jasper had locked only a short time before. They both slipped inside and quietly made their way to the manufacturing floor. Polly led the way, and Elsie stayed close behind. That way, if Linus should surprise them, Elsie could ask him why he was still in the building. He might question her too, but she didn't have to give him an answer. Her position as sister of the boss gave her an authority that Linus, even with all his years on the job, did not have. Would never have.

That thought pierced Polly's brain. Was that the motivation behind Linus's strange behavior? Did he believe that he deserved a say in the operation of the business? It wasn't that far-fetched an idea. Longevity at an occupation tended to give people, especially a valued employee such as Linus, an expectation that they knew as much or even more than the owners. That they could make the decisions, run the company, and deserved a share of the profits. After all, they too possessed institutional knowledge.

They found Linus, head bowed and shoulders slumped, sitting on a squat barrel near the glazing stations.

Polly and Elsie exchanged puzzled glances, and then Elsie pulled the cap from her head. "There's no need for us to look like we're doing something we shouldn't," she whispered to Polly as she removed the bobby pins she'd used to tame a few loose strands. Her light brown hair, only a shade or two darker than her brother's, fell in loose waves to frame her petite features.

After Polly removed her own cap and fluffed her hair, Elsie tilted her head in Linus's direction. "Let's find out what he's up to. And pray it isn't anything we can't handle."

Polly didn't mind praying that Linus wasn't up to no good, but she was fairly certain she could handle anything he tried to dish out. After all, she'd handled Jasper better than she expected when he found her snooping in his office. Linus was more than twice his age and not nearly as strong or agile.

Perhaps Elsie didn't know about that encounter. Polly hadn't mentioned it to her new friend and partner in crime-solving, because she didn't want to embarrass Jasper. Considering Elsie hadn't mentioned it either, it was probably safe to assume Jasper had kept the defensive flip to himself.

For now, though, Polly was content to let Elsie take the lead, since she'd known Linus practically all her life and he'd always been kind to her. Over the past few days, Elsie had told Polly stories about visiting the factory when she was a little girl. Back then, Linus always had a peppermint drop in his pocket to give to her. Those little moments were made all the more precious because they hadn't been grand gestures.

"Hi, Linus," Elsie called out as they drew near. His head shot up in surprise, and his eyes darted around the huge space as if he expected to see an army materialize out of the woodwork. "What are you doing here? Quitting time was at least half an hour ago."

"Sittin'." He worried the fabric of the hat clutched in his hands. "Thinkin'."

If he thought their presence there was odd or their attire strange, he kept those thoughts to himself.

"This is a good place to think." Elsie perched on another barrel and gestured for Polly to do the same. "You've met Polly, haven't you?"

As Linus switched his gaze from Elsie to Polly, his eyelids half closed, as if he didn't want to take a good look at her. "She asks a lot of questions about things."

"Yes, she does." Elsie's light laughter seemed to dispel a bit of the gloom that surrounded them. "Jasper asked her to, you know."

"I've heard that to be the case."

"So many things are different now with Father gone." Elsie's soothing voice seemed to create peace in the vast space. "We all miss him."

"I remember when we first opened this place," Linus said. "We'd done outgrown the stable behind Stone House where we started out. Didn't take too long to do that either, but this place, it seemed so big. We joked that it'd always be bigger than us. But then it got to be just right, and it's been just right ever since. Don't need to get no bigger."

Polly shifted her gaze to Elsie, but she never took her eyes off Linus. Did Elsie understand what he meant? Polly couldn't be sure, but she didn't dare interrupt. Linus was talking, and Elsie appeared to know how to fill in the silences. Polly didn't need to do anything except listen.

"But we can't stay the same forever. If we do"—Elsie shrugged— "we might lose everything. Father worked so hard to keep the factory going through these years. You worked hard to make that happen too."

Linus pressed his lips together as he nodded. "That we did. Worked hard and thought hard. Mr. Edmund used some of his own money to be sure not a one of us here ever went without."

He bowed his head and twisted the brim of his hat. "I always thought I could trust Mr. Edmund to tell me the truth. It done near broke my spirit that he didn't do so at the end."

At this, Elsie's shoulders jerked back and her expression hardened. Linus's accusation about her father's trustworthiness seemed to stun her. A moment later, her features softened again. An almost inaudible sigh escaped her lips as she rose from her perch and placed her hand on Linus's arm.

"How did he break his trust?" she asked gently.

Linus simply shook his head.

Elsie knelt before the older man, bending her head to try to catch his gaze, but he looked away. "Please tell me, Linus. It's important I know."

"I spoke out of turn, Miss Elsie. An old man's ramblings, that's all that was." He stood, and she rose with him, her hands clutching his forearm as he twisted the brim of his hat.

Polly realized she'd also stood, though she wasn't sure why. The interrogation she'd expected had taken a bizarre turn, and instead of filling the role of interested observer, she now felt like an interloper. But she couldn't draw attention to herself by leaving. In truth, she didn't even want to. Something important was about to be revealed. She felt it in that deep place inside that one of her instructors had said gave her good instincts.

She needed to know what Linus knew. She needed to know why Elsie reacted as she had.

"I trusted him too." Elsie's voice, now desperate, seemed on the point of breaking. "But he didn't tell me the truth either."

Linus looked at her then. "I'd rather he lied to me every day than to have him lie to you once, Miss Elsie."

Tears sprang to Elsie's eyes and slipped down her cheeks. "Tell me. Please."

For the first time, Linus gazed in Polly's direction with kindness. "Tell her," she mouthed to him, and he responded with a barely perceptible nod.

"Mr. Edmund said he intended to give me a part of the company in gratitude for all my years and hard work. Not a big share, mind, but a little bit to call my own. It was supposed to be set out in that last will of his." Linus spread his hands. "But you were there when that lawyer read all the therefores and whichevers." He released a long, heavy sigh. "I know I should be glad for the bequeathing I got. But the disappointment doesn't leave me be."

"I'm truly sorry." Elsie's voice wavered, and she brushed away her tears with her fingertips. "That was a cruel thing for him to do. Did you tell Jasper?"

"No, miss. I'm ashamed to say I blamed him for it. Easier to blame him than Mr. Edmund, I guess." He turned again to Polly. "I know why you're here, and it's not to write no book. I heard you and young Jasper talking that night you snuck in."

"You were here?" Polly widened her eyes, more stunned at this revelation than anything else she'd heard.

Linus didn't bother to answer. "I want you to know I regret what I did. Messin' up the glazes and changin' the settings. It was the wrong thing to do, and I was just sittin' here, thinkin' how to make it right again. But there ain't no way at all, is there?"

"Of course there is," Elsie said. "We'll talk to Jasper. The three of us. Polly told me earlier today that Roy and a few of the others think they're helping my brother by not telling him what's happening around here. That they're protecting him. They mean well, but they're mistaken. He needs to know the truth."

She paused and stared into a far corner of the vast space, as if she needed a moment to make up her mind about something. Neither Polly nor Linus interrupted her. Finally, she released a deep breath. "As difficult as it may be to hear, Jasper needs to know the truth about Father too."

"Perhaps you and Mr. Vaughn should go without me," Polly said. It was one thing to be an accidental interloper. It was quite another to be one on purpose.

"Nonsense," Elsie said firmly. Her decision to talk to Jasper seemed to have strengthened her in a strange way. Though her eyes were red, no more tears fell.

She'd said her father had lied to her too. Polly couldn't help but wonder what promise Edmund Kane had made to his daughter. What promise had he broken?

✒ CHAPTER TWELVE ✒

Jasper was disappointed not to find Polly at the boardinghouse, but the last thing he expected to happen that evening was to find her and Elsie at Stone House dressed as cat burglars along with Linus Vaughn. Since Polly first came into his life, however, the unexpected seemed to happen more often. Perhaps he would have been more surprised *not* to find his sister with the unlikely detective and their most trusted employee.

Except their most trusted employee had made a confession. One that was hard for him to admit and perhaps even harder for Jasper to hear. His disappointment was palpable but, strange as it seemed, Jasper was relieved to know that Linus was behind the small acts of sabotage that had taken place and doubly relieved when Linus denied stealing any of the designs. Jasper showed them the tracings that Paul had given him.

"I couldn't draw a straight line with a ruler," Linus declared. "Laying that thin paper on top of another sheet of paper wouldn't have done me no good at all. If I was intent on stealing those designs, I'd have taken them straight and simple."

"That's what most people probably would have done," Polly said. "The only reason not to take the original sketches would be to keep you from knowing the theft had occurred. It's a diabolical way to think."

"But it doesn't bring us any closer to identifying the thief." Jasper released a heavy sigh.

"I'm afraid not," Polly admitted, her voice saddened by defeat. Jasper clasped her hand in his and momentarily wished they were alone so he could tell her that it didn't matter. They'd found each other and, for him, that was enough. He prayed that she cared the same way about him. Since she didn't pull her hand from his, he had reason to believe his prayer had been answered.

"Linus has more to tell you," Elsie said, breaking into Jasper's thoughts. "It's about a promise Father made to him. One he didn't keep."

"I don't want to tell that story again, Miss Elsie," Linus said. The poor man looked like he'd rather be anywhere else than in the Stone House parlor.

"Do you mind if I tell it then?" Elsie asked him. Linus merely shook his head.

Jasper's heart pounded, alternating between anger and sorrow, as Elsie shared their father's treachery to his longtime employee. No wonder Linus had stopped whistling while he worked.

"I don't understand," Jasper said when Elsie had finished. "Why would Father do something so cruel?"

"There's something else you should know," Elsie said.

Jasper wasn't sure how much more bad news he could take. But he owed it to Elsie to listen to whatever she needed to tell him. He'd seen himself reflected in a metaphorical mirror—one that Polly held up to her brother. Their relationship was much like his and Elsie's. And even though Polly was careful never to criticize Isaac, she'd made a few little comments that had made Jasper realize he was prone to be as overprotective of Elsie as Isaac was of Polly.

Their sisters were strong, capable women with God-given gifts and paths to walk. Who were they, as brothers, even with their well-meaning motives, to stand in their way? To tell them *no* and *you can't*? Jasper had promised himself that he'd change. He just wasn't sure how to do that.

Mrs. Bennett chose that moment to bring in a tea cart complete with the silver tea service, a tray of triangular sandwiches, and a plate of decorated sugar cookies as if they were hosting the King and Queen of England. She pretended not to notice Elsie's and Polly's strange attire or Linus's glaze-stained pants.

Although Mrs. Bennett and her husband would probably know the details of their conversation before it was over, Elsie went along with the pretense that family discussions were private and waited for the housekeeper to return to the kitchen.

Once she was gone, Elsie wasted no time.

"Father misled me just like he misled Linus," she said. "He told me that half of his estate would be left to me."

Jasper's stomach dropped, and his grip on Polly's hand tightened. When he spoke, his voice was a mere whisper. "He never said anything like that to me."

"Never?" The pain in Elsie's voice was heart-wrenching.

Jasper cleared his throat. "He only said that Stone House should always be your home and that I needed to provide for you. I always planned to. I always will."

"That's not what I want, Jasper. It's not what I need."

Of course it's not.

As if scales had fallen from his eyes, Jasper knew exactly what he needed to do to fulfill the promise he'd made to himself to change only a few minutes before. Somehow, he needed to give Elsie the financial independence she craved. He wasn't sure how to make that possible when their cash reserves were so low. He only knew that the plan had to be one that the two of them worked out together.

"It won't happen overnight," he said. "But I promise you'll receive what Father promised you."

A relieved smile lifted Elsie's features. "Half of the estate is more than I want or need," she said. "But the pittance Father left me is too little."

"We'll work together to make it just right," Jasper assured her. Then he turned to Linus. He didn't see how it was possible to keep the promise that Father had made to him. Or even if it would be wise to part with a percentage of the company to anyone who wasn't family. Linus must have realized Jasper's struggle from his facial expression.

"I don't deserve nothin' from you, young Jasper," he said. "I done betrayed your trust with what all I did, yet here you are givin' me these fine sandwiches. It's more than I should have."

"A bite to eat is little compared to what you've given our family over the years," Elsie said.

"I agree with Elsie," Jasper said. "Father betrayed your trust, but I don't want you to leave us. We need your expertise and your knowledge. Please don't go."

"I'd never go unless you kicked me out the back door," Linus declared.

"There's nothing more to say then, is there? At least not tonight. In the next few days, though, we need to discuss the possibility of developing a new line. In fact, multiple new lines. Otherwise, Vernon Spears might steal all my designs while we disappear into obscurity." Polly spoke up. "That's not going to happen. We're going to find that thief, and Linus is going to help."

When all eyes turned to her, Polly bit the inside of her lip. She'd spoken with such confidence, and now they looked to her for a solution. But she had nothing that could be called a plan. Only a tiny inkling of an idea that she prayed would lead to another idea and then another and then another.

"Tell me what to do, miss." Linus's voice sounded hopeful for the first time since Polly and Elsie had found him sitting on the barrel in the factory. "I'll do whatever I can to be of help."

Polly believed he was genuinely sorry for the trouble he'd caused and wanted to make amends. She counted on that.

"Earlier you said you heard Jasper and me talking when we were in his office late that night."

"You mean when you broke in? Sure. I remember."

Elsie's eyes widened, and she stared at Polly. "You did what?"

"I broke into Jasper's office. He found me there." She gave in to a sudden urge to shoot a grin in Jasper's direction. *Should I tell them I flipped you on your back?* His eyes sparkled with amusement, but his jaw might as well have been set in cement. His response was clear. *Don't you dare.*

Polly shifted her focus to Elsie. "You heard him say it too. That he heard Jasper and me talking the night I 'snuck in.'"

"You're right," Elsie said. "I did. But with everything else that was said, I missed that little detail."

Another inkling of an idea suddenly presented itself. With enough inklings, maybe they'd identify the thief before he disappeared. And there it was. A third inkling.

"Polly?" Jasper said, his voice reaching her as if from a faraway place. "What are you thinking?"

She took a moment to gather her thoughts then answered him. "A few things. For one, what Elsie just said about little details. She heard Linus say I 'snuck in' but was surprised when I said I had broken in. Her mind was on other things, and that little detail from Linus didn't matter to her then. What other little details could we be overlooking because they didn't seem important at the time?"

"I don't know." Jasper narrowed his eyes, and Polly could almost see his mind churning over the events of the past several days to find a significant detail he'd missed.

"I was also thinking that we need to find the thief before he disappears. But maybe he already has. Have any employees quit lately? Or gone away?"

"None that I know of," Jasper said without hesitation. "Linus? Do you know of anyone?"

The older man gave the question only a second more thought than Jasper had. "I've seen everyone doin' what they're supposed to be doin'. Don't know of anyone missing."

"That sounds risky, doesn't it?" Elsie asked. "Though I suppose he doesn't want to draw attention to himself by leaving, he's also risking arrest by staying around."

Inkling!

Polly inwardly smiled. They were making progress, slowly but surely. "He may be staying because he's greedy. He made a successful sale to Vernon Spears, but what if one sale wasn't enough?"

"Paul Nolan said no," Jasper said. "We don't know yet if anyone else was contacted."

"Why those two, I wonder." Elsie tilted her head in thought. "The thief must have expected Paul to be interested in the designs. He surely didn't foresee Paul telling Jasper about the offer."

"You're right," Polly said. "There has to be a reason he went to those two men first. Since the three of you know them and I don't, you'll need to think of what they have in common."

"I can't think of much exceptin' they run a factory just the same as young Jasper does." Linus awkwardly balanced a porcelain teacup and saucer on his lap. "Miss Polly, were you wantin' to ask me somethin' about that night in the office?"

Her first inkling. Somehow it had gotten lost as she followed her others. But now that he'd brought it back up, her stomach clenched at having to ask the question. "I don't believe you stole the designs," she said, holding his gaze. "But can you tell us what you were doing at the factory that night? And why Jasper and I didn't see you?"

Elsie threw up her hands. "This is why I'm never able to solve any of the mysteries in the novels I read. It didn't even occur to me to ask that question." At the sight of Linus's crestfallen expression, she leaned forward. "Don't you see, Linus? That's because I trust you. If you were at the factory, it's because you had a good reason to be. I would never wonder why."

"The same goes for me," Jasper said. "But since Polly asked…"

Linus carefully set the fragile cup and saucer on a nearby table. "Not for anything nefarious. I got what I've heard called insomnia. Sometimes I can't sleep, so I go for a walk. And more often than not that walk takes me to the factory, so I wander around. Make sure everything is as it should be. No other reason than that."

"You walk all the way from your house to the factory?" Elsie asked, her tone bordering on disbelief. "At night?"

"I don't want to saddle up Penny again, not late at night. Besides, it's only a bit of a hike if you follow the road, but I don't do that. I go by way of the tunnel."

"The tunnel," Jasper and Elsie exclaimed at the same time while Polly stared at the three of them.

"What tunnel?" she asked.

"It's an old one," Jasper said. "Stories go around that it was part of the Underground Railroad. There's one that connects the train depot to Reed's Mansion. The boardinghouse where you're staying."

"Miss Marla had her end of it bricked off though," Elsie said. "Another tunnel goes from the depot to the cellar at the factory. I thought it was closed too."

"Used to be." Linus chuckled. "Still looks like it is if you don't look at the boards too close. They open up like a door if you know how to do it."

He cast an amused look at Jasper, whose ears suddenly flamed red.

"Mark and I did that one summer." He smiled as he seemed to get lost in the memory of two mischievous boys looking for an adventure. "I hadn't thought about that in ages."

As he reminisced about how they'd managed the feat, Polly's mind fixated on another inkling. She'd intended to ask Linus if he'd ever seen anyone else at the factory during his late-night visits, but the conversation kept veering off in other directions.

At least now she knew of one other person who knew about the tunnel. Mark Gleason. Jasper's boyhood friend who'd left Crooksville when his father ended his partnership with the Kanes to open his own factory in North Carolina. A factory that failed, leaving Mark without a business of his own. Without an inheritance. Without any prospects unless he married money, which he seemed willing to do. He'd practically said as much at dinner the other night.

Polly gathered other threads from the conversations and stories told that evening she'd dined at Stone House. Threads that wove themselves into a tapestry and told a story of expectations, resentment, stolen dreams, and a friend betrayed.

Mark had come to Crooksville for the reading of Edmund Kane's last will and testament. Had Edmund promised him an inheritance, as he had Elsie and Linus, and then broken that promise? Had Mark, believing in the depths of his heart that the Kanes owed him for his father's contribution to their success, entered the factory through the tunnel and traced Jasper's designs?

The conversation surrounding her had grown raucous as Jasper and Elsie told hilarious stories about their childhood exploits with Mark. Even Linus had shared two or three, and each of them had tears of laughter streaming down their faces.

"How much longer is Mark staying in town?" Polly asked during a break in the conversation. She tried keeping her tone as neutral as possible, but Jasper's eyes flickered, and his jovial mood faded.

"We had breakfast this morning at the Bisque Biscuit," Jasper said. "He's waiting for a bank transaction to arrive. Something about an old debt someone owed his father's estate. Once he receives the money, he plans to go west."

"We'll have to throw him a going-away party," Elsie said. "I'll bake my blackberry mint tart. He seemed to enjoy it at dinner the other night."

"That's a fine idea." Jasper caught Polly's gaze and shifted his eyes to the door.

"It's getting late," she said. "We should talk again tomorrow."

"I agree." Jasper rose and returned his cup to the tea cart. "I'll take you home, Linus."

"Penny is at the factory, but I wouldn't mind if you took me there."

"That's fine," Jasper agreed. "Polly, if you'd like to come along, we can go by the boardinghouse after I drop off Linus."

Polly readily agreed. She and Jasper needed to talk in private. She knew, and she was certain Jasper did too, that Mark was waiting for money that had nothing to do with an old debt.

They'd identified the thief, but they had no proof. What would Jasper choose to do now?

CHAPTER THIRTEEN

Jasper and Polly followed Linus and Penny, the swayback mare, to the mounting block. Other than the scuffle of their feet along the dirt path, all was quiet at the factory. A three-quarter moon reflected pale light upon them, enough for Linus to adjust the saddle before getting astride the horse. He'd refused Jasper's offer to drive him home. He didn't want to leave the mare in the outbuilding all night even though they'd found her resting in a stall.

Once Linus and his mare were out of sight among the trees near the road, Jasper reached for Polly's hand, and they sauntered back to his Packard. From a nearby pond, the night creatures performed their musical overtures, and a few fireflies, up past their bedtime, flitted among the shrubs lining the drive.

"It's so peaceful here," he said. "And yet…" His voice cracked, and he pressed his lips together. He couldn't put off his suspicions any longer. "You think Mark stole my designs, don't you?"

"It seems likely." She ran her free hand along his arm, a sweet and comforting gesture that warmed his heart. "Did your father leave him anything?"

"Only a box of memorabilia. Photographs, newspaper clippings. That kind of thing." Jasper released a heavy sigh. He'd never understand why his father had made promises he didn't intend to keep. "My guess is he was promised something more substantial."

"Perhaps your father intended to change his will but died before he had the chance."

"That's a generous viewpoint, and I'd like to think it's true. His death took us all by surprise."

"But you have your doubts."

Jasper halted and turned so he and Polly faced each other. She looked lovely in the moonlight, her fair skin radiant beneath her blond waves. "Did they teach you mind reading at the Pinkerton Academy? You seem to always know what I'm thinking."

"I could say the same about you."

He glanced at her black outfit, the same clothes she'd worn when he caught her snooping in his office, and a mischievous idea blanketed the gloom caused by his father and supposed best friend. Why not? She was already dressed for an adventure.

"Can you read my mind now?" he challenged.

Polly searched his eyes, and her expression shifted from curiosity to excitement in the space of two heartbeats. Gripping his hands, she hopped up and down. "The tunnel."

"I have a flashlight in my car."

Within a few minutes, they were inside the factory. Jasper opened the cellar door and twisted the switch. A series of light bulbs flickered then remained on in the room below.

"Be careful on the stairs," he warned Polly. "They're old and steep."

"I will be," she promised.

He preceded her, testing each step as he went. "I don't even remember the last time I was down here." With each step, more of the room came into view. Old furniture, shelving, equipment, and boxes lined the walls. More boxes formed piles, though a meandering path made it possible to reach the door that connected to the tunnel.

"Perhaps I should ask Linus to sort through whatever we've got stored in these boxes and clean it out," Jasper said.

"It might also be a good idea to put a lock on the cellar door."

"I think I'll put a lock on the tunnel door too." He laughed. "It may sound strange, but I don't mind the idea of Linus wandering around here at night. Keeping an eye on things. Maybe we could fix up a couple of rooms for him so he could live here."

"Do you think he'd want to do that?"

"Maybe." Jasper reached the bottom step and turned to take Polly's hand. "The place he lives in now isn't much more than a shack. It must be miserable in the winter, but it's land that's been in his family for a couple of generations. He might not want to leave, but that would be his decision to make. I can at least offer him a choice."

Polly rested her palm on his cheek. "He sabotages your factory, and you reward him with a home. You're too good to be true, Jasper Kane."

He placed his hand against hers, enjoying the touch of her soft palm against his cheek. "I have more faults than I care to admit. If I thought Linus meant any genuine harm…"

"But he didn't."

"I can't give him what Father promised. But I need to do what I can."

His gaze went from Polly's eyes to her red-tinted lips. Overwhelmed by the desire to kiss her, he slid his arm around her waist and brushed his fingers along her neck. Her soft curls fell against the back of his hand. His mouth hovered less than a heartbeat away.

Loud applause echoed in the room, followed by heavy footsteps. "Congratulations," a familiar voice shouted.

The spell broken, Jasper turned and sheltered Polly behind him as Mark emerged from behind a stack of boxes, one hand behind his back.

"You'll lose your factory in a horrible fire," he said. "And each other too."

Fear raced up Jasper's spine, but somehow he managed not to let it show on his face. "What are you doing here?" he asked, as if delighted with the surprise of seeing his old friend. "Earlier tonight I told Polly about the tunnel. I see you remembered it too."

"You're not fooling me, Jasper." Mark came closer. "I don't know what game your father was trying to play, but it doesn't matter. You'll die here, the factory will burn, Elsie will inherit everything, including the insurance benefits for this old place, and I'll be here to mourn with her and dry her tears."

Jasper's chest roiled with fear and anger. The slight pressure of Polly's hand on his back calmed him even as she pushed him a step forward. He didn't know what she intended, but despite all his inclination to keep as much distance between her and Mark as possible, he trusted her. That realization both surprised and strengthened him.

"None of that will ever happen," Jasper said, his voice firmer than he would have dreamed possible in such a situation.

"But it will." Mark's eyes gleamed with hatred. "I have the matches in my pocket to make it so. And I have this."

He held up a steel pipe he'd been holding behind his back.

The pressure of Polly's hand on Jasper increased ever so slightly. He took another step forward, and doubt flickered in Mark's eyes. But only for a moment before the hate and an eerie calm returned.

"You don't think I'll do it," Mark said. "I might have been able to save my father from drowning in that accident." He pointed the pipe at Jasper's chest. "If I'd wanted to."

Jasper struggled to keep his face impassive, but it was impossible. He'd always known that Mark and his father didn't get along, but the elder Mr. Gleason wasn't a horrible person. If anything, he was too indulgent with his son. Mark could do no wrong in his father's eyes. Apparently, he'd paid the ultimate price for never forcing Mark to face the consequences of his actions.

That ended now.

Polly's hand on Jasper's back unleashed an iron resolve that braced him for the fight he now faced. A fight he had every intention of winning. His future, Polly's future, and even Elsie's future depended on their victory. What Mark, in his hubris, didn't know was that Jasper didn't fight alone.

Mark placed the pipe on his shoulder as if it were a baseball bat he was readying for a pitch. "Go down easy, Jasper, and I'll see to it that Polly doesn't suffer too much. Or Elsie either when it's her time to go."

"Left," Polly whispered.

Jasper lunged that direction, drawing Mark's surprised attention, as a black-clad human dynamo sprang into action. Polly, head bent, rammed into Mark's ribs, knocking the breath out of him. Jasper grabbed hold of the steel pipe, and the two men wrestled for control of the weapon. Meanwhile, Polly pressed her fingers into Mark's throat, maneuvered into position, and flipped him onto his back. The sound of his head hitting the cement floor made a sickening sound Jasper hoped never to hear again.

He wrenched the pipe from Mark's grip then pulled Polly into a tight hug.

"I'm fine," she assured him as she rubbed the top of her head. "Maybe a little bruised here and there, but all in one piece."

"Same for me." Jasper prodded Mark with the end of the steel pipe. A soft groan emitted from his lips, but at least he wasn't bleeding. "We need to tie him up before he regains consciousness."

He looked around the room and spied a coil of clothesline on a shelf. Perfect.

As soon as Mark's hands and feet were bound, Polly raced upstairs to phone for help. It didn't take long for the police chief and Crooksville's only deputy to arrive, followed by the fire chief, most of the fire department volunteers, and the editor of the *Crooksville News*. Roy Watkins, Vivian Ayers and her fiancé, plus other Kane Pottery employees somehow heard the news and showed up too.

No one wanted to miss out on the most excitement there'd been in Crooksville since Farmer Bailey's old Hereford cow gave birth to a two-headed calf.

Before Mark, who'd regained consciousness and complained about a pounding headache, was hauled off to the town jail, Elsie arrived with the Bennetts. Vernon Spears dared to show his face, apparently hoping to make quick amends so he didn't get caught up in what could turn out to be a nasty scandal.

Jasper took great satisfaction in ordering him out of the factory.

When the furor died down and everyone was finally on their way home, Jasper and Elsie insisted that Polly come home with them. They had plenty of extra rooms, and Elsie was certain she'd get more rest there than at Reed's Mansion. All the other boarders no doubt would be pestering her to share the story again and again.

Jasper agreed, though he simply wanted her nearby.

Always and forever.

CHAPTER FOURTEEN

After a better night's sleep than she'd expected to have, Polly joined Jasper and Elsie in the breakfast room. The charming space was beautifully decorated in blues, yellows, and muted pinks. The early morning sun shone through the east-facing windows, forming rectangles of light on the patterned rugs in front of the fireplace.

Though they'd stayed up late rehashing everything that had happened, the experience was still too new to ignore. Especially when Mrs. Bennett brought Jasper a special edition of the *Crooksville News* along with his pancakes and bacon.

"Front page coverage." Jasper held up the newspaper for Elsie and Polly to see the photo spread that took up most of the page. "You can't buy that kind of publicity."

"I'm not sure it's the kind of publicity we want," Elsie said as she added two sugar cubes to her coffee. "I, for one, hope to never see Mark Gleason again as long as I live. Or another photo of him."

She was horrified when Jasper had told her of Mark's plans. But that horror quickly turned to angry indignation that Mark had ever imagined she'd have sought him out in her grief. "I never liked him," she declared. Jasper had shared a glance with Polly that clearly said he wasn't sure that was true, but he'd wisely kept the comment to himself.

"May I see it?" Polly asked. Jasper handed her the newspaper. The photo spread included pictures of the factory, of Jasper talking to the chief of police, and one of Mark glowering at the camera that somehow ended up appearing pathetic.

Jasper glanced over her shoulder. "They should have included a photo of you," he said to Polly.

"I specifically asked the editor not to," she said, spreading jam on her toast. "A good detective seeks anonymity, not fame."

"Tell that to Sherlock Holmes," Jasper teased.

Mrs. Bennett appeared in the doorway a few moments later. "There's a gentleman here to see you, miss," she said, but the words were scarcely out of her mouth when a ginger-haired man with freckles and a bookish air pushed past her.

"Which one of you two ladies is Miss Elizabeth Kane?" he demanded to know.

Jasper rose to his feet. "Now see here…"

A second later, Elsie rose and placed her hand on Jasper's shoulder. Her eyes sparkled, and dots of pink highlighted her cheeks. "I'm Elizabeth Kane."

The man rushed forward to within a few feet of Elsie, a huge smile stretching from one ear to the other. "I knew it had to be you." He glanced at Polly. "No offense to you, miss."

"None taken." Polly shot an amused glance in Jasper's direction. At his questioning look, she shrugged. She'd never seen this man before in her life.

The stranger started to extend a hand to Elsie then changed his mind and removed his hat. Holding it in front of him, he made an awkward bow. "I know we said we'd wait to meet each other until after your mourning. But when I heard what happened at the factory...is it true? Was it burnt to the ground? Were you injured? I had to see for myself that you'd escaped."

Elsie, who seemed to be in a state of shock, quickly recovered. "Oh, no. It wasn't burnt at all. And I wasn't even there."

Relief washed over the man's features, which Polly found both odd and adorable. After all, Elsie stood before him in perfect health. And yet he still needed her reassurance before he could believe she hadn't suffered any harm.

"I came as quickly as I could," he declared. "You will forgive me?"

"Of course I will." Elsie stretched out her hand, and he took it in his as if she'd given him a great treasure. The look of adoration in her eyes was exceeded only by the same look in his.

Jasper cleared his throat then resumed his seat. "Perhaps you'd like to join us for breakfast, Mr....?"

Elsie stepped away from the table to tuck her hand into the stranger's arm. He couldn't seem to take his eyes off of her. "This is Mr. Aloysius Abernathy of the Ross County Abernathys," she said. "And we're engaged to be married."

The hubbub from that announcement continued throughout breakfast as both Elsie and Aloysius talked over one another in their excitement at finally meeting face-to-face. They took turns sharing how their pen-pal relationship had developed into a friendship and then love. Even though Aloysius somehow worked up the courage to propose and Elsie somehow worked up the courage to accept the proposal, they hadn't found the courage to meet—until today.

"At least now I know what was behind all the secret letters and telegrams," Jasper said. "And why you're embroidering new pillowcases."

Elsie blushed as profusely as any young bride.

All things work together for good, Paul wrote to the Romans in the New Testament letter. Polly mused that even Mark's plans for destruction had done so. She doubted Elsie had ever been as happy as she was right now.

Both couples left the breakfast table to enjoy a stroll in the garden, but as they were leaving the house, another young man arrived, his brow tense with worry.

Isaac.

Polly flew into his outstretched arms, reassuring him over and over that she had escaped unharmed. Introductions were made, and everyone gathered with glasses of iced tea and lemonade on the veranda to tell the story once again.

When Jasper recounted how Polly had flipped Mark head over heels, Isaac beamed at her. "I should never have doubted you," he said. "Never again. I promise."

The pride shining in his eyes warmed her heart, but his words burrowed deep into her soul. Just like Elsie, Polly didn't know when she'd ever been happier.

Chapter Fifteen

A few weeks later

Polly studied her reflection in the mirror in the guest room at Stone House and adjusted the lace headpiece into a more flattering position. She was honored when Elsie asked her to be a bridesmaid, but that didn't stop the butterflies from flitting around in her stomach.

A knock sounded at the door. "Come in," she called as she smoothed the skirt of her tea-length dress. The rose-colored fabric shimmered with the movement.

The door opened wide enough for Jasper to poke his head in. "Are you sure you don't mind? There's no strange superstition about a groomsman not seeing a bridesmaid before the wedding, is there?"

"Not that I know of, but I still wasn't expecting to see you." She smiled at him. "I am glad though. I need to go to Elsie's room soon, and I imagine the rest of the day will be joyful madness."

"That's why I came now." He slipped inside, and his gaze swept over her. "You look lovely."

Polly's cheeks warmed as she reveled in the joy of this moment. She'd come to Crooksville to find a thief. She hadn't expected to find a beau.

"Have you seen Elsie?" she asked.

"We talked earlier this morning. She's ecstatic with her wedding present." He took both of Polly's hands in his. "I'm sure that she and Aloysius will be very happy growing old together in Stone House."

"It was a kind gesture on your part. And a generous one."

"It was the right thing to do. Especially after I talked to Father's attorney."

Jasper had told Polly about the conversation over lunch at the Bisque Biscuit immediately after leaving the attorney's office. His father's scheduled meeting never took place, and though the attorney didn't know Edmund's intentions, Jasper chose to believe his father meant to make the promised changes to his will. Rather than taking a larger share of the business, Elsie was ecstatic when Jasper gave her full ownership of Stone House.

"At least Elsie is allowing me to live here. And Linus is happy with the plans for his new home at the factory." Jasper's eyes twinkled. "Which reminds me. I have a present for you too."

He disappeared into the hall and returned moments later with a large box wrapped with silver ribbons. He set it on a nearby table. "This is for you."

"What is it?"

"A surprise for the girl of my dreams."

Intrigued, Polly untied the ribbons and removed the lid. Inside the padded box rested the loveliest vase she'd ever seen next to a sealed jar holding bits and pieces of something she couldn't identify. She gave Jasper a curious look then removed the vase. The glaze was a blue so muted as to be almost white. The rounded base tapered upwards to a slender "waist" then tapered out again to a beautifully flared rim. Lovely bluebirds and vines rose and angled upward, winding from base to rim. The aesthetic was calming and breathtaking at the same time.

"You made this?" she said, awestruck by its beauty and the talent behind its creation. This was a gift she'd treasure for as long as she lived.

"For you." He removed the clear jar. "Then I broke the mold and encased the pieces inside here so there will never be another one like it. Just like there will never be, can never be, another you."

Polly stood with the other bridesmaids as Elsie and Aloysius said their vows, but she had eyes only for the handsome groomsman who'd somehow managed to steal her heart from the moment she'd flipped him on his back when he caught her snooping in his office. Considering how often he smiled at her, he didn't mind.

As she predicted, the rest of the day was joyful madness with toasts and good wishes, dancing and dining. Finally, it was time for the newly wedded couple to leave for their honeymoon trip to Niagara Falls.

Elsie had changed from her beautiful wedding dress into a sapphire-blue traveling outfit with matching hat. She halted halfway down the stairs that led to the foyer and looked over the crowd of well-wishers. A moment later, the bridal bouquet sailed over the banister.

And into Polly's arms.

MENDED BY LOVE

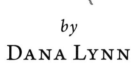

by

DANA LYNN

"E Concrematio, Confirmatio—*out of the fire comes firmness, through stress we pass to strength.*"

—CHARLES F. BINNS, KNOWN AS THE "FATHER OF AMERICAN STUDIO CERAMICS"
FIRST DIRECTOR OF THE NEW YORK STATE
COLLEGE OF CERAMICS

CHAPTER ONE

Crooksville, Ohio

Present Day

She didn't have time for a flat tire.

Claire Derrick stared down at the offending rear driver's-side wheel and barely controlled the urge to stomp her foot like a toddler in the midst of a tantrum. This was no minor issue. If the tire had merely been low on air, she could deal with that. She always had a portable pump in the back of the car.

This, however, needed more than a little air. The silver rim of the hubcap touched the ground, and the black rubber of the tire spread out like it had melted. She had a tire pancake. She bent and peered closer, her breath leaving her in a whoosh. Worse than that. There was no mistaking the long, gaping hole in the side of it.

Her tire had been deliberately slashed.

Why? Her stomach sank and quivered. What about the other side?

She walked around the front of the vehicle, the three-inch heels of her shoes clicking a determined beat on the cement driveway. The front passenger tire was in perfect condition. The rear tire, however, was an exact twin of the one on the driver's side.

She peered down the street both ways, looking to see if there were any strangers lurking around. She didn't see anything out of place. No strange vehicles. It was only seven o'clock on a Friday morning. Most people were inside, getting ready to head to work. Wrapping her arms around herself to ward off the October chill, she considered her options.

What was she supposed to do now? She had an eight-fifteen appointment she could not skip. Her gaze flicked back to the tire.

She only had one spare. There was no way she could change two tires, drive to her office to pick up some papers, and then head to one of her properties to finish prepping for tomorrow's open house. Not on her own.

Whipping out her phone, she called the only person she knew who would help her. The only person she'd ever willingly ask for help.

"Claire!" Suzanne Nelson's normal sunny greeting chirped through the cell phone. "I didn't expect to hear from you until later. I thought you had errands to run."

"I do." Claire kicked the tire. "I have a problem, Suze. Someone slashed my back tires."

"No!" Shock dripped from Suzanne's voice. "Did you park it in the garage last night?"

Claire winced. She had a perfectly good two-car garage but had not used it. "No. The battery on the remote died, and I didn't have any more. And then, once I got inside, I got too busy and forgot."

"For someone who likes to be in control…"

"Yeah, yeah. I know. Anyway, I need a ride to my office."

There was a slight hesitation on the other end of the phone. "You need to report this, Claire. I'm serious."

"I know." Tears pressed against the backs of her eyelids.

"Listen, I'll drive you to the office. Then we can stop by the police station and make a report. How does that sound?"

Claire sighed. "You don't know how much I appreciate this."

"Who else would you call but your bestie? I'll be over in thirty."

True to her word, Suzanne pulled up in her sporty little car twenty-five minutes later. The trip to Claire's office would take just a few minutes. When she plopped back down in Suzanne's passenger seat, she groaned and stretched her legs. "I should know better than to wear heels on days like this."

Suzanne curled her lip. "I'm totally jealous that you can. If I wore heels of any size, I'd tower over Phillip."

Claire chuckled, gazing at her friend with affection. While Claire was barely five foot five and often felt the need for more height so those she worked with would take her seriously, her dark-haired best friend was five foot nine and so was her spouse.

"I owe you. How about a trail ride this weekend?" Both women had been in love with horses since they could talk. In fact, that was how they'd met. They had both signed up for summer riding lessons at Brooks Hollow Stables right outside of Crooksville. Suzanne was nine, and Claire had just turned eight. They were a year apart in school, but their love of all things equine sealed the bond between them. A bond that grew when they entered the same equine 4-H club. Years of training and competing together made them sisters in all but blood.

"Um. I don't think I can," Suzanne said, her voice unnaturally high. As if she was nervous about something. Odd.

Claire shifted in her seat to get a better look at her friend. Suze would not meet her eyes. Her hands clenched and unclenched on the wheel. Both were signs that Suzanne was hiding something.

It was on the tip of her tongue to push, but something held her back. Suzanne had never kept anything from her. Which meant she would tell Claire in her own sweet time. Claire would never forget how Suzanne had stood beside her during the worst time in her life. She could wait a little while longer, give her friend the time she needed.

"Should we go to the police station first?"

Immediately, Suzanne perked up. "Absolutely."

The Crooksville Police Department, like many of the other official buildings, was made mostly of brick. The bottom third consisted of gray stone. Above that, the construction of the building had been completed with smaller bricks of varying shades, although red-colored bricks made up the majority. The sign on the building proudly referred to Crooksville as "The Clay City." Which made sense, since Crooksville's claim to fame was her pottery-crafting heritage.

Claire and Suzanne signed in at the front desk. The receptionist had them wait until an officer was available to talk with them. Claire tapped her shoes impatiently on the floor while they waited. It wasn't that long. Fifteen minutes at the most. However, Claire's nerves were already rattled. The idea that someone was targeting her was not something she wanted to dwell on.

Finally, they were called back, and the young officer greeted them and brought them both a cup of ice water before he began talking to Claire.

"What line of work are you in?"

"I'm a Realtor. I also dabble in renovating historic homes that were abandoned after the flooding nearly a decade ago. In fact, I have an open house scheduled for one of them tomorrow."

"Do you have any enemies? Anyone who might want to hurt you?"

Claire frowned. "I can't think of anyone. You don't think it's just a kid's prank?"

He took off his glasses and set them on his desk. "Ma'am, I don't think we can rule anything out. Unfortunately, right now, we have no suspects or motives. We will investigate though."

Clearly, he did not believe they would find the person responsible. She should have known it would be like this. "I see. Well, thank you for your time."

He walked them out to the front door and handed Claire his card. "Call me if you think of anything else."

She glanced down at it. *Sergeant Barry Stonis.* She followed Suzanne to the car.

"What a bummer." Suzanne started the ignition. "Look, why don't we go grab a bite to eat? It's almost ten thirty."

Claire opened her mouth to decline then changed her mind. Suzanne was biting her lip. She wanted to talk but wasn't sure how to begin. Realizing her friend might need her, Claire nodded. After all Suzanne had done for her, it was the least she could do.

"I didn't eat breakfast. I could do with an early lunch."

An hour later, they had both finished their chicken and cranberry salads and were on their second cups of coffee and dessert. Claire scooped her last bite of red velvet cheesecake into her mouth while her friend played with her pumpkin cake.

Finally, she ran out of patience.

"Out with it, Suzanne." Claire set her fork down on her plate and pushed it to the side. She waited while the server removed the empty dishes and set the check on the table. When the teenager left,

Claire clasped her hands on the table and leaned forward, catching her oldest and dearest friend with a level stare.

Suzanne squirmed, her cheeks flushing. She twisted her wedding band, still shiny after eight months of marriage.

Claire gentled her tone. "Come on, Suze. Whatever it is, you know you can tell me."

Finally, after what seemed like an eternity, Suzanne released a gentle sigh. "I know. Clary, you're my best friend ever. You've had such a horrible day, and I feel guilty. Maybe this can wait."

"Are you sick?" Claire clenched her hands so hard, her nails dug into her palms. She'd been sick and would not wish it on anyone, especially not Suze.

"No!" Suzanne burst out, shaking her head and making her ponytail swing. "It's not that. It's just, I'm so happy, but I don't want to hurt you."

That was when she knew.

"You're pregnant."

She truly was happy for her best friend. Suzanne and Phillip both wanted a large family. At the same time, however, the knowledge hit her like a physical blow. This was one experience she'd never be able to share with her best friend. It had been more than a decade since the chemotherapy had eradicated cancer from her body and destroyed her hope of becoming a mother. The medical advance that saved her life had destroyed one of her biggest dreams at the same time.

She'd considered becoming a foster mother. She'd gone through the approval process but had never gotten the courage to take in any children.

In time, she had decided she wasn't meant to be a mother.

She thought she'd gotten past the dream and the pain.

Until now.

Suzanne, though, didn't need to know this. Claire would be pleased for her friend and not dampen her joy. Reaching across the table, she grabbed Suzanne's hands. "That's wonderful news! Do I get to play Auntie Claire?"

Suzanne said through her tears, "Of course! The only aunt, since both my brother and Phillip's brother aren't married yet."

"I call dibs on godmother."

"You got it."

Laughing, Claire grabbed the bill and insisted on paying. They were turning away from the cash register when the newscast on the television caught her gaze. Horror crept into every pore and chilled her blood. The pretty anchor smiled as she gestured to the once gorgeous structure smoldering behind her.

"Unfortunately, this house, slated to be opened up for public viewing tomorrow, is a total loss."

"No!"

Claire didn't hear any more as she stared at the ruin of her beautiful house. The one she'd spent months renovating was now nothing but ash.

Everything about this fire screamed arson.

When his pager went off at five a.m., Jason Pierce had flown from his bed. He'd been a volunteer firefighter and EMT for nearly two years. While he couldn't attend all calls, he had more flexibility than many of the members, thanks to owning his own business. When he heard the dispatcher announce a structure fire, he didn't hesitate. Every available person would be needed. He had heard the address and decided against heading to the station, knowing the trucks would have already left. Instead, he hopped into his four-door sedan and drove to the scene. The fire was a fully involved out-of-control blaze when he arrived. Structure fires were always bad. And, on a day like today, when there was a stiff, cold breeze, there was the risk of the fire spreading. They usually burned slower though. This one burned like an accelerant had been liberally used. He had seen enough fires while serving in the army to know the looks of an unnatural burn.

And then there were the other arsons. A string of buildings and houses on the market in Perry County had been set on fire in the past year. This house made number six. To his knowledge, the police had no leads. The houses weren't all listed by the same real estate agencies, so it was hard to pinpoint a target. Technically, any structure up for sale was in danger right now.

Jason and the other volunteer firefighters worked efficiently, gathering the four-inch hose and other equipment and replacing it on the trucks. Three departments had responded to the early morning fire, including Harrison Township, Bearfield Township, and Clayton Township. The fire chief ambled from one area to the next, giving advice and encouragement, his white helmet bobbing like a beacon.

Now, if only the news crew would leave and let them complete their work. He scowled at the blond anchor who kept getting in their way. If this had been the first fire, she might not have been so persistent. But, like a shark scenting blood, she was on the trail of something bigger.

When she approached him and shoved the microphone in his face, he dodged it. "Sorry, ma'am. I can't talk now. You'd best find the chief and talk to him."

"Well! How rude."

He ignored her and continued working. At least no one lived in the house. That was the only positive in a situation like this.

A car roaring up the road caught his attention. Even as his mind identified his sister's new car, the vehicle screeched to a halt. The passenger door opened, and a short, slim figure with shoulder-length light blond hair, held back with some kind of clip, bounced out of the car, striding toward the house in a power walk on red shoes with ridiculous heels. It was a wonder she didn't trip.

Claire Derrick.

He hadn't seen his sister's best friend since Suzanne's wedding. Before that, it had been nearly two years. He would recognize her anywhere though. The pretty blond was a regular fixture in his house growing up. He had never paid too much attention to her before now. After all, she was only his baby sister's friend.

She headed straight to the house.

"Claire!" He jogged over and cut her off before she got too close. "You can't go near it. It's not safe."

Her wide green eyes had a wild look he didn't like. It took her a moment to look past his firefighter gear. Recognition dawned, and she seemed to calm a bit. Her shoulders relaxed.

"Jason. I–I…" She stumbled over her words before pointing to what was left of the structure. "That's my house."

What?

"I didn't think anyone owned it." A chill swept through him at the thought that she could have been in the house when it burned down. Too many people didn't have smoke detectors in their homes. He shook the grim thoughts away. She was standing safe in front of him. No need to worry about what-ifs. "It's a good thing you weren't home."

She shook her head. "I don't mean I live here. I'm the one who bought it and renovated it. It's a hobby of mine, flipping historic homes and selling them. This one was ready for an open house tomorrow." A tear slipped down her cheek. She swiped it away with a jerky motion. "I want to talk to the fire chief."

He hesitated. "I understand. But he might be another hour or so. I think he's called in a fire and explosion investigator. So it might be even longer than that."

"I don't mind waiting. But—" Her glance slid to Suzanne. "Do you think you, or one of the other firefighters, could give me a ride home?"

"Oh!" Suzanne blinked. "I'll be fine waiting, Clary. Really. I can wait in my car…"

Claire shook her head and glared at his sister. Were they fighting? "You will do no such thing, Suze. You have to take care of yourself. Waiting on the scene of a fire, with all this smoke, won't be good for you. Or the baby. Phillip would have my head if I allowed it."

Jason whirled to his sister. "Wait. You're pregnant?"

Claire winced. Obviously, she thought he knew. He returned his gaze to his sister.

She crossed her arms over her chest and narrowed her eyes. "Yes, I'm pregnant. But that doesn't mean I'm weak."

He held up his hands. "I never said it did. But I also don't want to risk having you here and possibly getting sick. Look, Sis, go on home. Rest. I have my car here. I'll make sure Claire gets home in one piece. All right?"

Huffing, she gave in. "Fine. But I want a phone call when you get home, Claire."

She hugged Claire, kissed him on his soot-covered cheek, and returned to her car. She gave them both a jaunty wave as she drove off.

"She can't be too mad with a wave like that," he commented.

Claire didn't respond. Glancing at her, he frowned. The flash of pain in her expression vanished quickly, but he knew he hadn't imagined it. Something disturbing was happening in her mind. Jason wasn't one to meddle, though, so he pushed it aside.

"Look, I have to help the others get the equipment loaded up, and then we have to make our reports."

"Okay. I'll wait and won't get in the way."

He started to walk off when he saw the over-eager news anchor headed their way. He heard the word "Realtor" and quickly reasoned Claire was her next target. He turned back to her.

"Come with me. We need to get you out of sight before the news lady attacks."

She gave him a surprised glance then peeked over at the approaching anchor. "Lead on!"

Grinning, he tugged her over to the fire engine and had her sit inside while they loaded their gear. Twenty minutes later, he spied the fire chief and a couple of police officers talking. He motioned for Claire to join him.

"I think the chief will be available in a few minutes," he said.

One of the officers, a young man with glasses, looked their way and did a double take. Before Jason knew what was happening, the fire chief and both officers were making their way over to them.

"Miss Derrick," the younger officer said, "I'm surprised to see you here."

"Sergeant Stonis." She dipped her head in acknowledgment. "This house is the one I was telling you about. The one I was showing tomorrow."

Her voice was low, but Jason caught the threads of anguish and anger woven together in her smooth alto tones.

"This is quite a coincidence. First someone slashes your tires, and then they burn a property connected to you."

"Slashed your tires! Claire!" Jason stared at her, shocked to his core.

She didn't respond. Her gaze remained glued to the young sergeant.

"I hate to say it, but I think we need to consider that this arson may be more than merely a random event. It's possible that you've become a target," the officer said.

Jason straightened. This wasn't his business. He shouldn't interfere. He peered at her out of the corner of his eye.

She seemed to wilt as he watched.

"How will you protect her?" The words burst from his mouth without his brain's permission.

The young sergeant shifted his stance.

They weren't going to do anything. What could they do? He knew as well as anyone the police department was small. This arson spree had taxed the city's resources to the limit.

"I'll be fine. I don't need protection." She straightened her posture, and all emotion drained from her expression.

"We do need to talk with you for a few moments, Miss Derrick."

Her flinch was well controlled, but he still saw it. Jason set a hand on her shoulder. "I'll wait for you and give you a ride home."

She nodded. The corners of her mouth tipped up in the tiniest smile he'd ever seen.

The bravery in that smile nearly gutted him.

His determination to not interfere started to crumble.

CHAPTER TWO

Jason distracted himself by assisting the other volunteer firefighters to clean up the scene. As much as they could, anyway. Most of the equipment was already cleared away, and two of the assisting departments had returned to their stations.

"Chief!" A shout had everyone spinning to face the house. The chief hurried over. Within minutes, Jason heard the murmur "accelerant" spread through the group. A heaviness like a rock settled in his gut.

It came as no surprise when the fire chief declared the house fire was indeed arson and the police called in the Fire and Explosion Investigation Bureau. They worked with every sheriff in the state, investigating and ultimately arresting arsonists.

He shook his head. Poor Claire.

The sassy ringtone he'd assigned to his sister broke into his thoughts. Around him, several of the other firefighters chuckled at the sound. He moved slightly away from them to have some privacy. Suzanne was bound to want to talk about Claire.

"Hey, Sis. Did you make it home all right?" Suzanne was forever telling him she was an adult and didn't need to be treated like a baby. It always got her back up when he asked her where she was and what she was doing. He couldn't help himself. That was what brothers did.

A heavy sigh blew down the line. He grinned. That was the other reason he enjoyed checking on her. Heckling his baby sister never grew old. Her reactions always amused him. Deep inside, they both knew they weren't truly annoying each other. She'd miss it if he stopped checking on her welfare.

"Yes, yes, I made it home. And I'm being well tended. As we speak, my husband is making me a cup of hot chocolate and I'm bundled up on the sofa with a book. Happy?"

"Yep. That's what I wanted to hear."

He waited patiently while she pulled the phone away from her mouth and held a muted conversation with her husband. Phillip was a good man. His sister could have done far worse. Part of him envied her. Jason wasn't an extrovert. His time in the military had left him with scars, both physical and emotional. He wasn't sure he could ask a woman to take on someone with his issues. He'd returned home a different person than the adventure-seeking nineteen-year-old he was when he enlisted.

These days, the company he preferred most was his own. He'd long grown used to the knowledge that marriage and family weren't meant for him. And most days, he was a hundred percent on board with that. Until he saw a loving couple like Suzanne and Phillip and knew his own future stretched out long and lonely ahead of him.

"Sorry." Suzanne came back on the line. "I had to talk with Phillip for a second. Listen, did you stay with Claire? Did you get her home? How is she doing?"

He swung his head to peer over his shoulder. She was still being monopolized by the investigators. "Actually, we're still here."

"Still there!" She sounded appalled. "Aren't you done cleaning up?"

"It's not that. The fire chief decided the house fire wasn't accidental. It was arson." Normally, he'd never reveal that information. However, the news anchor had heard and delightedly reported on it. They'd all see it on the six o'clock news that night.

Dead silence fell between them for a moment.

"Arson? Jason! Is she in danger? Oh, why did I let you guys convince me to leave?"

He heard rustling over the phone. "Don't you dare come out here, Suzanne. You hear me? Claire is fine. I'm not leaving without her."

She sniffed.

"Aw, don't cry, Suze. She's fine."

"Did she tell you about the slashed tires? This can't be a coincidence."

"I heard about them. The police and I agree with you."

"So?"

He blinked. Removing the phone from his ear, he frowned down on it for a moment before replacing it and resuming the conversation. "So what?"

"So, what's being done about it? My best friend is under attack. She needs protection, right? Is that happening?"

He rubbed his chin. She was not going to like his answer. "I don't know if anything is being done."

"What?" Her shriek hit his eardrum. He winced.

"Ouch. Take it down a notch, Sis." He switched the phone to his other ear. "Look, it's a small department. They're already stretched. And she hasn't asked for protection. In fact, she pretty much told them she didn't need it."

"Of course she did! She's stubborn. Claire never asks for help. You know that." He could hear her telling Phillip what was going on in the background.

He thought about her words. She was wrong about one thing. He didn't know Claire as well as his sister believed he did. Why should he? He was four years older. By the time she'd entered high school, he was beginning his first full-time job. A short time later, he decided that job wasn't for him, and he went into the army. He'd never paid that much attention to her. Although he had admired her spunk when she'd gone through cancer when she was a teenager. That was when he'd also realized his sister wasn't the shallow girl he had thought she was. She gave up almost everything to spend what time she could with Claire.

His sister was a woman of substance. He was proud of her.

When he said nothing, Suzanne sighed again. "Jason. I know you have your own life and you're a busy man. But could you help her out? You run a security company. Surely you can provide her some protection."

"Suze—"

"Don't say it, Jason. I do not want to hear that she didn't ask for protection. She won't ask. Even if she wants it."

Jason closed his eyes and pinched his nose. He didn't have a choice. There was no way he was going to let his sister down. And, if he was honest with himself, he knew he couldn't walk away from Claire when she needed him. That wasn't who he was. Shame filled him for even considering leaving her to fend for herself.

"Relax, Suzanne. Of course I'll help your friend. How could I turn my back on someone I've known most of my life?"

Immediately, her tone changed, and he listened to her praise his good sense for the next two minutes.

"Enough. Look, I need to make some phone calls. I'll be in touch."

He disconnected the call as soon as he could. Monitoring Claire, he called his company and began making plans to protect her. From where he stood, she looked so small, sandwiched between the officers and the investigator. Even with her heels, all of them stood five or six inches above her.

Who would target her? What could the motive possibly be? He'd promised his sister he'd stick by her.

Jason Pierce never went back on his word. He just hoped Claire would be okay with him hanging around.

Claire dug the heels of her palms into her eyes and rubbed them, trying to get rid of the scratchy feeling. If she had dived headfirst into a sandbox, she doubted her eyes would feel this gritty. Between the tears and the exhaustion and the stress, she was in bad shape. She'd give anything to be able to snap her fingers and start this day all over.

"What about any relationships that have gone poorly?" the investigator from the Fire and Explosion Investigation Bureau asked her. The man was relentless. He had already gone through her entire family, not that there was anyone except for her mother, her stepfather, and her little sister to be considered. And they all lived in Florida.

She sighed. She might as well just get it all over with, and then he might let her go while he completed his investigation. Besides, it wasn't as if he wouldn't find out everything anyway. That was his job. Claire knew that very little of anyone's personal life was truly private these days in the age of social media.

"I was engaged to be married two years ago. He had political aspirations and didn't feel I fit the qualifications of a politician's wife."

"What qualifications would that be?"

Of course, he couldn't just let it go. She lowered her glance so she was looking over his shoulder and not directly at him. It was the only way she could talk about such a private topic with a strange man. Even if he was an officer. "I'm not able to have children. He felt it was important for a politician to have a family to gain the public's trust."

"I'm going to need his name."

"Adam Hunter." That name had not crossed her lips in over a year and a half. It always left a bitter aftertaste in her mouth.

The investigator nodded and made a note on his tablet. She was glad he didn't offer her any sympathy. She just wanted the conversation to be done. "What about rivals at work?" He tilted his head and raised his eyebrows at her.

Claire started to shake her head and stopped. "I want to be clear. I don't think she's involved in any way. But there is a real estate agent from another company who went through some kind of personal issue last year. I don't know what, I never asked. We weren't friends. Whatever it was, it affected her business, and she wasn't able to keep some appointments. That's all I know about it, but a couple of her clients came over to me. I ended up selling them their homes. When I saw her after that, she was a bit cold. No surprise there."

"Her name, please."

"Margaret Ecklin."

It had been a while since Claire had spoken with Margaret, who preferred to be known as Meg. Meg was at least fifteen years older than Claire. When they did chance to meet, they were civil to one another. She couldn't see Meg having anything to do with this whole sordid business. Meg was always gracious, polite, and professional. Other than whatever issues she'd had the past year, Meg was the ideal real estate agent.

Finally, they released her. Claire swung around, intent on going to search for Jason. To her surprise, he stood twenty feet away, casually leaning against a tree, watching her. When he saw her heading his way, he pushed himself away from the tree and moved to meet her.

"Are you all done? Or do you need to do something else?"

For the first time in the past few hours, her smile felt genuine. There was something about Jason that eased her mind. He was so calm and steady.

She shook her head. "Thanks for all your help. I don't want to be a bother."

"That's not exactly what I asked, you know." His voice held the faintest tinge of amusement.

She turned to stare at him. "What?"

He chuckled. "Man, Suzanne was right. You don't enjoy asking for help. I asked if you need anything else. You didn't say no, you needed nothing else. You just said you didn't want to bother me." He leaned toward her a bit. Not too close, just enough to meet her eyes without her having to tilt her head back. "It's no bother. I want to help. What else do you need?"

She dropped her gaze. She hated crying in front of others. However, her emotions seemed to be connected to her tear ducts today. It seemed she was constantly on the verge of tears. Blinking fast, she took a deep breath to settle herself. There was something she wanted to do. Something she needed to do.

"Can we stop by someplace on our way back to my house?" she asked, her voice strained. It pained her to ask, but surprisingly, not as much as she would have thought. Probably because she was so desperate to ensure she had not lost everything she had worked so hard for.

"Absolutely." He opened the door for her. She let a small grin escape.

"What's so funny?" He slid into the driver's seat and buckled himself in. His deep brown eyes caught her gaze.

She shrugged, feeling a bit flushed. "Nothing, really. Except you sounded like Suzanne. Every time I ask her a question, instead of a simple yes, I always get 'Absolutely!'"

She emphasized her words by making air quotes with her fingers.

He chuckled. "Yeah. That's a habit we both got from our mother."

"I know. It just makes me smile." And a smile was something she needed so very badly today.

He pulled around the U-shaped driveway and stopped at the street. "Which way?"

She gave him directions one turn at a time, never actually telling him where they were going. Less than seven minutes later, they pulled up in front of the house, her newest love.

"Wow. This place looks ancient." Jason whistled.

She looked up at the two-story redbrick house. The doors and windows were white, and a full wraparound porch swept the entire front of the building. Large columns held up the balcony on the second floor.

"This house was abandoned after the flood a decade ago. This morning I picked up a report from a historian I'd hired to dig into the past of this place. In 1938 a couple named Jasper and Polly Kane bought it. Jasper was a well-known potter in the area. The story is, he would create something then break the mold so no one could duplicate it. So his vases and pots were literally one of a kind."

"Did their descendants live here at the time of the flood?" Jason turned off the ignition.

"No. Their family hasn't lived here for nearly forty years."

He nodded, and they both got out of the car and walked up the sidewalk to the steps. "Okay, this place feels like a classic."

"Right? I have to admit, I fell in love with this house immediately. More than any other house I have ever flipped or renovated. This is a house I could live in myself."

"Have you considered that?"

She hesitated. Then shook her head. "It's a big house, Jason. And there's just me. To keep a place like this when a family could enjoy it, it feels selfish."

She saw doubt crawling over his face, but he didn't argue. Instead, he said, "Why don't you give me a tour?"

Eagerly, she agreed.

She led him into the front parlor. "This is one of my favorite rooms. I can just imagine a family sitting together and reading or watching a movie."

He glanced around. "It does have plenty of potential."

She smiled, pleased with his assessment. "I bought it three months ago for a song. I hope to start restoring it soon and finish sometime in January."

She led him through the house, describing what she wanted to do in each room. The second floor needed the most work. Floors were in need of sanding and some of the wood needed to be replaced. The walls needed to be patched, and the roof above the closets leaked.

"Hey, what's this?"

She hurried over to Jason. "What did you find?"

"This board is coming up. But I think it was deliberate." She peered closer and saw what he meant. The edges were straight and smooth.

"Someone made a hiding place." She helped him lift the board up. Underneath was a small wooden chest. Her heartbeat quickened. Her fingers trembled as she lifted the chest out and opened it. Inside she found a vase, in mint condition. It was almost hourglass shaped. The vase was painted white with a bluish cast. Bluebirds and vines wound around each other from the base to the rim.

"The artwork is exquisite," Claire breathed. Excitement stirred in her veins.

"I wonder if this was a vase made here at Hull's Pottery?"

She pursed her lips. "Maybe. I don't think we'll ever know. But I wonder if this was one of Jasper Kane's." She looked on the bottom. "I don't see any markings. Well, it's a special find either way. I think this needs to be on the mantel."

She carefully made her way down the staircase to the first floor, aware of him at her back the entire time.

"Claire, why are we here? Do you need to do something?"

She slowly rotated in a circle, scanning the walls for any sign of mischief. "No. I just needed to see that this house hadn't been destroyed or damaged."

He stepped closer to her. "Claire, I think I can help you protect it."

She whirled to face him, hardly daring to believe him. Could it be true? A spark of hope took root in her soul.

CHAPTER THREE

Jason saw the hope shining in her eyes and swallowed. He couldn't call the words back. Not that he wanted to. But he worried about being overcommitted and disappointing her. What if his security wasn't enough to protect her? Or this house that she obviously loved?

She was watching him.

"I run a security company. I've already made arrangements to have a security system put in at your house. It wouldn't be difficult to set one up here as well. You would know if anyone broke in. The police would be called if anything happened."

She bit her lower lip and slowly paced the perimeter of the room. She hadn't outright dismissed the idea, which he found encouraging. Although it had taken him a little bit of time to warm up to the idea, now that he had decided on his course, he was eager to have the security system set up.

All he needed was for her to agree to it. His sister had said Claire didn't like accepting help. He could see that in the way she was thinking so hard about his offer, probably looking for the hidden angles.

"I don't expect anything from you in return," he blurted. "I'm offering as a friend, that's all."

She glanced up at him with a strange little half smile playing about her lips. "Are we friends, Jason? I don't think I've ever had a conversation this long with you before."

He shrugged. "I'm not going to lie. Hanging out with you and my sister wasn't exactly my top priority when I was a senior in high school. You two were kids."

She smirked. The expression faded as she made one last circle around the large room, her heels clicking on the hardwood floors. Finally, she stopped in front of him. "Thank you. I appreciate your offer, and…" She swallowed. "I accept. But only if you're sure this won't harm your business in any way."

He laughed. "It can't hurt my business. In fact, it might even help my business if you display one of my signs in your yard. Not that I expect you to. Totally up to you. Regardless, I'll be fine."

Once she agreed, it was a familiar process. He drove her to her home and brought his laptop inside. At her kitchen table, they discussed the different options and he waited for her to choose which she wanted. Then he drew up a contract. After she read it and signed, he left to gather the necessary equipment. He could have let one of his employees install the system, but he didn't want to make her uncomfortable having someone unfamiliar going through her house. He started with the home where she lived. It took almost four hours to get everything up and running. By the time the system was installed, it was dinnertime.

It had been a grueling day, and he'd been up since five. Going home to fix dinner sounded as appealing as running a marathon, but he needed to eat.

"I'll swing by in the morning and get the system set up in the other house." He paused as a yawn caught him unawares. "Sorry!"

"You don't need to apologize. Look, Jason, the least I can do is fix you dinner. Why don't you go lie down on the couch for a few minutes. It won't be fancy. Probably macaroni and cheese and a salad."

He was tempted to argue. A second yawn convinced him to take her offer. He'd close his eyes for a few minutes. That was all. When he reclined on the couch, his head sank into the pillows tucked against the armrest.

The next thing he knew, someone was shaking his shoulder.

Startled, Jason jumped up off the couch. It took him a few seconds to remember where he was. Embarrassed, his heart pounding and his face covered with sweat, he lifted his gaze to Claire, steeling himself for her reaction. Instead of appearing alarmed or bothered by his reaction, she calmly remained seated in the armchair beside the couch.

"Sorry. You surprised me."

She nodded and moved past it. "Dinner's ready."

He blinked at her. That was all? One of the major reasons for his reluctance to become involved with any woman was a moment like this. Yet she reacted as if nothing out of the ordinary had occurred. Amazed, and not a little humbled, he followed her into the kitchen.

He looked at the kitchen clock. "Wow. I didn't realize I was asleep for so long. It's been over an hour."

"Yes. I figured you needed the sleep. And it gave me time to whip up a quick dessert."

That piqued his interest. "Really? What are we having?"

She tossed him a sassy smirk. "Uh-uh. You'll have to wait and see."

Grinning, he joined her at the table.

When she bowed her head to say grace, he followed suit. His faith had been the cornerstone of his life since he was a child.

The macaroni and cheese melted in his mouth. It was a simple meal, but no less satisfying than if she'd served him steak and potatoes. The company wasn't bad either.

He picked up his glass and took a deep swallow of ice-cold milk. Just the way he liked it. "This is the house you grew up in, right? Does the rest of your family still live here too?"

She stood and walked to the counter. She cut into something he initially thought was a pie. But the crust looked different. When she set it before him, he got an eyeful of dark berries in a golden-brown crust.

"What is this?" It smelled divine.

She had already gone to the freezer and pulled out a half gallon of vanilla ice cream. "This is a blackberry and mint tart. It's a recipe my mom makes frequently. I don't make it often, but some days you just need something sweet."

She returned the ice cream to the freezer and resumed her seat.

He took a bite. It was rich and creamy. He dug in with relish.

She glanced around the kitchen. "As to your question, yes, this is the house I grew up in. Mom remarried several years back. She and Lizzy live with my stepfather in Florida. I chose to stay here because I had a job and thought I'd be getting married. It didn't seem worth the hassle of finding my own place when I'd be moving after the wedding."

She shrugged one shoulder as if it no longer bothered her, but he could see it did. He tried to recall the name of the man who had hurt her. Andrew—no, Adam—something or other.

"I remember Suzanne ranting about this guy for a full month. Then one day, I asked her how you were doing, and I started to mention the loser's name. My sister cut me off and told me his name was off-limits."

A gorgeous grin broke across her face like the sunrise, causing his brain to come full stop. "Your sister is the best. I was so lucky the day our parents decided to enroll us for lessons at the same stables."

He smiled back, his eyes never leaving her face. "Yeah. She's pretty special. Although I think she'd insist she's the lucky one." He finished his dessert and stood. "I'll help you clean up, and then I have to leave. What are you doing about your car? Do you need a ride tomorrow morning?"

She appeared startled. "I forgot about my tires. Sergeant Stonis said he'd stop by and take pictures of my car today. When we were at the fire scene, he told me he'd done that. I need to have it towed to the tire place and have the tires changed."

He frowned. "That could take forever, depending how backed up they are. They might be booked with cars that need to be inspected by the end of the month."

"Can't be helped. I don't have two spares."

His own schedule was packed pretty tight, but he couldn't leave her like this. "Look, I can get the tires in town. Then tomorrow morning, after we do the system install at the other house, I'll bring you back and change your tires for you. How about that?"

"Are you assuming I can't change my own tires?" Her right eyebrow arched. He could practically feel the acid of disdain dripping from her words.

Oops. He hadn't meant to offend her. The tips of his ears burned. "Um. Sorry. I didn't mean to sound arrogant. I was—"

Her eyebrow dropped, and she laughed. "It's all right. I can change a tire, but it's not easy. I think I'll take you up on the offer, just so I can have my car back sooner. Thanks."

He blew out a breath. "You had me there. I thought I'd gotten myself in serious trouble for a moment."

"Nah. I get it." She walked him to the front door, snagging her purse on the way. "How much do tires cost?"

He waved it away. "I don't know. I'll give you the receipt, and we'll deal with it later. Make sure the system is on after I leave."

Jason had some time to think on the drive to his apartment. He would stop by and get her tires in the morning. He would also read up on the other arsons from the past year and see if he could find a pattern.

He let out a huff of laughter, snorting at his own conceit. As if he'd find a pattern that the investigators and police missed. But there was one thing he could do for her. When he reached his apartment, he bowed his head and fervently prayed that Claire would not be targeted again.

Claire set the alarm for the night and then loaded up the fireplace, making sure there was enough wood to last through the night. She'd probably have to rebuild it in the morning, but maybe if there were enough coals left, it would be easy.

She closed the damper enough to keep the fire from burning too hot then grabbed her Bible and her journal and headed to her room. On the way there, she paused.

If she slept upstairs, she'd be too far from an escape route if someone did do something to her house. She eyed the couch. She could sleep there or on the recliner, just for one night. Immediately she pushed the idea aside, calling herself ridiculous. She had never let any concerns or worries keep her from sleeping in her own bed before, and she wasn't going to cave in to them now.

Besides, if anything, she was safer tonight than she'd been in the past. She and Jason had run a safety test on the system after he'd installed it. He'd called the police station, letting them know they were running a test. When the alarm went off, an officer called back to acknowledge an alert had come through. Not only that, but anyone on the property would immediately know an alarm had sounded.

Jason assured her that would be enough to scare any villains off. They wouldn't have time to do any harm before the police arrived on the scene.

Jason Pierce. She shook her head and smiled. She'd always liked his sense of humor and admired the way he looked after his sister. Although she hadn't known him that well. And he was too old for her to have developed a crush on when they were younger. She'd been too involved with her horses to even notice boys before she was in high school. And by the time she did, he'd moved out and joined the military.

She recalled the way he'd startled and then froze when she'd tried to wake him earlier, and sighed. It would be too much to hope that he hadn't seen any ugliness while in the service. His reaction told her better than any words that he was still deeply affected by what he'd experienced.

Her phone rang. She checked the display. Suzanne.

"Hey, Suze."

"Claire! I can't believe all that happened today. Are you all right? Do you need to come over here for the night?"

"I'm fine. Your brother just left a few minutes ago. He installed a security system, and it's up and running, so I'm good. Besides, I still have two flat tires. You would have to come and get me."

"You know I would."

"I do. But don't worry. I'll be fine." They chatted for a few more minutes, but Claire's mind was too scattered to hold up her end of the conversation. The temptation to ask her friend about Jason's time in the service was great. She opened her mouth to ask but then closed it so fast her teeth clicked. She didn't have the right to ask for such personal information about him. If he wanted her to know about it, he'd tell her. She would respect his privacy.

Besides, if she started asking questions, Suzanne might get the wrong idea and try her hand at matchmaking. Claire definitely didn't want to leave herself open to that. It was almost a relief when she hung up a minute later.

Sitting on the edge of her bed, she opened her Bible randomly and began to read. After a few verses, she stopped and reread Romans 8:28 aloud. "'And we know that in all things God works for the good of those who love him, who have been called according to his purpose.'"

Closing her eyes, she held her Bible close to her chest. All things work together for good. How did her cancer fit into that category? Or the fire and the slashed tires? If she could have children, would she have married Adam? They would have been miserable together. She knew that now. She still didn't understand everything, but she needed to trust that God knew what she needed. That was the hard part.

She loved God. She had chosen to live according to His truth. She bit her lip. But did she truly do so? She had spent so long trying to be independent, she'd effectively isolated herself from most friendships, except Suzanne. Although, truth be told, Suzanne was a force of nature. No one could stand against her.

She'd all but accused Jason of being arrogant, but she had been just as bad. She hadn't allowed herself to acknowledge that God's plans for her life might not align with hers. She needed to repent and trust in His providence.

Sleep was slow in coming as she mulled over everything that had happened until well into the night.

CHAPTER FOUR

On Saturday morning Claire woke an hour before her alarm was set to go off. Groaning, she tugged the covers tighter and snuggled deeper, shivering when the wind rattled the windows. It was going to be another chilly day.

After fifteen minutes, she gave up. She was wide awake now. After putting her slippers on, she padded to the kitchen and made herself a cup of vanilla chai tea. When it was done, she held the steaming mug between her hands and moved to the living room to rebuild the fire.

When the flames sputtered to life, she sat back on her heels.

It was going to be a busy day. Jason said he'd pick her up around nine to go to her house and install the system. She winced. She needed to stop thinking of the place as her house. It wouldn't be a good thing if she became too attached to the property. After all, in January it was going on the market. And hopefully, it would sell fast. Not because she needed the money. No, she needed it to sell so she could move on. It was strange. She had never gotten attached to a house she worked on before. They were all fun projects, nothing more. This house, however, seemed to call to her.

She pushed it out of her mind and moved on with her agenda. She and Jason would get her car back to working condition. Well,

Jason would. She'd be there to supervise. She snorted and took a sip of her tea.

By seven o'clock, she was dressed and ready to start her day. She decided against any cosmetics, as she had no business appointments that morning. She brushed her hair out, scowling at the static electricity crackling while she brushed it. The heat of the fireplace and the cold air of the fall and winter months didn't always agree with her. Whipping her frizzy hair into a messy bun, she concluded she was ready to face the day.

At five minutes past eight, her phone rang. She strode to the kitchen and grabbed it off the counter, disconnecting it from the charging cable. Her pulse hammered in her veins. Sergeant Stonis. Maybe he'd found something.

"Hello?"

"Claire Derrick, please."

"This is she." Her fingers cramped. She loosened her grip.

"Good morning, Claire. I was wondering if you would be available to stop by the station this morning. We found something at the fire scene and thought maybe you'd come and see if you recognized it."

She glanced at the clock. "Yeah. I don't have my tires fixed yet. But my friend Jason will be picking me up around nine. Could we stop by then?"

"That'll work. I'll be here until around lunchtime." There was nothing in his voice to give away what he was thinking. What had he found?

"I'll be there as soon as I can. Thanks." She hung up and hesitated. It was only ten minutes after eight. Jason was pretty tired when he left the night before. Common courtesy demanded she wait until nine before calling. But he'd be there at nine, so obviously he needed to get up earlier. Her mind argued that she could tell him about the phone call when he arrived. She paced the length of the living room for a full five minutes before giving in and dialing his number and hitting call. Immediately, she wished she hadn't. She was being needy.

"Hi, Claire." He didn't sound like she had woken him.

"Hey. Sorry for calling at the crack of dawn."

His warm chuckle floated into her ear. "Hardly. I've been up for two hours."

She sagged against the wall, relieved. "Good."

"So, what's wrong?"

She bit her lip, feeling silly now that they were talking. "Well, nothing. Not really. It's just that I got off the phone with Sergeant Stonis a few minutes ago. He said they found something at the fire yesterday after we left. He wants me to stop by this morning. I didn't know if that would work with your schedule."

"Excellent. This could be good news for you if they can identify the person."

She heard a door slam shut.

"I'm going to my car now. I'll be at your place no later than eight thirty, and we can head to the police station."

"Are you sure you don't mind?" His car engine roared to life in the background.

"Not at all. See you soon."

He ended the call. She put the phone in her back pocket and grabbed her coat and sneakers. By the time he pulled into her driveway, she was watching out the window. She slipped out the front door and set the alarm then bounded down the steps and met him at the passenger-side door of the car.

The drive to the police station was silent. Claire had too much on her mind to focus on conversation. Jason seemed to understand this. He reached out once to where her arm rested on the center console and squeezed her hand. It was amazing how much that small bit of human consolation settled her queasy stomach for a moment. When she glanced his way, he smiled at her.

"It'll be okay," he assured her.

She nodded, but she couldn't force any words from her throat. It was too tight. Although she was happy the police had found some sort of clue, the idea that she might know the person targeting her had her feeling off-kilter. She really hoped it was a stranger. Someone she'd never actually spoken with. If it was someone she knew, that would be devastating.

Mentally, she went over the list of people she had talked about with the investigator the day before. Despite the breakup, she had trouble seeing Adam doing something vicious like this. Mostly because he would be so afraid of getting caught and harming his precious political career. Adam was a very cautious person. This didn't feel like something he would do.

What about Meg? Even as the question surfaced in her mind, she shook her head. She just couldn't see it. The older woman had too much class to do something like this.

But how well did she really know her? Or come to think of it, Adam? She never would have guessed that he would dump her like he did.

"You're getting very tense over there." Jason's voice interrupted her musings. "Anything you want to share?"

She shook her head. Then thought better of it. "I've just been thinking about my conversation with the police and the investigator yesterday. Trying to go over the people that they thought might be on the suspect list. I'll be honest. I think they're looking in the wrong place."

He reached out and adjusted the heater. His brow furrowed like he was considering how to respond to her question. "I don't know. Sometimes it's the people we know who can shock us most."

He flipped on his blinker and let a car pass before turning into the parking lot of the Crooksville Police Department. They walked together to the door. He held it open for her, and she walked through, regretting drinking the entire cup of tea that morning. It sloshed around in her stomach and made her queasy. Although she knew it wasn't really the tea.

Jason walked at her side and gently took her hand in his. "I'll be with you if you need me."

This time, she didn't have to wait. Sergeant Stonis was waiting for her. He led them back to a small conference room and shut the door. Gesturing to the table, he offered them coffee or water. She declined both, knowing her stomach couldn't handle anything.

He placed a clear bag on the table. Inside was a tube of lipstick.

She recognized the brand. It was a very high-end one. "This was at the scene?"

He nodded. "Yes. Do you recognize it?"

She shook her head. "No. But I have heard of that brand before. It's not available at drugstores. You'd have to go to a cosmetic store or order it online." She listed the cosmetic chains she knew of in the surrounding area. "It's pricey. You'd probably pay thirty or forty dollars for that one tube."

Jason's eyes widened. Obviously, he had never been shopping with a woman at one of those places before.

"Do you know anyone who uses this brand?" Sergeant Stonis asked.

She frowned. "I don't know. I don't usually ask women where they got their cosmetics. Can I touch the bag?"

He gestured for her to proceed. She picked it up and flipped the item around so she could see the top of the tube. The cap was clear at that end. Peering into it, she looked at the contents. "It looks like your average rose pink."

"I take it that's a common color."

She shrugged. "Yeah, I guess so. Probably every makeup brand ever invented has a similar shade."

He leaned forward, placing his elbows on the table and clasping his hands together. "Would you say Margaret Ecklin might wear this shade?"

Her breath caught in her throat. She didn't want to implicate Meg, especially since her gut said the woman was innocent. But she also couldn't deny the possibility that she was, in fact, the person they were looking for.

"I don't know. I've seen her wear several shades of lipstick. This might have been one of them. I can't say for sure."

He nodded. "I expected that answer."

She thought of something. "I also don't know if that means the arsonist is a woman. That house has been listed for sale for months.

So if someone wants to view it, they just go to an agent and make an appointment. I know for a fact several agents and prospective buyers have walked through the house this past week."

He pursed his lips, considering her words. "Valid argument. For the time being, we'll continue searching for suspects and leads. I intend to question Margaret Ecklin today though."

Five minutes later, they were on their way to her house, or rather the house she was getting ready to sell. An aggravated breath escaped her.

"What?"

"I keep thinking of this place as mine. I need to stop it, or I won't have the heart to sell it."

He smiled. "That would be a problem."

She snorted at his understatement. "Ya think?"

He parked in front of the garage and immediately went to his trunk and began to gather the tools to install the system. She felt a surge of relief. After today, she wouldn't have to worry about her security issues any longer.

The area between her shoulder blades prickled. Spinning around, she scanned the area. When she spied two familiar faces on the sidewalk, a smile bloomed across her face.

"Good morning, Brody. Good morning, Emma. You two are out and about early."

Jason twisted to see who she was talking to. His body posture relaxed as the two small children approached. They were adorable. She'd first met them about a week ago. They were playing in the front yard, and she shared her lunch with them. Since then, they regularly came to visit when she was here. She hadn't met their parents yet.

She frowned as they came closer. "Emma, where's your coat? It's cold today."

Emma ducked her head into her brother's shoulder. "Emma doesn't like her coat, Miss Claire," Brody informed them.

"Jason, this is Brody and Emma. Brody is seven, and Emma is five. They live on this block and have become my pals while I work. Kids, this is my friend, Mr. Jason. He's going to help me today and put in a system so people won't be able to break into my house."

Brody's eyes grew wide. "You can do that?"

Jason chuckled. "I can. If it's okay with your parents, you can stick around and watch, if you want to."

The child bobbed his head up and down in an enthusiastic nod. Claire couldn't hold back her smile. They were too cute for words.

She made her way up the walkway to the house and opened the door, humming under her breath. The first room she entered was the front parlor. Her breath stopped and her lungs froze. For a moment, she stood gasping for air as her brain registered what she was seeing.

The beautiful vase she'd fallen in love with the day before now lay shattered on the floor.

"Jason!"

Claire's scream ripped through the air. Jason dumped the box of equipment back into the trunk and charged up the sidewalk. He halted beside her, his arms instinctively wrapping around her while he scanned the room for threats.

The moment he saw the broken pottery, his heart dropped. He had failed her already.

"Claire, I'm so sorry. If I had put the system in yesterday—"

She pushed her way out of his arms. He let her go, letting his limbs fall to his sides at her rejection. She spun to face him, and her finger jabbed into his chest. He winced.

"This. Is. Not. Your. Fault." She spat the words at him. "You spent hours installing the security system at my house. That was the more important place. This is sad, and I'm angry that someone wants to hurt me, but I'm not angry with you."

"But if I had come out last night—"

"Jason, you were exhausted. You were on the scene of the fire for ages, and then you were with me the rest of the day. No. This isn't on you. We'll call the police and then move on."

"Do you want me to clean up the vase for you?" He was desperate to redeem himself and remove the sorrow from her gaze.

"No," she drawled out, lengthening the word. "I think I want to try and repair it."

He gave her a skeptical glance. "Um, Claire? It's in a lot of pieces."

"Yeah. It's probably not possible. But I want to try. It'll be cathartic for me."

He doubted it but kept his opinion to himself. She'd been through the wringer. He was not about to add more stress or pain to her life. And if she thought trying to mend the smashed vase would bring her some sort of inner healing, he was all for that.

"Still, we should call Sergeant Stonis. Let him know about the break-in."

She nodded. "I will. Do you think they'll come back? Is it worth setting up the system now?"

"It's always worth protecting yourself." He turned and spied Brody peeking in at them, his face pale. "Come on, buddy. How about helping me install the security system?"

Brody pressed closer to the doorway, almost as if hiding himself, his gaze glued to Claire's wet face. It probably petrified the poor kid seeing an adult cry.

"She's fine, Brody. Claire's not hurt."

She pivoted to face them at his comment, swiping her arm across her face to dry it. "Jason's right. Why don't you go ahead and help him?"

Her tender smile took in both kids as Emma appeared in the doorway behind Brody. He was only on the edge of it, but that sweet glance made his heart race. What was wrong with him? He never got mushy like this. The sooner the arsonist was found, the better. He didn't want to become emotionally attached to a woman he could never hope to have a relationship with. But if he stayed near Claire too long, he might be in danger of falling for her. Already, he could sense himself wanting to be in her company.

Only this morning, his first thought when he woke up had been whether she'd managed last night being alone in that big house after the horrendous day she'd lived through. He had to convince himself not to call her first thing to check on her.

When his phone rang and he saw her number pop up, he practically snatched it off his nightstand. Hearing her soft voice on the other end eased some of the tension. No, he was becoming way too attached far too quickly. Forcing himself to turn away from her, he walked to the door, waving for Brody to follow him. Brody cast one last look at Claire and his little sister and then took off after Jason.

He thought Brody would become bored after a few minutes, but the boy stayed right with him, peppering him with questions about how the system worked. It quickly became apparent that he was gifted. He understood concepts that most twelve-year-olds wouldn't understand, much less a seven-year-old. And the kid was fascinated by how things fit together. Jason found himself explaining every minute detail about what he was doing and why. It was hard to remember the last time he had enjoyed his work so much.

They took a break when the police cruiser drove up to the house. Sergeant Stonis stepped from the car and took in the surroundings with a narrow-eyed gaze.

Brody and Emma took one look at him and headed home. Jason shrugged. Maybe they found cops intimidating. He moved inside in order to support Claire during her conversation with Sergeant Stonis. The officer acknowledged him briefly, not fazed by his appearance at Claire's side.

"I need you to walk me through what happened, exactly as it happened."

Claire took a deep breath. Jason rested his hand on her shoulder and gave it a gentle squeeze. It wasn't a romantic gesture. It was just his way of letting her know that he was there if she needed him.

"Jason and I had made plans to come here this morning so he could install one of his security systems. He installed one at my own house last night, and we figured since the arsonist had burned down one of my houses and my tires were slashed, it was better to be safe than sorry." She paused, biting her lip. Jason could almost see the wheels go around in her head as she tried to figure out how to explain what happened next. "We came straight from the police station to here. I didn't notice anything wrong at first. The front door was still locked. It wasn't until I walked inside and saw the vase on the floor that I realized someone had been in here." She pointed her shaky finger at the parts still lying on the floor.

"Any idea how they got in?" Sergeant Stonis asked.

"I'm not sure. I checked the back door, and it was still locked."

"Did you check the windows?" the cop asked her with a level stare.

"It never occurred to me to check the windows."

Jason was already moving. "I'll check the kitchen and the back porch."

The house had enough windows, that was for sure. The enclosed porch alone had seven windows and a door. All three outside walls had windows beginning thirty inches from the floor and reaching to eight inches below the ceiling. After checking the windows on the top floor, he opened the door in the hallway beside the entrance to the kitchen. It led to the full basement.

That was when he noticed the mud on the top stair. It wasn't dried and crusty as if it had been there a while. It was still damp.

At the bottom of the staircase was the laundry room. He found a clothesline stretching from one corner to the other. At the far end, nearly blocked by a small homemade cupboard, he found another door.

This one was unlocked, and he could see tracks leading into the room.

"I found it!" he yelled up the stairs.

Footsteps stomped across the floor above. Sergeant Stonis crashed down the stairs, followed by Claire at a more sedate pace.

Claire gaped at the tracks and the door. "I forgot this door was here," she said. "It's so well hidden, I didn't even think of it."

"Install that security system," the officer told them. "Make sure you keep all your personal property with you, and don't leave anything of value here. I suspect this house was vandalized on purpose. Someone knows it means something special to you, and they wanted you to know they could get in here to scare you. To let you know they're in control."

She shuddered.

Jason looped an arm around her shoulder and drew her close. She barely seemed to notice his presence.

"Did you get the chance to check on the leads you had?" he asked.

"Some. Adam Hunter wasn't available, but I'll track him down. Margaret Ecklin is no longer a suspect."

Claire raised her head and quirked an eyebrow at him.

"When I called her home, her husband informed me she is in the hospital and will be for the next few days."

It was clear he wasn't going to discuss her health history. Jason respected that. He would not want someone talking about his scars and the wounds he had from his days as a soldier. That information was his to share.

Sergeant Stonis left after taking down the information regarding the vandalism. He had called a couple of officers to come and dust the premises for prints and take any evidence into custody. This included the broken vase.

Claire didn't like that at all. Jason could practically see the steam hissing from her ears. "Can I have it back as soon as you're done with it?"

One of the officers nodded. "If there are no useable prints on it, we'll return it to you next week."

Once things quieted down, Jason returned to installing the security system. It went faster without his little helper, but it also wasn't as much fun as before.

When he was finished and ready to test it, he found Claire staring out the window in the kitchen. Her closed posture ate at him. He hated seeing her so hurt and bewildered.

"Come on." He nudged her with his elbow. "Let's go out and grab a bite to eat."

She sighed. "I should say no. But I don't want to cook tonight."

They ended up at a cute little mom-and-pop family restaurant right on the main street of town. The food was rich and filling. Jason told her stories about growing up with Suzanne and some of the tricks they'd played on each other. Hearing her laugh warmed him from the inside out.

They were enjoying brownies topped with ice cream and caramel syrup when Jason suddenly remembered Claire's car.

"I completely forgot to change your tires today. I still have to go to the tire store and buy new ones."

Claire licked her spoon and set it on the ice cream dish. It was empty except for smears of syrup and brownie crumbs. "Don't feel bad. You've done so much for me already. Honestly, Jason, if you don't have time to help with the tires, I completely understand. I feel like I'm monopolizing all your time, and that's not right."

He reached over and tapped the back of her hand. "I want to help. Don't worry about it."

He was surprised to realize how much he meant it.

She gazed at him for a moment before nodding.

"If you really want to, whenever you can do it is fine."

"Great! Let's plan on tomorrow after church. Did you want to stop by the hospital and see your friend?"

Her eyebrows rose. "Meg? I hadn't thought of it. We're not friends. More like associates. Still, it would be the right thing to do. If you don't mind? I feel guilty that she ended up on the suspect list."

"To use your line to me this morning, that's not your fault."

She shrugged and sighed. "You're right. But if I were in the hospital, I would want people to visit me. It's grim, staring at the walls with no one to talk to."

That was when he remembered who he was talking to. He would never intrude on her privacy, but if there was anyone who would understand the anxiety of being stuck in the hospital, it would be Claire.

"I tell you what. Tomorrow, I'll play chauffeur one more day. We can go to church together, and then afterward we can go see your Meg. And if you're lucky, I might even remember to change your tires."

She glanced at the time on her phone. "Yeah, I guess it's too late to stop by the tire store and pick up new ones today."

He grinned at her. "It's a date then."

She flushed and glanced down at the table. He could feel warmth climbing into his cheeks. It wasn't a date. He knew neither one of them was in the market for romance. It was moments like these, though, when he wished he was.

CHAPTER FIVE

Jason dropped Claire off at her house well past dark. The sun set close to six in the evening. They had both watched the colors fan the horizon and fade. As it sank lower in the sky, the air chilled. When he stood on her front porch under the motion-detecting light, he saw little puffs every time he exhaled.

She disarmed the alarm and unlocked the front door. Even from where he stood, the soft current of warm air called to him. He shoved his hands in his pockets to keep them warm and rocked on his feet. He planned to wait until she was inside and had locked the door and reset the alarm before leaving.

She stepped inside and flipped the hall light on before turning back to face him. "Would you like to come in for a cup of hot chocolate? I have travel mugs. You can take it with you."

Although it sounded good, he declined. "I can't. I have a list of things I need to do before I go to bed tonight."

He doubted he'd get most of them done, but he would try.

"I understand. What time will you be here tomorrow morning?"

He couldn't tell if she was disappointed that he had turned her down or relieved. Was she just being polite, or did she want to extend their time together? He mentally shook himself. This was why he needed to go to his own home.

"Church starts at nine. Why don't we plan on eight thirty again?" That should give them plenty of time to park and find their seats with time to spare. Jason abhorred showing up late to anything, but especially church. In his mind, it was the height of disrespect. Plus, he liked to be able to sit near the front, but not in the first few rows.

She smiled and gave him a small nod before shutting the door. The lock clicked into place. He pivoted on his heel and walked back to his car. He was bone tired, but something told him he would not sleep well tonight. And it would all be because of a certain blond.

On the way home, his phone rang. It was Suzanne. He hit the button on his console to answer the call. "Hey, Suze. How's my favorite sister?"

She scoffed. "That joke is way too old."

He smiled. She sounded like her sassy self.

"So," Suzanne began, "did you get the tires put on Claire's car? Oh, and what about the security systems?"

"No to the tires." He paused. Then he huffed out a heavy breath. "I might as well tell you. The house she's been working on was vandalized."

Her shocked exclamation nearly rattled the windows.

"Exactly." He turned into the parking lot of his apartment building. After backing into his space, he tapped his fingers on the steering wheel as he listened to Suzanne rant against the audacity of someone attacking her friend.

"What are you doing about it?"

Here we go again. "Suzanne, I've been her escort for the past two days. I've installed security systems in both her house and the one she plans to sell. Tomorrow, I'll change her tires and get her vehicle working so she can be independent again. What more do you want me to do?"

She grumbled. "I guess you have a point."

"Look. She's had a rough time. Call her. It would cheer her up." Suzanne ended the call five minutes later, promising to call her friend. Something was bugging him. Making a split decision, he turned the car back on and drove to the house Claire planned to sell. When he arrived, he sat in his car for a moment, waiting to see if there was any motion. Seeing nothing out of the ordinary, he approached the house.

The alarms were still set. Using the flashlight on his phone, he aimed the beam at the ground and walked around the house, keeping far enough away not to trigger the alert. At first, he didn't see anything suspicious. He decided to make a second round, just in case.

That was when he saw it. Outside the dining room window, about ten or twelve inches from the house, a set of footprints were visible in the dirt of a large flower bed. They faced the window, and he could see that the print was much smaller than his, the entire foot narrower.

A woman's shoe?

Someone had been looking inside the window. Was it the neighbor, just being curious? It didn't look like anyone had gone in. Or maybe someone was planning some mischief but noticed the security signs and thought better of it.

One thing was for sure. This would require another chat with Sergeant Stonis.

On Sunday morning Claire hurried to answer the knock on the front door. It was only eight o'clock. Jason had said he'd be there at eight thirty. Her stomach clenched painfully. It did no good to tell herself not to worry. The anxiety continued to shoot through her veins, making her heart pump faster and her breathing hitch in her chest. The blood rushing in her ears muffled the sound of the person knocking a second time.

Standing on her tiptoes, she peered out the peephole in the wooden door. Jason stood on the porch, handsome and rugged while he burrowed his hands in his pockets against the bitter chill. She sagged against the door briefly to catch her breath and allow her heartbeat to resume its normal rhythm.

In control again, she opened the door with a flourish. "Jason! I didn't expect you for another thirty minutes." She motioned for him to come inside, quickly shutting the door behind him. "*Brr.* It's cold. Lucky for you, I have coffee made."

He set a hand on her arm. She paused. When she looked into his face, she knew something was wrong. She braced herself. He gently took her elbow and led her to sit on the sofa.

"What happened?" she demanded. "Is someone hurt?"

The fear that someone would be injured had hovered in the back of her mind every second for the past two days. She gripped his arms, anchoring herself in place and keeping his attention on her. She wouldn't let him sugarcoat the truth for her.

Not that he ever had. Jason had been up front with her about everything since this whole fiasco had started.

"No one is hurt," he reassured her. "And I don't know if anything has happened. But I found footprints outside your other house last night. Like someone was looking in."

"What?" She shook her head, confused. "Why would someone be standing outside looking in? And why wouldn't that fancy shmancy alarm we spent all that time putting in alert the police?"

He slid his arms back so that he held both of her soft hands in his work-roughened ones. His thumbs rubbed over her knuckles in a soothing gesture that she found more distracting than calming.

"The alarm didn't go off, because the footprints weren't right next to the house. No one actually tried to enter. In fact, it's possible it was just a nosy neighbor."

She quirked her eyebrows. "The neighbors' houses aren't that close."

He shrugged and grimaced. "No. But it's a house for sale. Lots of people assume that means it's okay to look inside." He glanced down, staring at their joined hands. When he looked up, she knew more was coming. "The other interesting thing is that the footprints were too small to be a man's. I think we're looking at a woman."

He squeezed her hands. "I called the police. There's not an actual crime here, so they can't do much. But your friend, Sergeant Stonis, did say his chief authorized a drive-by several times a day, just to make sure everything is okay."

She nodded. "I appreciate that. You know, in all the excitement over the house that burned down and this one, I nearly forgot that I have another property I'm doing an open house for on Wednesday evening. It's not a house I did any work on. Just a normal house a client wants to sell."

"I think we'd be wise to pass that information on to the police so someone will be there for you."

"I agree." She sighed.

Suddenly she felt the need to move. Shoving herself to her feet, she gazed down at Jason. She wouldn't have known what to do if it hadn't been for his presence these past few days. "Thanks for everything, Jason. I mean it. I would be lost if you hadn't stepped in to help."

He flushed. "You would've been fine. Why don't we grab that coffee, and then we can head to church?"

She rolled her eyes at his attempt to distract her from voicing her gratitude, but let it go. They went into the kitchen. She tried to keep the conversation rolling, but it was hard to focus. Despite Jason's assurances, Claire still wasn't completely convinced that the presence of the footprints was benign. Granted, he'd never said it was. In fact, all he had really said was no crime had been committed. Yet.

Her stomach continued to bubble and turn as her imagination ran wild. In her mind, she tried to picture who could possibly have been looking into the house and why. Was it the person who had set fire to her other project house? What if someone was planning something even worse? Up to this point, no one had been injured. She was truly grateful for that, but there was no guarantee that would continue.

"Are you ready?" Jason nudged her, a travel mug filled with coffee in his hand.

"Did you want creamer with that?" She pointed to the refrigerator. "I have several different kinds."

"Uh, no." He scrunched up his mouth like he'd tasted something disgusting. "I've seen what you call creamer. I'll take mine black, thanks all the same. All I need is the caffeine, and I'll be good to go."

"Coffee snob." She poured a healthy amount of French vanilla creamer into her own coffee.

"You got it."

She smiled at him. They walked to the car. He turned it on and adjusted his phone to play music through the speakers.

She recognized the song. "That's one of my favorites."

He nodded, glancing her way. "Mine too. Sometimes I need the reminder that no matter what happens, it's all in God's hands."

She leaned her head back and closed her eyes, soaking in the music. She'd spent too much time worrying lately. It was time she focused on giving the glory to God and letting go of some of the control. She had very little power over what happened, but God knew what was coming and what was best for her.

Lord, help me get out of my own way. Protect me and guide me so I'll truly walk in Your paths.

CHAPTER SIX

The notes of the final hymn lingered in the air. Claire replaced her hymnal in the rack on the back of the pew. She and Jason joined the congregants flowing out of the sanctuary to the main lobby.

"Claire!"

Claire spun around in time to see a head of dark brown hair before she was grabbed in a fierce stranglehold. Suzanne held her so tight, Claire had the brief thought that she might be the first person ever suffocated in a church.

"Okay, Suze. I can't breathe."

Laughing, her best friend backed up, giving her space. "Sorry, sorry. I'm just so worried about you with all that's been going on. When I saw you, all thoughts of dignity and decorum flew out the window."

Claire snorted. "As if you possessed those in the first place."

The two friends talked and laughed together for a few minutes. When Phillip and Jason joined them, the subject turned to Suzanne's baby. Claire did her best to ignore Suzanne's concerned glances. She said a quick prayer to reaffirm her decision to trust God in all things. She was determined that she would trust Him to do what was best for her.

"Hey guys." Jason broke into the conversation. "Claire and I need to go. I promised her I'd drop her off at the hospital to visit a colleague."

Of course, that prompted another round of queries about who was sick. Claire brushed most of these off. Suzanne and Phillip didn't know Meg. It took a full five minutes to extricate themselves from Jason's family and their friends.

Claire was still laughing when they got into the car. "You'd think we hadn't seen any of them in months."

He chuckled and shook his head. "Yeah. Well, that's family. Which hospital is she at?"

"Genesis." Crooksville wasn't that big. Less than three thousand people lived there. Although they had a health center for emergencies and surgeries, people often went to a hospital in one of the surrounding towns. Genesis was in Zanesville. "I hope they'll allow visitors, since I'm not family."

"There's only one way to find out."

Zanesville was less than fifteen miles away. They arrived in good time. Jason pulled under the awning at the main entrance. "Do you need me to wait until you find out about visiting hours or if you can see her?"

She smiled at him. "No. That's okay. If they say I can't visit, I'll read until you come back. If I can visit, I'll call you when I'm done. What will you do while I'm visiting Meg?"

"I'm going to go and buy those tires like I promised you."

Spontaneously, she leaned over and kissed his cheek. "Thanks. I owe you."

She grabbed the flowers she had bought in Crooksville and scooted out of the car, her cheeks burning. She refused to look back at him. What had possessed her to kiss him like that? Was he shocked? Amused?

She hurried into the hospital and focused on seeing Meg, which turned out to be surprisingly simple. Claire thanked the receptionist and made her way to Meg's room. Her footsteps slowed as she approached the door. What if Meg didn't want to see her? It wasn't like they were friends. And several of Meg's clients had left her to hire Claire.

Taking a deep breath, she approached the room and knocked on the door. Meg's voice, weak and tired, called out for her to enter. Claire threw her shoulders back, lifted her chin, and pasted what she hoped was a friendly smile on her face. She entered the room. Meg was the only patient present, although there was a second bed.

"Claire! I didn't expect you to visit me." Meg moved as if she planned to try and sit up.

Claire hurried forward. "Don't sit up on my account, Meg. You need the rest. I was sorry to learn you were in the hospital."

She placed the flowers on the bedside table.

"Those are lovely. Thank you." Meg sighed and settled back into her pillow. "It shocked me too. I was hurting for a few days. When I finally listened to my husband and went to see my doctor, I was shocked when they rushed me here in an ambulance. My appendix was about to rupture. At my age! Can you imagine?"

Claire made sympathetic noises. "I'm so sorry. You're okay, though, right?"

She didn't know much about appendicitis, except that it could be deadly if the appendix burst.

"Yes. I'll make a full recovery. I'm rather bored. But I'm alive."

Claire bit her lip, unsure what to say next. Before she could think of anything, Meg surprised her.

"My husband told me that the police called him. I was sorry when he told me about the house fire." A glint of humor appeared in her eyes. "I understand I was a suspect for a few hours. That's probably the most exciting thing that's ever happened in my life."

Meg gave a strange cackle. She seemed positively friendly this morning, unlike the other times they had encountered each other. Claire had always wondered if the older woman disliked her, but there was no hint of that now.

She shook her head. So much for all her worries.

"Did they tell him about the lipstick they found on the scene?"

"They sure did!" Meg chuckled. "As if I could afford to spend that much money on a single item of makeup. Everything I buy is from the dollar store."

"I told them I didn't think there was any way you could be involved."

"Thanks." Meg smiled. Then her glance moved to the flowers. "I'll have the nurse put those in water. Thanks again."

"I always thought you didn't like me." Claire closed her eyes, mortified. She couldn't believe she'd blurted that out. She was as bad as a schoolgirl who wanted to be in with the cool kids.

Meg frowned. "I think I was bothered that some of my clients left me. But that wasn't your fault. I was going through a rough patch, and I was off my game."

Claire murmured in sympathy. She understood how emotions could change your life. She had spent years letting fear and anxiety control her. She'd missed out on so much. Suddenly, she wanted to hear her mother's voice. When her parents and sister moved, Claire had allowed their relationship to suffer. She was so determined to be strong, she had neglected those who loved her most.

How her mother must have suffered! Shame filled her when she recalled how she had rebuffed her mother's attempts to show affection. That had to change. She'd wasted too much time.

After a few more minutes of conversation, Claire left. She called Jason to let him know she was done. When he responded he'd be back in fifteen minutes, she dialed her mother's cell phone.

The call went to voice mail, and her heart sank in her chest. Emotion clogged her throat. She swallowed. When she heard the beep, she started to leave a message.

"Hey, Mom. It's Claire."

Her phone vibrated. Her mother was trying to call her back. She quickly accepted the call. "Mom?"

"Claire? Is everything all right, honey?"

Claire winced. This was how far she had fallen. When she called, her family automatically assumed something was wrong. She closed her eyes, briefly saying a prayer of thanks to God for opening her mind and her heart and allowing her to see what she had done.

"Hi, Mom. I'm fine. I just realized how dumb I've been over the past few years."

Her mother choked out a laugh. "Oh, honey. Don't say that. You know I'm proud of you no matter what you do."

Claire smiled through a haze of tears. "I know. I just realized that I've been pushing you away. I don't know why I did that."

Her mother was quiet for a few moments. When she spoke, Claire could hear the tears in her voice. "Sweetie, you went through one of the most traumatic things anyone can go through when you were a teenager. That would change anyone. And I think I came so close to losing you, I was afraid to try too hard. I didn't want to push."

They chatted for a few more minutes. Claire looked outside and saw Jason drive under the awning. She stepped through the sliding glass doors, and when he looked at her, she pointed to her phone and mouthed *Mom*. He nodded and gave her a thumbs-up.

When she got off the phone, she felt lighter than she'd felt in months. In a matter of minutes, she had made huge steps to mend her relationships with her family. Relationships that, until now, she hadn't realized were dysfunctional and unhealthy. Guilt stirred in her heart and began to rise up inside her like a cobra uncoiling. She smacked it down. Such feelings would only harm the progress she had begun to make.

Climbing into the car, she smiled. Until she recalled what had happened right before she exited. Immediately, color rushed to her face.

She met Jason's eyes. He grinned at her. "Are you going to kiss my cheek again?"

Groaning, she sank into her seat. "I didn't mean to do that!"

He laughed. "I knew that the moment you backed away. I've never seen anyone scramble out of a vehicle so fast."

"I don't know what to tell you. It was an impulsive move. I still can't figure out what I was thinking."

He chuckled and left the parking lot. "Don't sweat it. I thought it was kind of sweet."

She blew out a breath and relaxed against the seat. "I may never live this down."

Their eyes met. Electricity sparked between them. She was in so much trouble.

He had been so determined to avoid entanglements. And he had failed. Every moment he spent in her presence, she intrigued him more and more. If he wasn't careful, he'd end up with a broken heart. But how did she feel? Sure, she had kissed his cheek. But it was clear she'd immediately regretted her action. What he didn't know was why. Was it because, like him, she wanted to avoid a relationship, or was it because she saw him as too old for her, or even worse, as a brother?

He mentally recoiled at the last idea. If she saw him as a brother, there was nothing he could do, ever, to change her mind.

Now he was confusing himself. He'd already determined he didn't want a relationship. He needed to let the matter go and move on. Except he found he couldn't.

"I talked to my mom." She broke the silence.

He raised his eyebrows. "Okay?"

She sighed. "I know. It doesn't sound like such a big deal. But trust me, it was a huge moment. I haven't really allowed myself to be close to anyone except Suzanne since I had cancer. I realized last night that I didn't want to cut myself off from people anymore. So I called my mom to start reconnecting."

He smiled at her, finally understanding. She was so brave. She made a decision and immediately moved to follow through on it. That took courage. "I'm assuming she was receptive."

She smiled back. "She hadn't understood why I pushed them away. It won't happen again."

He held his question in for a moment. He didn't want to be rude. But she was opening up to him. "I want to ask you something, but it's personal, so I'll back off if it's something that bothers you."

She tensed beside him.

Maybe he should stop now.

"You can ask. I don't know if I'll answer."

Fair enough. "I noticed the other day"—was it only two days ago?—"that you seemed to be sad when you were talking to Suzanne. You didn't make it obvious. I just wondered if you two were fighting or something."

For a moment, she didn't answer. He wished he hadn't asked, because it was obviously a question she didn't want to answer. He nearly apologized for bringing the subject up, but then she began to respond, slowly, as if the words were being dragged from the depths of her soul.

"You didn't imagine it." She turned her head to look out the window. "Suzanne had just told me about the baby. She didn't want to tell me, because she didn't want to hurt me."

"Hurt you?" He hadn't expected that.

Keeping her head against the back of the seat, she rotated it until she faced him again. "I can't have children, because of the chemotherapy. It's why I don't date. Ever. My one foray into romance ended when my fiancé"—her lip curled on the word—"decided it was bad for his political image to have a wife who couldn't give him kids."

Disgust for Adam Hunter sprang up inside him. "That's ridiculous. What about adoption? I'm sorry, Claire, but I dislike the man more every time you talk about him. You're better off without someone like that in your life."

She finally smiled a tiny smile that said she agreed. "Thanks. I figured that out for myself."

The atmosphere inside the car grew thick with too much emotion. It was almost hard to breathe. He needed to change the subject.

"I got your tires. Which means I'll be able to fix your car when we get back to your house."

"Super! It'll be great to be able to come and go when I want to again."

"I still think you need to be cautious. We don't know who's after you or why. So far, they've not struck out at you physically, but we can't be sure things will stay that way."

"I know," she said. "I'll be careful. It just feels good knowing that something positive has happened after all the bad stuff that's gone on."

He understood that.

They made it back to her house in good time. His stomach growled like a caged animal as he turned off his car. Grimacing, he looked at her out of the corner of his eye. There was no way she hadn't heard that. Her shoulders shook, and a chuckle escaped.

"What? I haven't eaten since this morning."

She laughed. "I'm hungry too. I'll tell you what. You change my tires, and I'll make us lunch."

"It's a deal."

By the time he walked into her kitchen forty minutes later, the growls had become a constant rumble. She pointed imperiously at the kitchen table. "Sit!"

He gave her a mock salute and dropped into a chair. She placed a plate in front of him.

"I hope you're good with cheeseburgers and salad. I don't have much in my fridge."

"It's perfect. Trust me."

It was the best cheeseburger he'd ever eaten. Maybe because he was so hungry. Or maybe it was the company he was keeping. Either way, he had no complaints.

They were cleaning up the remains of lunch when someone knocked on her door. She tensed next to him. "Are you expecting someone?" he asked.

She shook her head. "No."

He walked with her to the door. When she lifted herself on the tips of her toes to look out the peephole, he grinned despite the tension. She was adorable. She scowled at his expression and opened the door.

"Good afternoon, Sergeant Stonis. Won't you come in?"

CHAPTER SEVEN

Claire stepped back to allow the law enforcement officer room to enter. She frowned. Unlike other times he'd talked with her, his expression was closed and somewhat forbidding. Something new must have happened. She could feel her stomach muscles begin to cramp and had to fight to remind herself that she needed to trust God to deal with whatever bad news the man brought this time.

"Won't you sit down?" She gestured toward the sofa and the two chairs in the living room.

"No, thank you." He stared at her, his gaze like flint. Her heart faltered. Something weird was going on. "Miss Derrick."

She swallowed. Yesterday he'd called her Claire. Was he dragging this out on purpose? It was worse than a suspense novel.

"Yes?"

"Where were you between nine o'clock last night and eleven this morning?" He barked out the words.

She blinked. "Well, Jason and I got back late from dinner. I was here alone after he left. Then this morning, we went to church, and then he dropped me off at the hospital to see Meg."

"Hmm." His expression didn't shift. "You didn't leave your house last night? Can you prove it?"

"I couldn't have. My tires were still slashed until Jason changed them an hour ago."

Some of the sternness melted from his gaze.

"Sergeant," Jason broke in, "she set the alarm when we returned last night. If she had left and come back, she would have needed to enter her pass code. That sort of information is logged into the system and can be checked out."

He finally relented, raising a reassuring hand. "Okay. I'll check on that, but I believe you."

"What's this about?" Claire asked, although she wasn't sure she wanted to know.

"Another house was vandalized last night. It wasn't set on fire, which is how we managed to find this." He pulled a clear plastic bag from his pocket. Inside, she saw a gold necklace. She knew that necklace. Her name dangled from the chain in calligraphy-like script.

"That's mine!" she said. "I haven't seen it in years."

"It was found on the floor," he said. She jerked her head up and stared at him. "It looks like someone is trying to frame you for these crimes."

"How did you know? That I didn't do it?"

"The person who dropped this necklace at the scene didn't bother to clean it. If you look at it closer, it looks like it was packed in dirt. Now, I realize I don't know you that well, but the little I have seen of you, you've never worn anything that wasn't spotless. Nor have I seen you with this necklace on. You've always worn that one." He gestured to the small golden cross she wore around her neck on a delicate chain.

"This is the only necklace I wear most days."

"I thought as much. So, my guess is, someone found this and decided to use it to cast suspicion on you. It was very clumsily done."

Clumsy or not, she wondered who she'd angered so much that they would go through the trouble. "What does this mean?"

"It means we're widening our search. I had originally knocked your ex-fiancé off the list of suspects. He's officially back on."

That surprised her. "I thought you said you were looking for a woman."

"We were," he said. "But now I wonder if everything that made us think it was a woman was actually someone wanting evidence to point at you."

"Yeah, but the lipstick? I've never bought that brand before." And now she never would, just on principle.

"But you said yourself it was a common enough color. If I look at pictures of you, will I find you wearing a similar color?"

She thought about it and had to admit he had a point. "Yes, but wouldn't that lipstick have DNA evidence on it?"

She had watched her share of crime shows.

"No. It's brand new. Never been used. I have my partner checking the stores to see if we can get a list of people who have bought that particular brand and shade, but it might take a while. Especially if it wasn't bought locally."

She felt a tension headache coming on and rubbed her temples. A strong arm slid around her waist and pulled her close in a comforting embrace. Once again, Jason offered his support, letting her lean on his strength.

"What makes you think my ex-fiancé might be a suspect?" It had been two years since she had last seen Adam. And he'd dumped her, not the other way around. If anyone held a grudge, it would be her.

"I've been looking into Mr. Hunter," Sergeant Stonis informed her. "He ended your engagement because of political aspirations. Did you keep track of him after that?"

She shook her head. She hadn't wanted to hear his name, much less follow his career. "I wanted nothing to do with him."

"When he ran for office, a reporter dug up his engagement photo. The reporter snooped around, asking people what had happened to his fiancée. She found someone you had talked with who was willing to talk. The media had a field day with it. Politician dumps cancer survivor and breaks her heart. There were several articles along that vein."

"I'm glad I didn't see any of them."

To have her pain splattered all over the newspapers made her feel physically ill. That was her private life. No one had a right to see it without her permission. She wrapped her arms around her middle as if that would settle the chaos inside her.

"Did the articles mention my name?" She braced herself for his reply.

Jason squeezed her silently. She wasn't alone.

"They didn't, but the picture made the rounds." He looked at Jason. "You never saw it?"

"Not that I recall. I might have skipped over the article without realizing Claire was the woman in the photo. We hadn't seen each other for several years at that point. I might not have recognized her at a quick glance."

"That would explain it. I have one more order of business." Sergeant Stonis walked to the door and went out onto the porch. He returned carrying a plain brown box. "I was told I could give this to you."

She took the box and heard a tinkling noise. She felt her heartbeat speed up and handed the box to Jason. When he grabbed it, she carefully lifted the flaps to open it. "My vase! I didn't think I would see it for weeks."

The stern police officer smiled at her. "I rushed it for you. There are no prints on it, so it didn't provide any evidence."

"Thank you!" she said fervently. "I've been itching to begin repairing this."

"You're very welcome. I plan on speaking with Hunter today if I can, tomorrow at the latest. I'll keep you informed. For the time being, I would still avoid going places alone."

She nodded, too happy with the return of her vase to complain about the restriction. Looking at the pieces in the box, she knew it would be a challenge. But then, anything worth doing was a challenge. She was done being passive while life sped by.

Claire practically vibrated with joy. Jason watched her face as she lifted a shard from the box and inspected it. She radiated energy and enthusiasm. She made him smile.

"Do you want to start putting this together on the kitchen table? Or maybe in the dining room?"

She paused, the piece of broken pottery still clutched in her hand.

"Jason, I know this will sound strange, but I don't want to put it together here."

His eyebrows climbed his forehead. "No? Where will you assemble it then?" As soon as the words left his mouth, he knew. "At the old house?"

"At my house."

She really was getting attached to that place. He could deny her nothing. "All right. I'll drive you over. Will you let me help?"

He had never glued a vase together in his life, but he was a big fan of puzzles. She lifted her gaze to his. A soft smile played around her lips. "I'd like that. I'd like that a lot."

So would he.

Gathering their coats, they carefully made their way out to his sedan. He placed the box in the trunk and packed blankets around it to keep it from shifting too much. The less it moved, the better the chances that the vase wouldn't break any further.

He couldn't help the grin spreading across his face as they drove. She jiggled her legs so fast in her seat, he was surprised the entire car wasn't vibrating.

"You must be fun to watch on Christmas morning," he teased her.

She wrinkled her nose at him. "Yeah, yeah. So I get a little excited. I can't help it. I seriously didn't think I would get the vase back so soon. Possibly never at all. So, yes, I'm a little more animated than usual."

"A little?" He cleared his throat to hold in the snicker. "I'd say more than a little. But that's fine. It's nice to see you in such a good mood. I know these past few days haven't been easy."

"Yeah. When I saw Sergeant Stonis's expression earlier, I was really scared for a few minutes. And when he started asking me where I'd been, I could almost see the headlines. It was not a fun experience."

"I'll bet. But I think he knew all along it wasn't you. He went pretty easy on you."

"That was easy?" Her voice climbed an octave. She shook her head. "I still can't believe someone would plant my necklace at a crime scene."

"When's the last time you had it?"

She leaned her head back against the seat. "The very last time I remember putting it on, I was on my way to dinner at Adam's house. That was the night his mom hinted that he and I had something to discuss. She was never warm, but this time, her smile was positively icy. That's when he told me I wasn't good for his image, and he needed to end our engagement. I didn't hang around. I left right away and haven't talked to him or anyone in his family since."

"Wow. I'm sorry I asked."

She shrugged. "Don't be. I'm glad I found out how much his image controlled his life before we married. Anyway, that's the last time I remember seeing the necklace. I thought I put it in my jewelry box when I got home, but I couldn't find it later."

He tossed her a smile and pulled up to the front of the house. "Honey, we're home."

She flushed.

Laughing, he ducked out of the car and grabbed the box from the trunk. It was too easy to joke with her and forget that they were just friends. She met him on the wraparound. When he approached, she pushed the door open for him. "Let's take it into the kitchen area. I have a couple of folding chairs in there. We can work at the counter."

They spent the next ten minutes laying out all the pieces as if the vase was a giant jigsaw puzzle. All the shards containing the vines were in one pile. If they had a part of a bird, they were in another. When the pieces were separated out, she opened her phone and found a picture she'd taken of the vase. He hadn't noticed her doing that but was glad she had. Especially if this was a one-of-a-kind piece.

They worked quietly for a few moments. When the door swung open, both of them whirled around, alarmed. They relaxed when two little faces stared in at them. Claire frowned. It took him a moment to realize what it was that bothered her.

The children wore the same clothes they had yesterday, and they were filthy. Emma was flushed. Not a healthy flush, but a feverish one. She wiped her nose with her sleeve. When Claire called out a greeting, Emma tried to respond. The moment she opened her mouth to speak, a harsh barking cough shook her small body so hard she began to cry.

Claire abandoned the vase and moved to the children, kneeling in front of Emma. She pressed the back of her hand against Emma's forehead.

"Emma, sweetie, you have a fever. Maybe you should go home and tell your mommy."

Tears ran down the little girl's cheeks. She fell into Claire's arms, sobbing between choking coughs.

Brody looked terrified. "Miss Claire, we don't have a mom or dad. Not anymore. We've been staying in your house every night cuz we figured you wouldn't mind. You've been nice to us. But last night we couldn't get in because of the alarm system."

Several things clicked in Jason's mind at once.

"It was your footprints I saw in the flower bed. You broke the vase." It wasn't a question. No wonder the child had been so interested in the security system. He must have wanted to find a way to get past it but didn't stay long enough to see the code Claire plugged in.

Brody hung his head. "It was an accident. We didn't mean to."

Emma coughed again, and Brody's face paled.

Claire hugged the children. "You guys were the ones who came through the door in the basement. I've seen you in different clothes. Where do you keep them?"

"In the cupboard in the basement."

It broke his heart. And he could see it broke Claire's too. "You can't continue living here. Someone will buy this house very soon. And Emma needs to see a doctor."

"We know. We want to stay together." Brody's bottom lip quivered. The poor kid was doing his best to be brave, but his whole body radiated fear. Jason's heart wrenched in his chest. He'd seen grown men and women dealing with the loss of a parent. It was never easy. But these two kids, they had no one. The chill in the air spoke of winter's eminent arrival.

They'd slept outside last night because the house was closed up.

He moved to Brody and put a hand on his shoulder. "I know you're scared, buddy. I don't blame you. But your sister is sick. She needs to see a doctor. And you can't sleep outside when the snow comes."

The little boy seemed to wilt.

"Brody." Claire's voice was a soothing whisper. "What happened to your parents?"

He looked at her. "I don't remember having a dad. My mom disappeared. I don't know where she is."

Jason met her gaze. They needed to find out what happened to the parents. He didn't think the children were runaways, but it was a possibility.

Emma coughed again. First things first. "We need to get her to the hospital," he said. "Then we'll figure out the rest."

Brody looked up at him. "Will you help us stay together?"

Jason's throat closed. He tried to never break his word. This child was asking him for a promise he couldn't give. As much as he wanted to tell Brody that he and Emma would be able to stay together, the truth was, until they knew about their family, he couldn't answer that question.

He couldn't give the little boy a promise without risking breaking his heart.

CHAPTER EIGHT

Claire picked Emma up and held her close. "Jason, can we use one of the blankets in your trunk? She's shivering so hard. We need to warm her up."

"Absolutely. Brody, come with me. We need to get your sister warm, and then I'm going to drive you both to the hospital."

She watched them disappear through the front parlor before returning her attention to Emma. She didn't like the dullness in her eyes or the listlessness in her expression. Placing her fingers on the child's forehead, alarm bloomed inside her. The girl was burning up. She didn't have a thermometer, but she was willing to bet that Emma's temperature had risen during the short time she'd been in the room. Chills continued to shake her slight frame.

Jason and Brody burst into the room and hurried to them. Carefully, Jason wrapped a thick fleece blanket around the child, tucking it under her and trapping it between Emma's and Claire's bodies. "Let's get moving. I turned the car on and cranked the heat to high."

"I'll ride in back with her." Claire gently passed Emma to Jason, momentarily disrupting the tight blankets while she put her own coat on. Emma shivered and burrowed into Jason but didn't utter a single complaint. The two adults exchanged concerned glances.

"I'll carry her out," Jason decided. "Then I'll hand her to you in the car."

Claire nodded. She took Brody's icy hand in hers as the small group made the short trip from the house to the car. After getting into the car, Claire took Emma into her arms and settled the girl at her side, still wrapped in blankets. She reached across and grabbed the buckle, securing it across Emma's lap over the blankets. Brody sat on Emma's other side. If the situation wasn't so serious, she would have made a joke about Jason being their chauffeur. But now was not the time for teasing. Jason backed out of the driveway and headed toward Zanesville. An oppressive silence settled over them.

Slipping her arm around Emma, Claire gripped Brody's shoulder, trying to comfort both children at once. Her heart ached for them. Brody was so brave. And resourceful. She knew it was only fear for his sister that had made him reveal their true circumstances. Had Emma not become ill, he might never have revealed that they had no parents.

How long had they been on their own? Did they go to school, or was the school district even aware of the two homeless children in their midst?

Despite the current urgency, Jason drove with extra caution. No doubt he was doing his best to avoid unnecessarily jostling them in the back seat. Keeping her hands connected with both children, Claire shifted her position to allow her to watch the scenery outside the window. She let out a soft sigh when they passed the sign at the edge of Crooksville that stated the founders established the city in 1874, calling it the "Clay City of Perry County."

Each minute seemed to crawl by. Her jaw ached by the time Jason drove under the carport at the hospital. She hadn't realized she was clenching her teeth. She forced herself to relax, opening and closing her mouth several times to ease the tension.

"Hang on!" Jason left the car running and hopped out. He dashed around to the passenger-side rear door. Claire unbuckled Emma and slid out of the vehicle when he opened her door. He leaned in past her and gathered Emma in his arms then stepped back. Claire waited for Brody to slide across the seat and exit next to her. She held his hand as they followed Jason, still carrying Emma, into the hospital.

"Brody, go sit with Jason in the waiting area," she whispered.

Jason headed that way with both children, and Claire moved to the reception area.

The woman behind the desk gave her a professional smile as she approached. "May I help you?"

"Yes. It's a complicated situation." She lowered her voice and leaned in. She didn't want Brody to hear what she had to say. "That little girl is really sick. Her name is Emma. I'm not sure of her last name. Her brother might be able to fill in other details. They say they don't have any parents or family. I don't know if it's true or not."

The woman's eyes widened. Otherwise, her professional mask remained in place. "Where are they living?"

She bit her lip and glanced back at Jason and the kids. None of them were looking her way. "They're homeless. I just learned they've been sleeping in a house that's being renovated. She's running a high fever and has a horrible cough."

At that moment, Emma coughed, her harsh spluttering leaving her gasping and gagging. Claire winced, her heart contracting as if someone squeezed it. From where she stood, she could hear the child's harsh breathing once the coughing spell ended.

The woman cast a glance at the children, frowning with concern. "I'll get a doctor to take a look at her. In the meantime I'll also put a call in to Child Protective Services. Someone from the county will have to come and take them into custody."

Claire bit her lip. She had known that would happen. It was a good thing, wasn't it? Brody and Emma couldn't continue living in abandoned or empty houses, or on the street. They needed to have a warm house and access to clothing and education. Family. She had no idea how long it had been since they attended school.

Slowly, she made her way back to the small group, her heart heavy in her chest.

Brody had pleaded that he wanted to remain with his sister. Of course he did. That was natural. Jason, she had noticed, had not promised him it would work out that way. She understood that. Once the county took control, she and Jason would have no say in what happened to the children. She would lose contact with them. Although she hadn't known Emma and Brody for long, they had burrowed into her heart. It bothered her that the connection would be severed. But what choice did they have?

One option crept into her mind. Was she strong enough to take it? She had always resisted it, to spare herself from potential pain. But that was before.

A nurse stepped into the waiting room and called Emma's name. As a group, they rose, Emma held in Jason's arms, and headed to her. She frowned. "I'm sorry. Only one adult can accompany her."

Jason turned and handed Emma to Claire. She closed her arms around the sweet bundle. "Where will you be?"

"Brody and I will stay here. Do you have your phone on you?"

"I do. I'll keep you posted."

It was a fairly bold promise, considering the sign on the door said no cell phones beyond the emergency room doors. The nurse, however, remained silent. She turned and led Claire and Emma to an empty cubicle divided from others by curtains hanging from the ceiling on a rolling track.

"Place her on the bed, please." For the first time, Emma whined. Bracing herself, knowing she needed to be strong for Emma, Claire laid her on the bed and then stepped back. When Emma stretched out her hand, Claire quickly grabbed it, glad she could provide that small amount of comfort. The bed was narrow, but Emma still appeared so tiny and lost in it. The nurse took her vitals and recorded them on a small laptop propped on a mobile cart.

"The doctor will be in shortly," the nurse said before departing. Claire gaped at the curtain. The nurse hadn't said anything about what Emma's vitals were.

The doctor arrived twenty minutes later. "I hear someone isn't feeling well."

He approached Emma. She pressed herself deeper into the thin mattress, and the doctor cast Claire a small, confident smile. Here was a man used to dealing with timid patients. Some of her anxiety left her, and she sagged against the hard back of the chair she rested on.

He calmly talked to Emma. Claire appreciated his soothing manner. Then he listened to her lungs and asked Claire a few questions. She could see his eyebrows shift up and down, no doubt at all the information she didn't know.

"I'm not her mother," she murmured, looking at Emma out of the corner of her eye. "I'm not familiar with her history."

He nodded. "I understand. I'm admitting her."

She sat up. "Admitting her?"

She didn't like the sound of that.

"Yes. She'd dehydrated. She needs to be carefully monitored."

Tingling erupted in her fingers and toes. The air felt thin. Claire struggled to control her breathing. *It's going to be fine*, she told herself. Everything would work out. Remembering her decision to trust God in all things, she began a silent litany of prayer. She barely knew what to say, so she just kept repeating *Help us, Lord. Be with us, Lord.*

"Mr. Jason, they've been gone a long time." Brody fidgeted in his chair. His legs dangled over the edge. He swung them back and forth.

Jason noticed the motion getting stronger and faster. The kid was getting worked up.

"Easy, buddy. I'll text Miss Claire and see what's going on. Okay? You good with that?"

The motion slowed as Brody considered his words. "Yeah. That sounds good."

Jason began tapping out a message. Before he hit send, a message came through from Claire.

They're admitting her.

He blinked, alarmed. That was not what he wanted to tell Brody.

Why? He typed out then hit send.

Come on, Claire. Answer.

Doc thinks she's dehydrated.

Jason sucked in a breath. That wasn't good. Suzanne had come down with the flu and gotten dehydrated once when she was in college. It was in March, her sophomore year. If he recalled correctly, she ended up dropping several courses because she was too exhausted to do all the work. She had to take summer school just so she wouldn't fall behind and have to stay an extra semester.

Emma wasn't as hardy as his sister. How would it affect her? Not only that, but she didn't have any consistent adults to care for her.

"What does Miss Claire say?" Brody interrupted his thoughts.

He was tempted to downplay what was happening so the boy didn't worry. But he couldn't. Jason made it a habit to never lie to anyone. Especially a child. Trust was a fragile thing. If he lost Brody's trust by lying, he might never get it back. Brody and Emma didn't have many people they could trust. In fact, he was fairly certain he and Claire made up their entire circle of trusted adults.

"Emma's really sick, Brody." The child's already pale face grew ashen. "The doctor wants her to stay here. I don't know what will happen."

Brody's jaw trembled, and his big brown eyes flooded with tears. But he didn't cry. He bravely sniffed them back.

Jason eased his arm around his shoulders, offering what comfort he could.

Twenty-five minutes later, Claire joined them, her shoulders tense. Her complexion was nearly as pale as Brody's. Between the agony in her eyes and her petite frame, if one didn't know her, they might think she was fragile. Ah, but he did know her. Or he was getting to know her. Claire Derrick had steel running in her veins. He had no doubt she would survive anything life dished out. It might change her, but it wouldn't destroy her. He'd known soldiers who would have broken under the stress she carried on her shoulders.

There was nothing about her he didn't admire.

The doors whooshed open, letting in a whirl of icy air. A woman in her late thirties or early forties swept in with the cold, her black pumps clicking out a rapid staccato beat on the tile floor. She swished past them, a thick cloud of perfume hovering about her, and approached the desk. He saw the receptionist lean away from the overpowering scent.

"I'm Stacy Boyd from the county. I'm here to take two homeless children into custody." She made no move to keep her voice down.

Brody sank into his chair, trying his best to be invisible.

"There's one of them." The receptionist pointed their way. "The other one, a little girl, is being admitted."

The county woman grunted then pivoted to them. Her gaze zeroed in on Brody. To Jason's surprise, contrary to the way she'd marched into the hospital, kindness shone on her face. She walked to where they waited, her steps less forceful than before.

"Are you Brody?" She smiled at the little boy. He turned his face into Jason's side. She didn't act surprised.

"Honey, I want to help you. Can you tell me your last name?"

At first, Jason didn't think he'd answer. Finally, the boy responded, his voice dull. "Mitchell. My mama's name was Zoe."

The woman took notes and asked a few more questions. Finally, she put her tablet back in her bag.

"What will happen?" Claire asked.

"They will be placed with a foster family while we search for any other relatives. If there aren't any, they'll remain in the system.

They'll go to school, have regular medical and dental care, be fed and given clothing."

"They want to stay together," Jason said, keeping an eye on Brody. He saw the boy flinch.

Her face became somber. "That's always the goal."

Jason and Claire's eyes met. They both understood what she didn't say. It might be the goal, but it didn't always happen. He knew of someone who had taken in a young girl. The family decided not to take her two brothers, saying it would be too hard for them. What if that happened to Brody and Emma? In his mind, nothing would be crueler than separating them.

"What if an approved foster mom volunteered to take them both?" Claire asked.

The woman blinked. "Such a placement would, of course, be evaluated. I can't guarantee it. I'm assuming by your question you have a possible foster placement in mind?"

"I do." Claire's chin rose. "With me."

CHAPTER NINE

Jason kept his jaw from hitting the floor, but it was a close call. Brody stirred and sat up, his gaze laser sharp on Claire, hope vibrating from him.

Stacy Boyd sighed, pity crossing her face. "It's not easy to get certified as a foster parent. It takes time. One must have the appropriate clearances, a health checkup, a home evaluation."

"Yes, I know. I have all those things." Claire shoved her hands into her pockets. "I started the process eight months ago."

A tiny smile worked its way onto Stacy's face. "Did you? How many children are you fostering currently?"

"None. Emma and Brody would be the first."

"Well, it would certainly be an option." She raised a questioning brow. "You are aware that if we find living relatives, they would have the right to take the children? I don't want to discourage you, but I can see that you've become attached to them. Having foster children leave is painful. I won't deceive you. It's a generous thing to do, but it's not an easy task."

"I get it," Claire said. "But I'm willing to take the risk."

His admiration for her soared.

Brody shot from his chair and threw himself at Claire, wrapping his arms around her waist. "Does that mean we can stay with you, Miss Claire?"

He swallowed past the lump that formed in his throat. Claire gently pulled the boy's arms loose. Once she was no longer entangled, she squatted down in front of him. "I don't know yet, Brody. I'm going to try, but I can't promise it'll happen the way we want it to. Do you understand?"

He nodded energetically, his hair flopping over his forehead with the force of his enthusiasm. Clearly, her warning had not dimmed his hope.

"I'll see what I can do," Stacy said. "Brody will have to come with me, though, until we get it sorted out."

Brody obviously didn't like that idea. He folded his arms across his chest and thrust his bottom lip out in a classic look of childish defiance.

"Hey, buddy." Jason got his attention. "If we want Miss Claire to do this, you have to follow the rules. Miss Stacy needs you to go with her so she can work on making it happen."

He hoped he hadn't just promised something that wouldn't pan out.

It wasn't easy to convince Brody. He seemed to believe the possibility of staying with Claire would vanish if he wasn't personally there to make it happen. Jason understood. It wasn't an easy thing, letting others decide your fate. He'd found that out during his military career. Sometimes that was the way things had to be.

Finally, the child allowed himself to be led away, constantly looking back over his shoulder at Claire.

It was one of the longest afternoons he'd ever spent, waiting with Claire for news. The hospital allowed them to stay with Emma after a phone call from Stacy confirmed she'd gotten permission to temporarily place Emma and Brody with Claire while the county searched for any living relatives.

Stacy and Brody returned to the hospital at seven thirty that evening.

Brody immediately snuggled against Claire and asked if he could see Emma.

"Can he?" she asked the nurse.

The woman pursed her lips. "He can see her from the door, but he can't enter. That little girl needs rest. And we want to minimize germs. Visiting hours will be over in twenty-five minutes."

Emma was sleeping peacefully when they opened the door. Already, Jason could hear she breathed easier.

"Those breathing treatments seem to be helping," Claire murmured, echoing his thoughts.

"She's on albuterol, an antibiotic, and a steroid to reduce the inflammation in her lungs," the nurse said. "When you return tomorrow, she'll sound even better."

When the door closed and they returned to the waiting area, all their spirits were lighter. Claire downloaded a book for Brody on her phone. Then the adults moved away to talk about the children.

Stacy referred to her tablet. "It's hard to know how the children got into this situation. As you can imagine, a seven-year-old doesn't understand a lot of what the adults around him are thinking." She sighed. "The best I can tell, from what Brody knows, the mother took the children and left the shelter where they were staying. Brody doesn't remember where the shelter is—he just knows they drove for a few days before they arrived here. He said they slept in their car for two nights before their mother moved them into the basement of the house."

Claire's eyes filled with tears. "I wish I'd known."

"Brody watched Emma during the day while their mom went out searching for work. And then one day she didn't come back. The children had some money she'd left behind, so they were able to walk to the store and buy bread, peanut butter and jelly, and cereal." She paused. "I called the police chief at home and asked him if he had any information about a Zoe Mitchell."

Jason could tell by the look on the social worker's face that it wasn't good news.

"He told me that their mother died of a heart attack a little over a week ago. That's why she never came back for them. We still haven't found any other relatives, but we'll keep looking. In the meantime, I checked on your foster parent status." She dipped her chin at Claire. "I'm happy to say it all looks good. I brought some paperwork."

Jason was amazed at how quickly the process went after that. By nine that night, Brody was on his way back to Claire's house.

"The doctor seems to think we can bring Emma home tomorrow afternoon." Claire glanced over her shoulder.

Seeing her smile, Jason looked in his rearview mirror. Brody had zonked out, his head against the window. "He's had a long day."

She bit her lip. "I hope I'm doing the right thing for him. For them."

He sent her an "Oh, please" glance. "How could it be wrong? They trust you, and you have a warm house with a new security system."

She opened her eyes wide. "Oh! But with all the attacks."

"Wait. We know the vandalism wasn't really vandalism. So there was no personal attack."

"Someone is still trying to implicate me in this."

"Yeah, but the cops are on to them. So that tactic will fail." He reached out and took her hand. "And you have a state-of-the-art alarm system at your house. I'll be there in fifteen minutes if you call me, and you have Sergeant Stonis on speed dial. You've got this."

Claire lifted her chin and took a deep breath. She could do this. God was in control. He had given her an opportunity to help two people who needed her desperately. When she had first started the journey to become a foster parent, her doubts had pushed her to stop the process before she'd taken any children into her heart and home.

The irony was, the two children being placed with her had already been living in her home, but she never knew it. It broke her heart—if that door in the basement wasn't partially hidden, she would have locked it tight. Then they would have truly been on the streets, like they were last night.

She shook her mind free from those morose thoughts. "You know, I should give Sergeant Stonis a call. Let him know what we found out."

They should have done that hours ago.

Jason turned the radio off. She dialed the number and put the call on speaker.

"Claire. It's after nine. Did anything happen? Do you need help?"

She smiled. She could hear the sounds of chatter in the background. He was at home with his family but still ready to assist at a moment's notice.

"Everything is fine. I realized we never updated you on what's happening."

Quickly, she summarized what had occurred earlier, starting with finding out Brody and Emma were staying in the house and had broken the vase. He asked several questions but seemed satisfied that they could classify the incident as an accident rather than any malicious activity. Strangely, he didn't seem to find her venture into the world of being a foster parent odd. She felt better when she got off the phone with him.

Scanning their current location, she saw they were approaching the road to take them to her house. "We should stop by the other house and pick up their clothes and any other items they have hidden there."

Jason flipped on his blinker and smoothly swerved into the right lane, slowing to make the turn. "Do we bring the vase back to your real house?"

She thought about it for a moment then rejected the idea. "Nah. I'll continue to·work there. I'll call my office tomorrow and tell my boss I'll be doing most of my work from home for the foreseeable future."

"Will he or she mind?"

"No. We have another agent who works from home almost exclusively. She won't care."

And if she did, Claire would look for a new job. Brody and Emma had to come first.

When he pulled into the driveway, she unbuckled and prepared to enter the house. His hand on her arm stopped her. She swung around, waiting to see what he wanted.

"Do you want me to go in first? It's pretty dark in there."

She hadn't considered that until now. She shook her head. "I'll just be a minute."

She dashed up the steps, happy when the motion detectors flicked the lights on. Inside the house, she ran down the basement steps, trying to block any fears or images of some unknown threat waiting for her at the bottom of the stairs. She couldn't deny it gave her goose bumps. She wasn't a fan of basements even during the day.

Clutching her phone, she continued, grabbing the bags of clothes as fast as she physically could. She wouldn't let herself fall prey to fear.

She was, however, touched by Jason's sensitivity. She had never seen that side of him while they were growing up. He'd intimidated her a little. She saw the older brother who enjoyed teasing his sister. His care and his kind heart weren't as obvious to her then as they were now.

That was when she knew she was in real danger. Not from some outside force trying to harm her or her career. A house could be rebuilt. And she had the help of Sergeant Stonis to assist her in minimizing the harm to her reputation.

No, the real danger was to her heart. She had only scraped the surface of the man Jason Pierce had grown into. It was enough, though, for her to know he was a strong man of strong principles. One who made his family a priority and took his responsibilities seriously. He was also a man of faith.

In essence, he was exactly the kind of man she could fall in love with if she wasn't careful.

She told her heart to be strong. To resist the temptation he represented.

Unfortunately, she strongly suspected the warning had come too late.

Chapter Ten

The following morning, Jason got up and forced himself to go into the office like he did every Monday. He didn't want to. If he had his druthers, he would spend the entire day with Claire and Brody. Emma was still in the hospital. He promised Claire that after he finished work, he would swing by and they could all go to the hospital together.

She didn't need him to drive her. Her car was completely functional now. However, he didn't feel right having her go by herself. What if the hospital had a rule against Brody visiting? He was, after all, only seven years old. Besides, he had become fond of the kids and wanted to see Emma for himself.

Suzanne called him before he'd been at his desk five minutes. He had a feeling he knew what she would say.

"Good morning, Suzanne," he greeted her.

"Good morning! Jason, Claire is by herself, after the fire and the vandalism."

His eyebrows rose. "You haven't talked to her since yesterday, have you?"

A thick silence followed his question.

"No." She drew out the word, ending on a high note, making it sound like a question. "I haven't talked to her since we saw you guys at church. Has something changed?"

"Well, first, the vandalism wasn't actually an attack."

He proceeded to tell her about Brody and Emma. When he got to the part about Claire deciding to try her hand as a foster parent, he was shocked to hear a muffled sob coming from his sister. "Suzanne? What's wrong?"

"Oh, Jason. You have no idea what a huge step this is for Claire." She sniffled in his ear.

"Um, no? I guess I don't. I was surprised to hear she had all her documentation ready to go, but apart from that, it didn't seem that odd. Claire is a generous person."

She laughed, a shaky sound filled with tears. "She is. But she's also a person who has kept to herself for years. Has she told you why her jerk of an ex-fiancé dumped her?"

"Adam? Yeah, she told me about him." He couldn't argue with his sister's assessment.

"When he dumped her because she couldn't have children, she shut part of herself away. She hasn't dated in the past two years. At all."

"I know. She told me." He sighed. "So, she decided to be a foster parent—"

Suzanne cut him off. "No. She thought about it. And she did all the groundwork so she could do it. Then she let it go before she could even try it. She didn't want to fall in love with a child and then have to let the child go. It would be heartbreaking, and she didn't think she had the strength to do it."

And then she met Emma and Brody.

He had only known them a few days himself. But he could easily understand how she'd fallen in love with them so quickly. They were great kids. It hurt, thinking about a loving woman like Claire closing herself away from love, or the possibility of love, because of

Adam's cruel and selfish nature. She was a woman who deserved to be cherished.

He froze. Why was he thinking of her like this? He knew better than that.

Suzanne wasn't finished. "Jason? She reminds me of you in some ways."

He pulled the phone away from his ear and stared at it for a moment before placing it against his ear again. "I don't see your point."

She sighed. "Seriously? You got hurt in action. I get that."

He straightened in his chair. "Suze."

"Oh, stop it. I know that voice. That's your 'We're not having this conversation' voice. But we are. Because you're making the same mistakes she did. You think because you have scars, people will be disgusted. I've seen your scars. I still love you. You're an honorable and brave man."

She didn't understand. He didn't think he could explain it to her. She had one thing right though. He didn't discuss his wounds or his past. Not with her, not with anyone. And especially not with Claire. She had enough to deal with at the moment and didn't need him to go all emo on her.

The day dragged on. He had three meetings with prospective clients. Normally, he was hyperfocused during such meetings. Today? Not so much. He caught his mind wandering several times. When he was back at his desk, he found himself reaching for the phone so he could call Claire and check in.

Stop! She'd call if she needed assistance. He didn't need to check in on her every few hours. As she liked to remind him, she was an adult, fully capable of handling herself.

He would leave her alone.

That decision lasted exactly five minutes. The moment his phone dinged telling him he had a text, he grabbed it and eagerly scanned the message.

BRODY AND I ARE GOING HOME. EMMA WILL BE DISCHARGED AT FOUR.

He looked at the time. It was already half past one. He tapped out a quick reply.

GLAD SHE'S COMING HOME. I'LL PICK YOU UP AT YOUR HOUSE AT THREE THIRTY.

When he realized he was grinning, he groaned. He was acting like a lovesick teenager. Forcing himself to focus, he set his alarm and buried himself in work for the next two hours. When the alarm went off, he stood and stretched. Then he grabbed his coat and swung it on. He caught his reflection in the mirror as he did so. He was grinning like a loon again.

Hurrying out to his car, his made his way to pick up Claire and Brody.

They were waiting for him. He didn't even have to get out of the car. Brody dashed to it and let himself in the back, chattering away nonstop. Was this the same child he'd sat with silently the day before? He raised his eyebrows at Claire and nodded his head toward the talkative seven-year-old.

Claire snickered. "He's a bit excited about getting his sister."

A bit? "Ya think?"

She laughed, and his heart raced at the musical sound. He knew he wanted to hear her laughter every day for the rest of his life. But that was an impossible dream. His heart cracked. When they picked up Emma, the reunion between the siblings tore another hole in his heart. They both cried.

"I don't think they've ever been apart this long before."

"I think you're right," he said.

Claire told him she wanted to go to the old house. All the way, Emma and Brody talked over each other, their enthusiasm swirling around. If he let himself, he could believe this was like having a family. Emma still coughed, and her voice was hoarse. But she had more energy than the day before.

He sensed Claire observing him. He didn't know what to say. He'd already broken his promise to keep himself emotionally distant. Every moment seemed like a painful reminder of what he could never have.

It was a good thing Claire didn't know what he felt. If he could spare one of them pain, he would.

When they got to the house, he asked her, "Why did you want to come here instead of going back to your place?"

She unbuckled her seat belt. "Brody wanted you to see how far we've come on the vase."

They entered the house, and he followed them to the dining room area. She'd set up a sturdy square table. The vase wasn't complete yet, but she and Brody had managed to get about half of it reassembled.

"Wow. That is an amazing amount of work accomplished."

When he looked into her shining eyes, he sucked in a breath. All the emotions he was holding back were reflected in her gaze. He needed to tell her about his past. To let her know what was wrong and why they could never be more than friends.

Claire was not looking forward to whatever it was Jason planned to tell her. She could see it on his face. He had seen her feelings and was preparing to let her down easy.

Her heart ached like he'd reached into her chest and squeezed it with his fist. She wouldn't let him know how she felt. She had learned to hide her feelings. This afternoon, she'd forgotten to be guarded. But then she'd seen his face and remembered why it was important to protect herself.

She had to hold herself together until the kids were in bed. Then she would face Jason. It took all her acting ability to remain chipper and not show the cracks growing inside.

An hour later, she sat across the table from him, a mug of pumpkin-spiced coffee in her hands. She didn't feel like drinking it, but she needed something warm to hold on to. Inside, icy chills began to race through her blood. If she was right, her future depended on this conversation. And it didn't look good.

Jason stood up from the table and began to pace around the kitchen, combing his hands through his hair. Every sign of agitation he displayed reverberated in her soul.

Finally, he turned to her. "I don't know how this happened."

"How what happened?" she asked.

He shook his head. "I never planned to develop any feelings for you. Or that you would have feelings for me."

Wait. Was he saying he had feelings? A spark of hope lit in her chest.

"I spent six years of my life as a soldier. The first five years were great. I got to travel. I made friends. I felt like that was the life I could live forever." He began pacing again. "And then we were deployed to assist after a hurricane. I didn't think anything of it. It wasn't war. But it was bad. So bad."

He squeezed his hands into fists. "We hadn't counted on how devastating it could be. While evacuating a town, a buddy and I were ambushed and left for dead. I was shot four times."

He looked directly into her face and sucked in a deep breath as if bracing himself. "I have scars on my back, left leg and shoulders. And I have nightmares."

She stood and crossed to him and placed her hands on his cheeks. "We all have pasts. Jason, I can never have children, because of my cancer. I thought that meant I had to remain alone. But don't you see? I am more than that. And when I see you, you are more than your scars. You're a good man. An honest man who loves the Lord. The scars—and I'm sorry you had to go through that—but the scars don't matter to me."

"You say that, but if you saw them…"

A memory popped into her head. "I did see them."

He stared at her. "When?"

"At Suzanne's wedding. We were at your parents' house, and you ran outside in the morning to catch the dog. Someone had left the door open, and he escaped. You were wearing shorts and a sleeveless T-shirt."

He paled. "I was running on the treadmill in the basement. No one goes down there."

"I saw your scars. And I was sorry that you had suffered. But they didn't disgust me. Or shock me. They don't define who you are to me."

For the first time since the conversation began, a light kindled in his dark eyes. "They didn't disgust you?"

She shook her head, holding her breath.

"So, if I asked you on a date, a real date, you wouldn't let them persuade you to reject me?"

She shook her head again, letting her smile grow. "Nope."

He moved closer. "And if I confessed that I think of you all the time? That I'm always reaching for my phone to call you, just to hear your voice?"

"Call away. Because your voice is my favorite sound in the world."

"Claire Derrick, I think I'm falling for you."

"Same goes for me. I'm so thankful God brought you into my life."

He leaned down and placed a kiss on her forehead before drawing her close in a sweet and simple embrace. It was too soon for anything more, and she was blessed that she had met a man who understood that.

This time, she smiled with her whole heart. She would let herself dream and feel and trust in God's plan.

CHAPTER ELEVEN

Jason called a week later and asked if he could come over that evening. Claire's pulse kicked up. She agreed, joy and anticipation zinging through her. She hadn't seen him since their heart-to-heart due to a situation at his office. He came straight from his job to have dinner with her and the kids at her home. Brody told him all about his new class at Crooksville Elementary School. Claire had registered the children the week before.

After dinner, Brody and Emma asked to watch a movie. She set up the TV for them then joined Jason in the kitchen for coffee.

"I had a call from Sergeant Stonis this afternoon," she said as she carried his steaming mug to him.

"Oh?"

"They're trying to track down Adam. He's apparently out of town. I think he's suspect number one."

He took a sip. When he set the coffee cup back on the table, she met his stare. "How do you feel about that?" he asked.

She shrugged. "I can't see it. He's cold, but he's never one to get his hands dirty. If he's involved, I doubt he's the one actually committing the crimes."

"An accomplice. Hmm."

"And look at this." She grabbed her phone and pulled up Adam's social media posts. "He was clearly out of town during the past two incidents."

"Did you tell the sergeant this?"

She nodded. "He's trying to find whoever Adam might be working with."

She still didn't think he was involved, but that was for the police to discover.

The next day, she awoke to a robocall saying school was closed for the day due to a waterline break. She didn't mind. It gave them another day to be home together. Although she did have some chores she'd need to do later.

Her phone rang. She danced over to where it sat on her kitchen counter and picked it up. When she saw the name *Stacy Boyd* appear on the screen, her heart dropped to her stomach. She knew she should answer immediately, but she hesitated. There was a possibility this call would not be a pleasant one.

Stacy had been very direct when she told Claire that they were still searching for any other relatives who might wish to claim Emma and Brody. Claire hadn't talked to the children about it, but she suspected they wouldn't welcome an unknown family member popping into their lives any more than she would. They were all very happy the way things were right now.

Knowing she couldn't avoid talking to the social worker forever, she accepted the call. But not before uttering a quiet prayer for strength and guidance. Peace sifted through her soul. God had her and the children in the palm of His hand. She would trust in His will.

"Claire!" Stacy's voice bubbled on the other end. "I'm so glad I caught you. I hope this is a good time to talk?"

Claire grimaced. She wanted to say it depended on why Stacy was calling but knew she couldn't say that.

"Good morning, Stacy." She kept her voice serene with an effort. "Yes, this is a fine time to talk. I'm just cooking breakfast for the children."

"Good, good! Are things going well?" Stacy didn't seem like she planned on breaking their hearts today.

"Yes, very well." She held her breath.

"Great. I know you're busy, so I won't keep you long. I just wanted to give you the news personally."

Claire tensed but didn't reply.

"We've done a thorough search. You know Emma and Brody's mother died. We were able to find out more about Zoe Mitchell. It seems their mother was an only child whose parents had long since passed. We don't know who their father is. We found her previous two addresses and put advertisements in the papers at both places. Plus, we've done a DNA test to find matches. So far, nothing. We're fairly comfortable in saying there are no family members who will be coming forward to claim the children. I know that you seem to have formed a connection with them. I just wanted to check and see if you're still willing to keep them with you long term, knowing that no one is coming forth to claim them."

Claire blinked. Why would she mind?

"Of course I want to keep them with me. I'm not sure why you think I wouldn't?"

Stacy laughed. "I figured you would. But there was also the chance that you agreed to do this simply because you're a good person and hadn't expected it to be longer than a few weeks."

Claire decided it was time for her to mention something she'd been thinking of since she agreed to foster the children.

She cleared her throat. "To be honest, I hope to adopt them someday."

Stacy was silent for a moment on the other end. "I thought you might be leaning that way. I can't promise that will happen. There's still a chance someone will come forward. But if things continue going smoothly, I'll be in your corner."

It wasn't the ringing optimism she wanted, but there was a chance. She would hold on to it. After they hung up, she marveled at how her life had changed in such a short time. Only two weeks ago she was sure she would never marry or have children. Now she was a foster mom and had a wonderful friend in Jason.

And she expected they would continue to grow closer as time went on.

The timer dinged. She put the oven mitts on before taking the cheesy egg-and-potato casserole out of the oven. The rich aroma filled the air.

Running feet announced the arrival of Emma and Brody. Emma had completed her round of antibiotics. She still tired easily, but her cough had cleared up. She could be heard talking and laughing all day. Brody entered first and immediately began setting the table. She ruffled his hair as she walked past him.

The three of them sat down at the table to enjoy the tasty casserole. She had discovered both children were hearty eaters. It was a pleasant surprise, since she remembered being very picky as a child. They both had second helpings. Half the casserole was eaten before they left the table.

Breakfast had concluded and she was washing the dishes when her phone rang again. This time, she approached the device a little more cautiously. When she saw Jason's name and face on the screen, joy burst inside her.

She unlocked the phone and answered. "Hey, handsome! I didn't think I'd hear from you this morning. What's up?"

A deep rumble of laughter hit her ears. The sound curled deep inside her and warmed her from within.

"I heard a rumor that certain children don't have school today. How would you feel if I were to pick you and the kids up around noon and we could go to the new science exhibit over in Zanesville? A special movie will start at two."

Brody had been talking about the exhibit for the past three days. He loved science.

"That sounds great! I do need to go over to the house on Main Street for a little bit. And before one o'clock, I have to go to the post office. Would that still work?"

"That's not a problem. I'll tell you what. Why don't I meet you at the old house with a pizza? We can eat, and while the kids and I clean up, you can go run your errands, and then we'll all go to the new science exhibit."

"It's a plan!"

Brody whooped when she explained what they were doing.

"Listen, could you guys help me? I want to make a dessert for after pizza." She recalled how much Jason had liked the blackberry tart she'd served him. It wouldn't take long to whip up. She had just enough berries left to make one. She needed to use them up before they became freezer burned. When the children agreed, she hurried to make the dessert. They'd have to stop at the store on the way to the old house to pick up vanilla ice cream. That shouldn't pose a problem.

The tart was ready to go and they were in the car by eleven thirty. They arrived at the store and picked out two flavors of ice cream. Vanilla for the tart, and chocolate chip cookie dough for the kids, who looked at her with such sweet puppy-dog pleading eyes, she couldn't say no.

Jason was already at the old house when they arrived, and he had parked on the far side to leave room for Claire's car. Within minutes, they were ready to eat. Paper plates and napkins were on the table, the ice cream was in the freezer, and drinks were poured. The vase, which she had finished the night before, sat on the mantel. She couldn't help but admire it every time she walked into the room. It felt like God's promise to her.

"What a great meal," Jason said, smacking his lips. "I could eat pizza every night."

"Pizza's yummy," Emma declared.

Claire smothered a laugh before it could escape. Emma had pizza sauce smeared across both cheeks. There was even a tiny dab in her blond eyebrows. She was the most adorable little girl ever.

Jason's eyes twinkled as he looked at the kids. "It certainly is. Plus, I got to sit here and eat with two of the best-behaved kids I've ever met." Then he winked at Claire. "And don't we all agree that Miss Claire is the best dessert maker?"

Emma nodded dutifully, but Brodie scrunched up his face. "Well, I don't want to be rude. I love Miss Claire. And the dessert was okay. But the ice cream was much better!"

Claire laughed. "You're right, Brody. Ice cream is the best."

"On that note," Jason said, "you scram and do your errands. We'll hold the fort here."

She hugged the kids and gathered her purse. Before she left the kitchen, Jason walked over and kissed her forehead.

"I'll miss you. Hurry back."

She flushed and smiled as she headed for the door.

It didn't take long to go to the post office and take care of business. But while heading back to her car, she heard a familiar, and somewhat unwelcome, voice call her name. Turning slowly on her heel, she forced herself not to scowl as Adam drove up next to her. She had forgiven him, but that didn't mean she wanted to see him. Or talk with him.

But she would. If nothing else, it would show him that she had moved on.

"Hey," he said, rather awkwardly. "The police talked with me. They told me about the house fire. And about the vandalism."

"The vandalism turned out to be an accident," she said. "Don't worry about it."

"Good. I wanted to make sure you knew I had nothing to do with any of that."

She nodded. She opened her mouth to say something else, but then noticed a lipstick box on the seat next to him. It was the same brand dropped at the scene of the fire. "Why do you have lipstick?"

She kept her voice calm.

He rolled his eyes. "It's for my mom. She lost one like it recently and hasn't stopped complaining about it because it cost her a lot of money and she never even used it."

His mother. She was there when Adam dumped her—the last time she remembered seeing her necklace.

"Adam. Why did you break up with me?"

He gaped at her.

She waved her hand. "I mean, I know why. But why at that moment? You knew about the cancer and it hadn't bothered you before. What changed?"

Unease slithered across his face. "I didn't realize how it would look until my mother explained it to me."

His mother. Why hadn't she put it together before?

His mom burned down the house and tried to frame her for the incident at the other property. Sergeant Stonis was right. It was about anger over the way Adam's name had been smeared. Only it wasn't Adam who had done it.

Adam's phone beeped. He glanced at it and frowned.

"What's wrong?"

He shrugged. "Nothing. My mom said she'd be at an appointment all afternoon in Zanesville, but the app on my phone must be glitching."

She looked at the app. She'd seen the tracking app Suzanne had on her phone. It showed her where the members of her family were at all times. Claire had always thought that would be a handy app to have if one had teenagers. Then she saw the address and gasped.

Adam's mom was at the house she was renovating. Jason and the kids were there right now.

Jason picked up the phone on the first ring and put it on speaker. "Miss me already?"

"Jason! The arsonist was Adam's mother. She's at the house. With you. Get the kids out. I'm calling the police now."

She hung up. Alarmed, he whirled to find Brody and Emma. He hadn't locked the door or set the alarm, since they were in the house.

The door opened, and an older woman took two steps into the kitchen. Her gray hair was pulled up in a sophisticated swirl of curls. She wore pearls, an elegant coat, and slacks. And held a gas can in her hand. The dichotomy shocked him. Claire was right. Adam's mom was the arsonist.

The woman's astonished eyes met his. She hadn't expected anyone to be here.

The woman before him planned to burn down this house that Claire loved. Where were Brody and Emma? He could hear their muffled laughter in one of the upstairs rooms. They were safe. Would she try to harm them? She hadn't physically hurt anyone yet.

"The police are on their way. They know it's you."

She pressed her lips together, angry sparks shooting from her icy blue eyes. "This is Claire's fault. I regret the day she and my son met. They came to my house and questioned him about the fire."

"But you're the arsonist."

She scoffed. "And Claire has again ruined everything. Thanks to her, my son's reputation is in shreds. The media portrayed him as a heartless man who abandoned his fiancée when she got cancer. The first few houses burning down distracted the media from him, and his numbers went up. Then her name surfaced again in connection with his, and his poll numbers went down. All because of her."

The breath stalled in his chest. She had planned it all just to discredit Claire. She had destroyed hundreds of thousands of dollars' worth of property, all to redeem a man who had brought his problems upon himself.

"Police!" Sergeant Stonis's familiar voice called out from the doorway. "Sandra Hunter, put down the gas can!"

When she hesitated, a look of fury on her face, Sergeant Stonis said, "It's over, Mrs. Hunter. Don't make things worse for yourself."

Slowly, she set the can on the floor.

"Put your hands behind your head."

She made a low growling sound, like a caged animal, but complied. A female officer edged past Sergeant Stonis and approached the angry woman. With swift and efficient movements, she cuffed her and read her Miranda rights. Jason had never heard them read to a real person before. The moment the woman was out of the house, Sergeant Stonis collected the gas can.

Jason followed him to the door in time to see two cars pull up along the curb. Adam Hunter jumped out of one.

"Mom!" He hurried over to the officer coaxing his handcuffed mother into the back of a police car.

Claire hopped out of the second car. She cast a single glance at the drama between Adam and his mother then rushed to the house.

"Jason! Brody! Emma!"

Brody and Emma ran out of the house and stood on the front porch with Jason, eyes wide. He put his arms around their shoulders. "It's okay. She had a scare and needs a hug, that's all."

Brody and Emma tore down the front stairs and flung their arms around Claire. Jason followed. She was well. The children were safe. They no longer needed to worry about someone targeting her.

The small group watched the police cars leave. Claire waved at Sergeant Stonis as he pulled out of the drive. Adam raced back to his car and followed the officers. Jason wondered how his career would weather this scandal then put it from his mind. Claire was safe, and the arsonist had been caught. He wouldn't worry about the rest.

Because they'd promised the children, they went to the science exhibit. When they exited the car, Brody held Jason's hand and Emma held Claire's. When they entered the exhibit, Jason reached out and took Claire's free hand.

She smiled at him, tears misting her eyes.

It was an exhausted group that gathered at her house for supper that night. The kids went to bed without a whisper. As the evening drew to a close, Jason and Claire slowly made their way to the front door. He didn't want to leave, and she didn't want to send him home. As they lingered in the hall by the door, trying to find words to make sense of the day, someone knocked.

She looked through the peephole and gasped. "It's Adam."

He was tempted to tell her to ignore it. But they needed to know if Adam was a threat. "Let me."

Jason opened the door, and his eyes widened. The confident man he'd expected was humbled and dejected. Adam looked past Jason to Claire, and his throat worked. It took him a moment to speak.

"I didn't know," he finally said. "I would have stopped her. I promise."

Claire stepped to Jason's side and took his arm, her eyes narrowed on her ex-fiancé. "I believe you. What will you do?"

He shrugged. "It's time for me to drop out of the race. I can't run, not knowing what she did."

When he turned away, they watched him trudge back to his car. After he drove off, Claire sighed. "I hope he can find peace."

Jason took her in his arms and held her close for a moment. He looked down into her face. "Claire, I love you."

He hadn't expected the words to pop out like that, but he couldn't deny them. She smiled and touched his cheek. "I love you too."

Softly, he touched his lips to hers. For so long he'd held himself distant, thinking no woman could accept him as he was. But he was wrong. God had the perfect woman in mind for him. And he planned to hold on to her forever.

CHAPTER TWELVE

Four months later

Jason arrived at Claire's door five minutes ahead of time. He couldn't remember the last time he took a woman on a date on Valentine's Day. Brody and Emma were already at Suzanne's house. She and Phillip had agreed to watch the children so he could take Claire out on this special night. His sister had switched completely to maternity clothes. She glowed with joy and good health. When she'd hinted to know if he had plans, he'd kept quiet, although he suspected she guessed. He brushed his hands down the sides of his dress slacks before knocking on Claire's front door. He flexed his fingers while he waited for her, trying to work out the nerves suddenly plaguing him.

Then she was there. He forgot about nerves as he moved forward and brushed a quick, gentle kiss across her smiling lips. She was gorgeous in a red dress that swirled to her calves. Her hair was pulled back, but a few strands had escaped to frame her face.

It didn't matter what she wore. She'd always be the most stunning woman in the room to him.

"Jason! You're early." Delight rang in her voice. She laced her fingers with his. He gave her hand a light squeeze.

"I am. We have some time. Our dinner reservation isn't for over an hour. It'll only take us ten minutes to get there. Anything you want to do before we go to dinner? Any errands to run?" He knew what he wanted her to say. If she didn't pick the right one, he was prepared to persuade her.

Some of the light dimmed from her eyes. "Actually, yes. I found out today that my house sold."

He knew how much that house meant to her.

"You look so sad. That's a good thing, though, right?"

She sighed, nodding. "It is. I buy them and renovate them to sell. But somehow, I started thinking about that house as mine and not as a project for someone else to live in. Which is not smart, I know."

"Do you know who bought it?" He held his breath.

"No. Some man named George Chapman. I've never heard of him."

He made a sympathetic noise in his throat. If he said he was sorry, he wouldn't be telling the truth, although he was sorry that she was hurting. "Do you want to go by and see the house again?"

He shouldn't have framed it as a question. What if she said no? Then he'd have to work to change her mind.

Her expression brightened. "Could we? I want to see it one more time. And I want to collect the vase I left there. I should have kept it home, with me, but it felt like it went with the house. I don't want anyone else to have it though. Does that sound horribly selfish to you?"

He shook his head. "No. I get it. You spent a long time gluing that vase together. It's special to you." After glancing at his watch, he showed her the time. "Why don't you get your coat, and we'll head out."

A thin film of snow covered the driveway. It didn't look slippery, but one could never tell in the middle of February. The last thing he wanted was for her to injure herself. Funny, he'd thought those red shoes with the high heels were ridiculous the first time he saw them.

But now, walking next to the woman he had grown to love more than anything, he was grateful for them because they gave him a reason to be protective.

"Here. It might be icy." He placed her hand in the crook of his elbow and escorted her to his car. He opened the door for her. Once he saw she was safely buckled in, he shut the door and jogged around to the driver's side, whistling a random tune. He hopped in and backed out of the driveway. Joy and anticipation ping-ponged inside him. He didn't know how he'd keep himself still.

The heater kept the car toasty warm during the short drive to the house that meant so much to Claire. Once there, he pulled into the driveway and parked the car, killing the engine.

"Shall we go in?"

She sighed. "It feels weird entering when I know someone else has put a bid on it."

"That doesn't mean anything, right? They haven't closed yet. And you're not breaking and entering. You're the owner. And the Realtor. Until it sells, you can do what you want."

"True." She made to get out, but he was there first, opening her door and giving her his hand to help her from the vehicle. She rolled her eyes but allowed him to assist her.

Once they crossed the walk, they climbed the steps to the wrap-around porch. Claire put her hand lovingly on one of the white columns as she passed it. At the front door, she keyed in the pass code. The lock clicked. He stood beside her, watching her lovely face as she braced herself before entering the house. She stepped in, reached to her right, and flicked the light switch on the wall. The lights blazed, filling the room with warm light. He watched her glance skitter to the mantel. And stop. Her eyes widened.

Yesterday, the mantel had held nothing but the empty vase. Tonight, white roses covered the surface. And in the vase, a dozen deep-red roses were proudly displayed.

"What?" She gasped. "I don't understand."

Taking her hand, he led her farther into the room. He knew the moment she spotted the glittering diamond ring held in place by a ribbon wrapped around the vase.

She turned to him. He was already down on one knee. "Claire Derrick, I love you. My world was a dark, lonely place before you blew through my walls. I want nothing more than to spend my life with you. Will you marry me?"

Tears sparkled on her lashes. "You don't care that I can't have children?"

He heard the hope, and the fear, in her trembling voice. "I don't care. I love you. No matter what. What do you say?"

"Yes!" She fell to her knees and hugged him. "I say yes!"

He placed his hands on either side of her face and kissed her softly. After a few moments, he helped her to her feet. After slipping the ring off the ribbon, he placed it on her finger. She sniffed.

"How did you know my size?" She held out her hand to admire the ring. It fit perfectly, as he knew it would.

"My sneaky sister got it for me."

"Ah. I should have known." She looked around at the garden of roses. "I'm assuming my boss helped you get the roses in here. She's a romantic at heart."

"Well, about that…" He hoped he'd done the right thing. "She let me in because I'm the one who bought the house."

She stared at him. "You bought it?"

Heat crawled up his neck. "Yeah. George Chapman is my lawyer. I had him submit the bid. I know you love this house. So I put a bid in. Do you think you can stand to live here once we're married?"

With a squeal, she threw her arms around his neck and hugged him so hard, he heard his back crack. He laughed, kissing the tears off her cheeks.

He couldn't wait to make her his bride.

June came in with a scorching heat. Fortunately, Claire had chosen a reception venue with central air. Suzanne made a gorgeous matron of honor. Her one-month-old daughter, Melissa, slept straight through the ceremony.

Claire adored her soon-to-be niece by marriage. She had the love of a good man. One who had done everything he could to give her everything she wanted.

Including children. She grinned at Emma. The six-year-old was perfect in her flower girl dress. Jason had Brody stand up with him as one of the groomsmen. They had started the proceedings to adopt the children. Their home study would take place in two weeks.

The reception lasted until early evening. Jason and Claire left the celebration amid cheers and well wishes from the remaining guests including her mom, stepdad, and little sister, Lizzy.

Claire settled into the passenger seat of Jason's car.

"I'm a wife."

He grinned at her. "Better than that. You're my wife. I never thought I'd say that."

She smiled back at him, her gaze lingering on his face. They were off to Alaska for their honeymoon. She'd always wanted to go there. But it didn't matter where they went. As long as they were together, she was content. Jason's parents were keeping Brody and Emma while they were away. Both Jason and Claire had considered taking the children with them, but his parents wanted time to get to know their soon-to-be grandchildren. The kids were thrilled to have grandparents.

And when they returned, they would live in the house she'd worked so tirelessly to make a home for someone, never dreaming that would be them.

The future had never been so alluring as it was now that she had Jason at her side.

Six months later

Claire hurried into the kitchen and pressed the button on the stove to stop the timer. Humming along with the Christmas songs playing from the Bluetooth speakers, she slid her hands into oven mitts and removed the tray of sugar cookies from the oven.

A stampede of footsteps in the hall warned her that soon she'd no longer be alone in the kitchen. Fifteen seconds later, she was surrounded. Jason slipped his arms around her waist. She leaned back against him, smiling, while pulling free of the oven mitts so she could place her hands over his. As was his habit, he briefly touched her left ring finger where her engagement ring had been joined by a plain gold wedding band. She could hardly believe they'd been married for six months.

"Mom! Do we get to decorate these?" Emma bounced on her toes in excitement.

Mom. It melted her heart every time she heard it. She looked back and forth between the two shining faces of her children. The adoption had been finalized three weeks ago, and she still woke up each morning and went to their rooms to make sure it wasn't a dream.

"Yes, Emma. You and Brody will be able to decorate all of them tonight after dinner."

"But you can't eat all of them," Jason cautioned. He kissed Claire's cheek before stepping to her side. "Don't forget all the grandparents will be here tomorrow evening for the Christmas party."

"Will Aunt Suzanne and Uncle Phillip be here too?" Brody asked. "And Aunt Lizzy?"

"They will." Claire rustled his hair. "And your cousin Melissa too."

He wrinkled his nose. Emma squealed and clapped her hands in delight. Suzanne and Phillip's little girl was a nonstop bundle of energy. Emma adored the baby, but Brody preferred spending time with his dad and uncles. He'd been the adult for so long, sometimes he struggled just being a kid.

Both children were undergoing counseling to help them recover from the trauma they had survived.

Glancing at the clock, Claire saw it was nearly six o'clock. She took the plates down from the cupboard and gave them to her children to set the table. When the small family sat down to dinner, they joined hands for grace, thanking God for their many blessings. Some nights, Claire felt her heart was so full, it was difficult to eat.

After the dishes were done and the counters cleared off, she whipped together the frosting and divided it into six bowls. Adding food coloring, she soon had yellow, blue, green, purple, red, and white frosting ready to go. When she placed the cookies and frosting in front of the children, their eyes nearly swallowed their entire faces. They turned to look at each other.

To her surprise, Brody covered his face and burst into tears. Falling on her knees at his side, Claire drew the child into her arms. He sometimes acted so much older, it was easy to forget he wasn't even nine yet. The little boy snuggled into her shoulder. She held him until his tears faded into soft hiccups.

Emma jumped off her chair and ran to his side. "Brody. It's okay. Don't cry." She reached out and patted her brother's shoulder.

He lifted his head and smiled at his sister. "I'm fine, Emma."

She scrunched up her face and studied him until she was satisfied. "Good. We have cookies to decorate."

Chuckling, Claire and Jason helped the children back to their chairs.

Emma wanted to frost a bell first. She was adorable, sticking her tongue out of the corner of her mouth in concentration while she slathered the cookie with blue and purple frosting. Jason took several pictures. Claire had told him she wanted to document every precious moment, and he'd remembered.

While Emma was occupied, Claire moved close to Brody. "Brody," she whispered, "are you okay?"

Jason's head tilted in their direction. He was listening to the conversation.

Brody glanced at Emma, and then he responded in a low voice, "I'm fine. We used to decorate cookies with our first mom. I didn't think I'd ever get to do that with a family again."

Oh, the things that made her heart ache. She stood and leaned over to kiss the top of his head. "I never had children to do this with before. Sometimes the joy makes me cry too."

"Really?"

"Absolutely."

He thought about it for a moment before blessing her with a smile so sweet and pure, it took her breath away.

Later that evening, she sat on the couch snuggled up to Jason, a mug of fragrant hot chocolate in her hands. Thanks to her thoughtful husband, a fire crackled in the fireplace and the lights twinkled on the Christmas tree.

"Tomorrow will be our first Christmas Eve as a family," she murmured.

Jason kissed the top of her head. "The first of many. Two years ago, this would have been unimaginable. Now, I can't even think of a future that doesn't include the three of you."

She leaned over and set the mug on the coffee table. When she sat back again, she readjusted her position so her arms were around the man she had promised to love, honor, and cherish and her head rested on his chest. The familiar beat of his heart had become her favorite sound in the whole world.

Despite her battle with cancer and all the horror he'd witnessed during his tour of duty, they had found each other and created a small family. Emma and Brody might not have been born from their love, but the two darlings were the children of their hearts.

Her gaze flicked to the mantel. There, in a place of honor, sat the vase she'd pieced together. Just as she'd mended the broken vase, God had taken their brokenness and mended it with His love.

At long last, her heart was whole.

Dear Reader,

We hope you enjoyed our journey to Crooksville, Ohio, as much as we did!

When we first started researching this book, we were both struck by the fact that Crooksville was known for its gorgeous and unique pottery. As we brainstormed, the idea of the contemporary couple finding one of Jasper's one-of-a-kind vases appealed to us.

We liked the image of God as the Potter. We also really connected to the theme of God healing our brokenness. We may have cracks and suffer along our life's journey, but His love can mend our hearts if only we will trust Him.

We love hearing from readers! We can both be found on Facebook.

Blessings!

Dana R. Lynn and Johnnie Alexander

✒ About the Authors ✑

Johnnie Alexander

Johnnie Alexander is an award-winning, bestselling novelist of more than twenty works of fiction in a variety of genres. She is on the executive boards of Serious Writer, Inc. and Mid-South Christian Writers Conference, and she cohosts an online show called *Writers Chat*. She also teaches at writers' conferences and for Serious Writer Academy.

A fan of classic movies, stacks of books, and road trips, Johnnie shares a life of quiet adventure with Griff, her happy-go-lucky collie, and Rugby, her raccoon-treeing papillon.

Dana Lynn

Dana R. Lynn is an award-winning, *USA Today* and *Publishers Weekly* bestselling author of more than twenty romantic suspense and Amish romance books. She believes in the power of God to touch people through stories. Although she grew up in Illinois, she met her husband at a wedding in Pennsylvania and told her parents she had met her future husband. Nineteen months later, they were married. Today, they live in rural Pennsylvania and are entering the world of empty nesters. She is a teacher of the deaf and hard of hearing by day and writes stories of romance and danger at night. Dana is an avid reader, loves cats, and thinks chocolate should be a food group.

Story Behind the Name
⸜⸜∂ ᧖⸝

Crooksville, Ohio

A hundred years ago, the famed Pottery Capital of the World was located in Perry County, a rural area of picturesque hills in southeastern Ohio. At that time, the state was the largest manufacturer of clay products in the entire United States.

At its peak, seven pottery factories were located in Crooksville, known as Clay City, and its neighbor, Roseville, also known as Pottery Land.

Perhaps the most well-known of these factories is the famed Hull Pottery Company, whose historic figurines, vases, bean pots, pitchers, and dishware are sought after by modern collectors. The company, founded in 1905, survived the lean years of the Depression, and even a flood and a fire.

Though the company no longer exists, Crooksville remains the home of the Hull Pottery Association, a collectors club whose goal is to preserve the company's heritage.

Each July since 1966, Crooksville and Roseville have taken turns hosting the Crooksville-Roseville Pottery Festival, which begins with a plate-breaking ceremony. The broken plate is one of twelve specially designed for the year. The one is broken, one remains on permanent display, and the other ten are auctioned.

Crooksville is named for Joseph Crooks, who submitted the post office application. The name he suggested, Reeds Post Office, was already taken, so Washington, DC officials recommended Crooksville. The village was incorporated in 1894.

Blackberry Mint Tart

Ingredients:

1 unbaked piecrust

¼ cup thinly sliced mint leaves plus a few left whole for garnish

3 cups fresh blackberries

4 tablespoons granulated sugar

¼ cup freshly made nut paste (whatever is available, though almond paste is best!)

2 tablespoons butter, softened

2 large eggs

Directions:

1. Preheat oven to 400°F.
2. Gently combine sliced mint, blackberries, and 2 tablespoons sugar in medium bowl.
3. Beat nut paste, remaining 2 tablespoons of sugar, and butter until smooth. Add 1 egg at a time and beat mixture until smooth.
4. Spread nut paste mixture on rolled-out piecrust, leaving about 2½ inches free around the edge.
5. Top paste with blackberry mixture.
6. Fold crust edges over filling.
7. Bake 20 to 25 minutes (or until crust is golden brown).
8. Garnish with additional mint.

*Read on for a sneak peek of another exciting book
in the Love's a Mystery series!*

LOVE'S A MYSTERY *in*
LAST CHANCE, IOWA
by PATRICIA JOHNS & SANDRA ORCHARD

Love's Vow
By Patricia Johns

Last Chance, Iowa
May 1905

Last Chance's only church smelled comfortingly of polish, dust, and the faint pine scent of some towering trees outside. There were only a few guests, this not being a big, fancy wedding. There would be no wedding lunch, and only a few of the faithful from the congregation had come to witness the event. Anne York sucked in a breath, her chest rising above her corset. She tried her best to keep her mother's advice to not lock her knees lest she faint away in the middle of the service. There would be nothing quite so undignified as crumpling into a heap at Reverend Bogg's feet.

"Dearly beloved, we are gathered here together to witness the union of this man and this woman in holy matrimony..." the reverend intoned.

Anne wore her best sheer cotton shirtwaist and light blue linen skirt. Her finely woven straw hat was a little too broad to be fashionable this year, but she'd trimmed it with some turkey feathers, a brand-new piece of cream-colored ribbon, and a bit of lace that she'd bought at Wheaton's Millinery Shop where she worked three afternoons a week. It had cost her two days' pay, even with the discount Mr. Wheaton gave her on account of her being a hardworking employee, but it was worth the expense. She'd done her best on short notice for her wedding day.

Benjamin Huntington stood opposite her, his dark beard neatly trimmed and his slate-gray gaze locked on the ground a few inches from Anne's black leather boots. She wished he would look up, reassure her somehow, but he didn't. His expression remained solemn, and he stood with his broad, calloused hands folded in front of him.

This man would be her husband. Benjamin, the father of a five-year-old daughter who needed a mother. He had broad shoulders and the strong hands of a man who did physical work. And yet he looked refined too, for a woodworker.

That was one thing she liked about him. He'd moved to Last Chance a little over a year ago, and he'd set up shop right away. His work spoke for itself, and word spread. He made everything from furniture to wood paneling for a couple of wealthier patrons. With the railroad so close, he could ship his work all the way to Des Moines, if he could get the customers.

He had explained all of that when he proposed. At first, Anne thought he was offering her a job—maybe as his secretary. But no, he suggested something more permanent, and Anne's parents were already on board with the idea. Besides, Anne had been helping her mother care for Molly the last few months, and she'd grown fond of the girl. She was sweet, polite, well-mannered, and truly eager to please. With her little rosebud mouth and her dark glossy hair that curled on its own, she would grow into a beauty one day too.

"Therefore, if any man can shew any just cause why they may not lawfully be joined together, let him now speak or else hereafter forever hold his peace." Reverend Bogg paused and looked up.

The scent of talcum powder and lavender water lingered in the silence among the dancing dust motes that shone in the rays of sunlight slanting down through lead-paned stained glass. The church was furnished with row upon row of fine wooden pews, all polished to a glow and smelling faintly of furniture polish. The reverend's wife, Eleanor, polished those pews herself every Monday morning to give the wood time to absorb the polish, lest it rub off on the back of a man's trousers or a lady's Sunday-best dress during the Wednesday evening prayer service. This being Tuesday, there was a small risk taken in sitting on those pews, and Anne's mother had brought handkerchiefs for her and Anne's father to put beneath them, just to be on the safe side.

"Who gives this woman?" Reverend Bogg lifted his head from the worn, leather-bound book of common prayer and looked expectantly toward the front pew.

Anne's mother, dressed in a long, gray, puff-sleeved dress with a spattering of lace over her chest that bespoke of an earlier time, hooked a gloved hand under her husband's arm and helped him rise a few inches off the seat.

"I do," Father said, his voice quavering. The words slurred past the sagging side of his mouth. Then he slid back down into the pew. The apoplexy had ravaged her father, and Anne looked at him with a wash of love.

Her father might be the one giving her to Ben in marriage, but he was also the reason she'd agreed to this hasty union to begin with. He needed someone to care for him in his declining state, and she didn't have the means without a husband.

The sound of a distant clanging rang softly through the air, and the reverend frowned slightly. The old ladies murmured and looked toward the stained-glass windows, even though they couldn't see past the colored glass.

"Benjamin, repeat after me," Reverend Bogg said, turning to Benjamin.

Benjamin took a gold ring from the minister's hand. This would be the ring she wore for the rest of her life. Her stomach fluttered nervously at the thought. A marriage either made or broke a woman, and she could only pray that this hasty choice was the right one.

The wedding service continued. They repeated their vows—until death did they part—and they exchanged rings and plighted their troth. All the while, the clanging bell from town grew louder. Anne's gaze flickered toward the doors of the church. It sounded like a fire alarm. Fires did happen from time to time, the town consisting entirely of wooden structures, and that, combined with pipe smoking, cooking stoves, and inebriated farmers come to town, resulted in some tragic fires. The sound of the insistent bell was enough to tighten every one of her nerves. If only it would stop—the sign of a false alarm.

If a rainy day was considered good fortune for a wedding—a sign of showers of blessings to come—then what did a fire alarm mean?

But the wedding plunged forward, and Reverend Bogg read the final section of the service, his voice sonorous and echoing through the high-raftered building. "Those whom God hath joined together, let no man put asunder. Let us pray."

That was it. The ceremony was done. She and Benjamin Huntington were legally wed. Anne bowed her head, trying to focus on the reverend's words, but her heart had a prayer of its own today.

God, give us happiness. Please, give us happiness. Bless this marriage, and show us how to love each other truly.

Because right now, all Anne really knew of her new husband was that he was a talented woodworker, he was a widower, and he had a five-year-old daughter in need of a mother. She knew that Ben could afford to help her parents where she could not and that other single young women in this congregation would have jumped at this opportunity to become Mrs. Huntington, but they were not Benjamin's choice. Anne was, and her heart pattered at the thought. Ben was strong, handsome, and solemn, and she'd developed some hopeful feelings for him over the last year of helping care for his daughter. But what did he feel for her, beyond gratitude that he'd have a stepmother for Molly?

She wasn't sure. Benjamin Huntington was both the beginning of a whole new life, and a mystery.

Ben lifted his head as the reverend's prayer ended, and he met Anne's gaze for the first time as her husband. One thing he'd learned in his eventful life thus far was that a man needed to appear calmer than he felt—always—but looking into Anne's brown eyes, he felt a wave of uncertainty.

He'd been focused on getting to this point, the wedding, but now it was over. They were married, and he'd have to bring his new wife home and start life as a married man all over again.

What was Anne expecting? He wished he knew. The only thing he was certain of was that she didn't love him. Not yet. He was half-way in love with her from the start, watching her so kindly care for his little girl. But she hardly knew him, and he wouldn't push that.

The thunder of hooves sounded outside, and the front door to the church swung inward and banged against the wall. Joss Musgrave stumbled inside, his white shirt dirt-smeared and without a hat on his head.

"Fire!" Joss gasped. Everyone exclaimed and rose to their feet. "Ben—your shop! It's burning down!"

Ben's heart hammered to a stop. His woodworking shop—the business he'd poured his last few dollars into, and his very livelihood.

"Molly, stay with Anne!" Ben yelled, bolting for the open church doors.

"Mama, can you keep Molly with you?" Anne's voice echoed behind him. He didn't notice that she'd run after him until he got to his own horse and buggy and she clambered into the seat next to him.

"This might be dangerous," he said. "You'll want to stay here."

"Nonsense." She turned forward and braced herself in the seat.

"I can't take you into danger, Anne! I only just married you!"

Did he need another family blaming him for something outside of his control? Could his heart take losing another wife?

"And marry me, you did!" Anne retorted. "This is my future at stake too. Stop wasting time!"

Right. Her comfort was at stake as much as his. Ben opened his mouth then shook his head and whipped the reins. He looked back only once as his buggy lurched forward. The few witnesses to the wedding had come running outside, shading their eyes and staring in the direction of town. His father-in-law, Thomas, was just now coming out the church door, leaning heavily on a cane and his wife at his side. Joss wiped his forehead with a handkerchief, talking animatedly to the pastor and his wife. Standing on the church steps, a little bit apart from everyone else, was Molly in her green cotton dress. She shaded her eyes against the bright spring sunlight, and he felt his heart tug.

Molly...his reason for all of this. The reason he'd seen more in Anne York and had begun to look closer.

"My mama will take care of her," Anne said, as if reading his mind.

Abigail York, who'd been caring for his daughter the last several months during the day while he worked, would be Molly's new grandmother. Molly would be safe. He was confident of that.

The horse sped up from a walk to a brisk trot just short of a gallop as they headed out of the church lot and down the gravel drive that led to the town of Last Chance. Of all the names for a place... But it had seemed oddly appropriate when Ben was choosing a new home to melt into and disappear with his daughter. This little town had felt like his last chance too.

Smoke hung in the air as they rattled onto the main street. Wooden walkways lined both sides of the dirt road. Women with baskets on their arms, skirts swirling around their ankles, and men pushing their hats back as they tried to get a better look, all gawked in the same direction he was headed—toward his shop where the last year of hard work, dedication, acquired wood, purchased tools, and a small loan still owing on the place was going up in a billow of gray, choking smoke.

He passed the first intersection with Maynard's Drugstore on one side and Wheaton's Millinery on the other. Then there was Abner's Saddle and Tack, the Feed and Supply shop, Eaton Café, Saul's shoe repair shop…all his neighbors. The air was thick and heavy with the smell of fire.

Ben's prayer was a short one—*God, save my shop!*

The fire bells clanged, and he glimpsed a traffic jam of two automobiles with drivers shouting at each other and a farm wagon with a pair of horses rearing up and pawing the air at the scent of smoke and the sound of the honking horns. The horses were going to bolt—even Ben could see that, but there was no help he could offer as he kept a firm hand on his own reins, holding his horse back. Just beyond the melee, Huntington Woodworking stood between a bakery and the street, a fire wagon parked in front of it and water pouring from hoses into shattered windows.

The horses pulling the farm wagon took off when one of the cars backed up, providing an opening, and the wagon clattered over a pothole, the driver seeming to hold on only by some miracle as the horses galloped down a side street. His shouts of "whoa!" faded, and the crowd's attention was now split between the runaway wagon and the fire. There was no possibility for Ben's buggy to get any closer, so he tied off his reins and jumped to the ground. Anne followed him, and he reached up to catch her around her small, corseted waist and lift her to the ground. This was the closest he'd ever been to her, and his breath caught as her feet touched the dirt and her worried gaze met his.

But there was no time for anything more, and she brushed his hands away from her. Ben turned and led the way through the throng of neighbors, pushing his way to the front where the volunteer firefighters pumped the last of their water into a broken window.

There were no flames left that Ben could see, and a wave of relief surged over him. He looked back over his shoulder and saw Anne struggling behind him, people blocking her path.

"Let my wife through!" he barked, and surprised men stepped aside to let Anne pass.

Ben shot out a hand, caught her gloved fingers, and tugged her up next to him.

"Is the fire out?" he asked.

The volunteer firefighters were men Ben recognized. Henry Ager, both a deacon in the church and the postmaster, stood nearest him with a soot-smeared, sweaty face. Next to him stood the sheriff—Wyatt Miller—a tall man with a hooked beak of a nose and eyes that didn't miss much. He wore a cowboy hat and had a toothpick sticking out underneath a mustache.

"Ben," Henry said, "I'm sorry this happened today of all days. You just got married, didn't you?"

"I did," Ben replied. Anne slipped her hand out of his grasp, and he exhaled a shaky breath. "What happened? I know I banked the fire. I double-checked."

"I think I know what happened," Sheriff Miller said. "I'll show you."

The big man led the way to the front door, and Ben pulled out a key and opened the smoke-blackened lock. It swung open, and they all filed inside.

His dripping shop looked like it was only half burned—the wooden floors marred with black scorch marks, and the legs of his worktable charred too. His precious store of cherry wood that he'd acquired for a special commission was burned beyond hope, and his heart sank. But his tools on the walls were untouched by the flames, although smoke had smudged the whitewashed walls and ceiling. His desk at the far side of the room with his locked filing cabinet and wooden swivel chair were unharmed.

"I saw this through the window," Sheriff Miller said, nudging a broken liquor bottle with his boot. There were three in total, lying across the floor with burn marks surrounding them. "You don't drink, do you?"

"Not a drop. Those aren't mine."

"It's an arson tactic," Henry said. "An oiled or tarred rag is shoved inside a half-filled liquor bottle with part of it hanging out. You light the rag on fire and throw the bottle through a window."

Ben's stomach tightened. "Who would do that to me?" He glanced over at Anne. She looked like she was going to be sick.

"Do you have any enemies?" Sheriff Miller asked.

"I don't think so."

Except there were a few men who might not like him. Was there an actual enemy who would try to burn down his shop and his home over mild dislike?

"Wyatt would know more than me," Henry said. "I see fires, though, and one thing occurred to me."

"Oh?" Ben met the other man's gaze.

"We all agree that this fire was deliberately set, and whoever did it waited until they were sure you would be gone." Henry shrugged. "And what better assurance that you would be away than when you're getting married?"

Ben glanced at Anne again, his heart sinking. She looked so fresh and neat in the middle of this smoky mess. She stood with her feet together and one white gloved hand covering her throat as she surveyed the workshop. Just as she married him, someone tried to burn down his shop and their home together. Anger simmered inside of him.

Whoever did this might very well be targeting him, but they were ruining Anne's future too.

Ben ran a hand through his hair, and he looked toward the staircase that led up to the bedrooms. He could thank God that it appeared to be unharmed, and at least there would be a safe place to sleep tonight. He headed past the workshop and looked into the kitchen beyond.

The kitchen was small, but functional, with a medium-sized woodstove, some counter space, white wooden cupboards, and a small table. Nothing was burned here, although the scent of smoke lingered. A second set of stairs, narrower than the first, ran up to the upper floor so that the bedrooms could be accessed from the workroom or from the kitchen.

Ben returned to where Anne stood motionless.

"This could have been far worse," he said to Henry. "There is damage, yes, but I can clean this up. The kitchen is unharmed. If you and the fire brigade had not gotten here when you did, we might have lost everything."

"God is merciful," Henry replied. "I'll go gather up some wood to nail over your broken windows for today, at least."

"Thank you," Ben said, and he meant it.

"Think on who might have had reason to do this to you," Sheriff Miller said. "In my experience, this sort of thing is never random. Someone did it for their own reasons, and when we figure that out, we can press charges."

What would a man do without friends?

Ben watched as Anne plucked something off her skirt that left a black mark on her white glove. She looked down at the smudged fabric, tears welling in her eyes.

"I'm sorry, Anne," Ben said. He was sorry for all of this—that his promise to provide for her parents, for her, for her future, had all been threatened by someone's hatred. He didn't know who had done this, who he'd offended so badly that they would stoop to this kind of violence.

"It's not your fault," she said, but he saw the look in her eye as she surveyed the room once more. She was deeply worried, and she had every right to be.

But today, of all days, he needed his wife to feel safe with him. And he couldn't blame her if she didn't.

A Note from the Editors

We hope you enjoyed another book in the Love's a Mystery series, published by Guideposts. For over seventy-five years Guideposts, a nonprofit organization, has been driven by a vision of a world filled with hope. We aspire to be the voice of a trusted friend, a friend who makes you feel more hopeful and connected.

By making a purchase from Guideposts, you join our community in touching millions of lives, inspiring them to believe that all things are possible through faith, hope, and prayer. Your continued support allows us to provide uplifting resources to those in need. Whether through our online communities, websites, apps, or publications, we strive to inspire our audiences, bring them together, comfort, uplift, entertain, and guide them. Visit us at guideposts.org to learn more.

We would love to hear from you. Write us at Guideposts, P.O. Box 5815, Harlan, Iowa 51593 or call us at (800) 932-2145. Did you love *Love's a Mystery in Crooksville, Ohio*? Leave a review for this product on guideposts.org/shop. Your feedback helps others in our community find relevant products.

Find inspiration, find faith, find Guideposts.

Shop our best sellers and favorites at
guideposts.org/shop
Or scan the QR code to go directly to our Shop

**While you are waiting for the next fascinating story
in the *Love's a Mystery* series, check out
some other Guideposts mystery series!**

SAVANNAH SECRETS

Welcome to Savannah, Georgia, a picture-perfect Southern city known for its manicured parks, moss-covered oaks, and antebellum architecture. Walk down one of the cobblestone streets, and you'll come upon Magnolia Investigations. It is here where two friends have joined forces to unravel some of Savannah's deepest secrets. Tag along as clues are exposed, red herrings discarded, and thrilling surprises revealed. Find inspiration in the special bond between Meredith Bellefontaine and Julia Foley. Cheer the friends on as they listen to their hearts and rely on their faith to solve each new case that comes their way.

The Hidden Gate
A Fallen Petal
Double Trouble
Whispering Bells
Where Time Stood Still

The Weight of Years
Willful Transgressions
Season's Meetings
Southern Fried Secrets
The Greatest of These
Patterns of Deception
The Waving Girl
Beneath a Dragon Moon
Garden Variety Crimes
Meant for Good
A Bone to Pick
Honeybees & Legacies
True Grits
Sapphire Secret
Jingle Bell Heist
Buried Secrets
A Puzzle of Pearls
Facing the Facts
Resurrecting Trouble
Forever and a Day

MYSTERIES OF MARTHA'S VINEYARD

∽◌ ◌∽

Priscilla Latham Grant has inherited a lighthouse! So with not much more than a strong will and a sore heart, the recent widow says goodbye to her lifelong Kansas home and heads to the quaint and historic island of Martha's Vineyard, Massachusetts. There, she comes face-to-face with adventures, which include her trusty canine friend, Jake, three delightful cousins she didn't know she had, and Gerald O'Bannon, a handsome Coast Guard captain—plus head-scratching mysteries that crop up with surprising regularity.

A Light in the Darkness
Like a Fish Out of Water
Adrift
Maiden of the Mist
Making Waves
Don't Rock the Boat
A Port in the Storm
Thicker Than Water
Swept Away
Bridge Over Troubled Waters

Smoke on the Water

Shifting Sands

Shark Bait

Seascape in Shadows

Storm Tide

Water Flows Uphill

Catch of the Day

Beyond the Sea

Wider Than an Ocean

Sheeps Passing in the Night

Sail Away Home

Waves of Doubt

Lifeline

Flotsam & Jetsam

Just Over the Horizon

MIRACLES & MYSTERIES
OF MERCY HOSPITAL

Four talented women from very different walks of life witness the miracles happening around them at Mercy Hospital and soon become fast friends. Join Joy Atkins, Evelyn Perry, Anne Mabry, and Shirley Bashore as, together, they solve the puzzling mysteries that arise at this Charleston, South Carolina, historic hospital— rumored to be under the protection of a guardian angel. Come along as our quartet of faithful friends solve mysteries, stumble upon a few of the hospital's hidden and forgotten passageways, and discover historical treasures along the way! This fast-paced series is filled with inspiration, adventure, mystery, delightful humor, and loads of Southern charm!

Where Mercy Begins
Prescription for Mystery
Angels Watching Over Me
A Change of Art
Conscious Decisions
Surrounded by Mercy
Broken Bonds
Mercy's Healing

To Heal a Heart
A Cross to Bear
Merciful Secrecy
Sunken Hopes
Hair Today, Gone Tomorrow
Pain Relief
Redeemed by Mercy
A Genius Solution
A Hard Pill to Swallow
Ill at Ease
'Twas the Clue Before Christmas

Find more inspiring stories in these best-loved Guideposts fiction series!

Mysteries of Lancaster County

Follow the Classen sisters as they unravel clues and uncover hidden secrets in Mysteries of Lancaster County. As you get to know these women and their friends, you'll see how God brings each of them together for a fresh start in life.

Secrets of Wayfarers Inn

Retired schoolteachers find themselves owners of an old warehouse-turned-inn that is filled with hidden passages, buried secrets, and stunning surprises that will set them on a course to puzzling mysteries from the Underground Railroad.

Tearoom Mysteries Series

Mix one stately Victorian home, a charming lakeside town in Maine, and two adventurous cousins with a passion for tea and hospitality. Add a large scoop of intriguing mystery, and sprinkle generously with faith, family, and friends, and you have the recipe for *Tearoom Mysteries*.

Ordinary Women of the Bible

Richly imagined stories—based on facts from the Bible—have all the plot twists and suspense of a great mystery, while bringing you fascinating insights on what it was like to be a woman living in the ancient world.

To learn more about these books, visit Guideposts.org/Shop

.

Printed in the United States
by Baker & Taylor Publisher Services